HEAD WOUNDS

HEAD WOUNDS

MICHAEL McGARRITY

W. W. NORTON & COMPANY
Independent Publishers Since 1923

For information about permission to reproduce selections from this book, write to Permissions, W. W. Norton & Company, Inc., 500 Fifth Avenue, New York, NY 10110

For information about special discounts for bulk purchases, please contact W. W. Norton Special Sales at specialsales@wwnorton.com or 800-233-4830

Manufacturing by Lake Book Manufacturing
Production manager: Lauren Abbate

Library of Congress Cataloging-in-Publication Data

Names: McGarrity, Michael, author.
Title: Head wounds / Michael McGarrity.
Description: First edition. | New York : W. W. Norton & Company, [2021] |
    Series: Kevin Kerney
Identifiers: LCCN 2020019555 | ISBN 9781324002857 (hardcover) |
    ISBN 9781324002864 (epub)
Subjects: LCSH: Kerney, Kevin (Fictitious character)—Fiction. | Police—
    New Mexico—Santa Fe—Fiction. | Police chiefs—Fiction. |
    GSAFD: Mystery fiction.
Classification: LCC PS3563.C36359 H43 2021 | DDC 813/.54—dc23
LC record available at https://lccn.loc.gov/2020019555

W. W. Norton & Company, Inc., 500 Fifth Avenue, New York, N.Y. 10110
www.wwnorton.com

W. W. Norton & Company Ltd., 15 Carlisle Street, London W1D 3BS

1 2 3 4 5 6 7 8 9 0

HEAD WOUNDS

CHAPTER 1

Detective Clayton Istee stood at the edge of the hotel swim- ming pool and stared at a nude body floating facedown in red-tinged water. A large tuft of hair had been yanked free from the man's skull. Two semicircular knife cuts at the edges of the wound had penetrated the thin protective layer of skin and deeply scored the cranium. Clayton knelt and took a picture with his smartphone.

"Scalped?" Sergeant Armando Perez, the night-shift commander on duty, ventured.

Clayton rose up. "Seems so. I've never seen anything like it before."

"You will again, amigo," Armando replied, flashing the brilliant smile that dazzled the many ladies hoping to land a good-looking bachelor cop. He nodded at a partially ajar hotel room door with direct access to the courtyard swimming pool. "Inside you'll find victim number two. A nude female, throat cut, with the same head wound."

A round-faced middle-aged man stood next to Perez, shivering in the cold, moonless March night. The name tag on his short-sleeve shirt read JOHN COSGROVE.

"You found him like this?" Clayton asked Cosgrove.

Cosgrove nodded.

"And the woman also?"

"Yes," Cosgrove answered.

"When?"

"At three a.m. That's when I deliver invoices to the rooms of guests checking out in the morning."

Sergeant Perez consulted his notebook. "The deceased were registered as Tony and Linda Vaughn. According to Mr. Cosgrove here, they checked in at eleven-thirty p.m. They did not have a reservation."

Clayton raised an eyebrow. The killer had struck no more than four hours ago. Fresh homicides frequently led to credible suspects. "What do you have in place?"

Perez ran it down. Officers were posted at all exits to keep guests from leaving. A deputy was stationed in the hallway outside the hotel room to protect the second crime scene. Backup was rolling to seal the hotel parking lot, and the medical investigator was on his way.

"So is your new boss," he added.

Clayton nodded. "I heard Rodney's radio traffic as I arrived." He turned to Cosgrove. "Where do you keep the swimming pool equipment?"

Cosgrove pointed a shaky finger at a storage locker in a far corner of the courtyard. "There."

"Do you have a pool skimmer on a long pole?"

"I think so. Let me get the key to the locker."

Cosgrove scurried away just as Captain Frank Rodney announced his arrival to dispatch by radio.

"You need me here?" Perez asked.

Clayton shook his head. "I've got three detectives en route. Stick with Cosgrove, take his statement, and hold him for further questioning. Locate the CCTV system and secure it. And thanks for keeping things tidy."

Perez smiled. "Anytime. Good luck with Rodney."

Clayton stifled a groan. Cosgrove returned with the electronic key to the storage locker in his outstretched hand. Clayton took the key and Perez led Cosgrove away.

For a long moment Clayton stood at poolside and took a look around. The hotel was brand-new, just outside the city limits of Las Cruces. It fronted the interstate that skirted the south edge of town. A large illuminated banner hung from the rooftop parapet proclaiming the establishment's grand opening. Clayton figured a double homicide probably wasn't what management had in mind to mark the occasion.

From the upper-floor windows he caught glimpses of curtains stirring, smartphones flashing, people staring down at him. The killings would have satellite TV news trucks soon rolling from El Paso and Albuquerque.

The locker yielded a pool skimmer. Clayton put on gloves and used it to gently guide the body to the shallow end of the pool. He was about to turn it faceup when Captain Rodney appeared in the courtyard.

"Let the MI do that," he barked.

Clayton backed off and waited for Rodney to approach. The captain was new to the Doña Ana County Sheriff's Office, hired to modernize and improve the Investigations Division. With less than a month on the job, he was still observing and fact-finding. But back-channel scuttlebutt predicted changes were coming, and soon.

At six-four and beefy, Rodney towered over Clayton's athletic five-ten frame. A retired commander of a detective bureau in an upstate New York police department, he'd moved to Las Cruces at the urging of his wife, a New Mexico native eager to escape the frigid Northeast and return to the embrace of warmer weather and her extended family.

"What's with the head wound?" Rodney asked, peering at the body.

"Scalped, it would appear," Clayton replied. The captain was a smoker, and the stench of tobacco clung to him. "Apparently a female victim was killed the same way."

Rodney snorted. "Well, that's a new one. Only in the Wild West. I hear you're an Apache, so I'd guess you'd know."

"I've never tried it myself," Clayton commented, straight-faced. "But I read somewhere that scalping may have been introduced in the New World by the Europeans."

"Spare me the politically correct history lesson," Rodney grumbled. "Turn him over."

"I thought we were waiting for the medical investigator."

"Do it."

Clayton hooked the pool skimmer under the dead man's armpit and turned the body faceup. Whoever had cut his throat was a pro. A single swipe with a blade had severed both carotid arteries.

"Neatly done," Rodney commented. "You said apparently the woman had been killed the same way."

Staring into the face of a man Clayton recognized had partially stunned him. "What?"

"Have you viewed the female victim in the room?" Rodney demanded.

Clayton shook his head. "Not yet. That's James Goggin."

"You know him?"

Clayton nodded as he walked toward the hotel room door. "Unless he has an identical twin."

He stopped in the doorway and stared at the naked body of Lucy Nautzile, sprawled on the bed, head lolled over the edge, her throat cleanly cut. A tuft of her long dark hair had been torn from her scalp. A drying pool of blood soaked the new beige carpet.

He'd known her all her life, and now she was finished, but where were her two young daughters? Still with their grandmother on the Mescalero homeland, he hoped, and not waiting somewhere for their mother's return.

For a minute he couldn't remember their names, but they were young, not yet teens. Their natural father had been a Mescalero tribal member, now long dead from alcoholism.

Angie and Jennie were the girl's names. Eight and ten years old, if he remembered correctly.

Clayton made a fast visual sweep of the room. Two travel bags sat unopened at the foot of the bed. Two neatly folded sets of clothes were draped over the arms of an easy chair angled in a corner of the room. Men's boots and a pair of women's sandals were tucked under the built-in desk.

A whiff of tobacco scent told him Captain Rodney had closed in.

"Do you know this victim also?" he demanded.

"Lucy Nautzile," Clayton answered. "Two years ago, she left her two girls with her mother and ran away with James Goggin, after they'd embezzled two hundred thousand dollars from a casino on the rez, where they worked. The crime was never reported, and nobody had seen them since, until today."

"Not reported?" Rodney asked incredulously.

Clayton nodded. He wasn't inclined to explain to Rodney tribal attitudes about dealing with the outside world of the White Eyes. "That's what I understand, but I can't vouch for it."

"We'll need more information about the casino embezzlement from the tribal authorities," Rodney said. "And maybe NCIC has a perp on file who likes to scalp his victims."

"That would be nice," Clayton replied doubtfully.

Rodney scratched his chin pensively. "Do you kill first and then scalp, or is it the other way around?"

"You scalp first, I believe. Which could make it an act of revenge."

"Or an assassination sent to give a clear message," Rodney suggested.

"Yeah, but why and to whom?" Clayton said. "There's no evidence of a struggle, and no visible defensive wounds on the bodies."

"The victims knew their killer," Rodney speculated. "The male doesn't look Indian."

"He wasn't," Clayton replied.

"How come you know so much about these two?"

"Mescalero is a small, tight-knit community."

Rodney grunted. "I'll want a helluva lot more information about them from you later on. I'm rolling the CSI unit, the mobile command post, and putting SWAT on standby. The sheriff is on his way. I want every person in the building identified and interviewed. No one in or out except authorized personnel. No one leaves until they're cleared. Maybe our perp is still here."

"It's possible."

"Do you think your tribe had anything to do with this?"

Clayton shook his head. "I can't answer that question. An individual, perhaps. If we can't ID a perp, I'll have to find a reason why they were targeted."

Rodney nodded. "Don't start a commotion with the hotel guests."

"Understood. It's still my case?" Clayton had caught the case on the normal after-hours rotation schedule, but Rodney could yank it away if he chose to do so.

"Proceed, Detective. I'll brief the sheriff when he arrives."

"Tell him the media is most likely on their way."

"Undoubtedly."

Rodney stepped away and Clayton started a close inspection of the room, item by item.

———

Frank Rodney stood in the shadows outside the hotel entrance, lit a cigarette, and waited for the sheriff. This was the first big felony investigation for the department since his arrival, and the timing couldn't be better. The sheriff had hired him with the understanding that he could kick some butt and jettison deadwood if need be, and Clayton Istee was on Rodney's list as a likely expendable.

He didn't trust cops who had corrective or disciplinary actions in their personnel jackets, and Istee was one of them. He'd been forced to resign from the New Mexico State Police for botching a cold-case murder investigation and had almost lost his police officer certification, which would have cost him his career.

But dumping Istee, if it came to that, wouldn't be an easy sell. Despite his screwup, Istee had been hired soon after by the sheriff as a senior investigator. It was only after Rodney learned the two men had been friends and roommates in college that it made sense. During his twenty-six years on the job, Rodney knew that friendship and favoritism almost always influenced who got promotions, plum assignments, or a second chance to salvage a career gone bad.

He'd come to Las Cruces fully expecting to stay retired, discovered it didn't suit him, and was happy to be back on the job. Now all he had to do was prove his worth in order to keep it.

In the parking lot, a patrol deputy in her unit slowly cruised past parked vehicles, running license plate information. Two other deputies in units were stationed to block access to and egress from the property. A quarter mile away, four unmarked vehicles turned onto the hotel access road, emergency lights flashing, running silent code three. The sheriff, the MI, and several more of Rodney's detectives were about to arrive. He ground out his smoke and stepped into the bright entrance lights to greet them.

———

Clayton finished a short meeting with the three detectives who got the interviews of hotel guests and employees quickly under way. After briefing the CSI team, he walked to the hotel reception area mulling over questions. Who was the killer's first victim, James Goggin or Lucy Nautzile? Did it matter? There was one bath towel missing. Did the killer take it? If so, why?

No luggage had been unpacked. Did James and Lucy plan to stay the night or were they here solely to meet someone? Had they been waiting for their killer? Or for someone else? Nothing about the crime scenes suggested the victims were expecting any trouble. They'd been deliberately made to suffer before being executed. Whatever their transgression, it had to be a major fuckup. Was the perp a hired assassin?

They'd registered under the names of Tony and Melinda Vaughn, yet there was nothing in the room connected to any identity, real or fake. No wallet, purse, cash, credit cards, or driver's licenses were in the room. Their car, a Ford Explorer with Texas plates, was missing from the hotel parking lot. Why erase all evidence of their identities? Perhaps the plan had been to remove the bodies, and something went wrong. If they'd paid for their room in cash, proof of identity still would have been required.

John Cosgrove was at the front desk assisting the recently arrived general manager, an overweight man in his mid-thirties with a somewhat frantic smile stamped on his face. They were issuing refund vouchers to a long line of unhappy guests anxious to leave.

Cosgrove told Clayton the woman had paid cash and provided a valid driver's license that matched her name. He handed Clayton the registration form. It listed a home address and phone number in Eagle Pass, Texas, pertinent vehicle information, and a check-in time of eleven-thirty p.m.

"Did you see the Explorer?" Clayton asked.

"I saw a vehicle idling outside the entrance when the woman came in to register, but I couldn't swear it was an Explorer. I told all this to Sergeant Perez, who wrote it down. Now that my boss is here, I'd like to go home. He'll let me, if you will."

Clayton shook his head. "Not yet, Mr. Cosgrove. I may have a few more questions for you in a little while. I know it's been a tough night for you but hang in there."

Cosgrove grimaced. "Yeah."

Sergeant Perez had formed a queue of restless hotel guests waiting to be interviewed in a corridor that fronted a series of large conference rooms where detectives where taking statements. Captain Rodney had brought in more help and the process was moving smoothly.

"All present and accounted for?" Clayton asked as he pulled Perez aside.

"Only Elvis has left the building," Perez answered with a grin. "Seriously, no one has tried to bolt, and all exits remain secure."

"Good. Has anybody piqued our interest?"

"Not yet, but killers come in all flavors."

Clayton groaned at the cop cliché. "Tell me about it. Cosgrove said he gave you a statement. Fill me in."

"He didn't see the male victim, couldn't positively ID the vehicle, and said there was nothing unusual about the woman's behavior. She paid for the room with cash and took the luggage directly from reception to the room."

"That pretty much jibes with what he told me. What about the CCTV?"

"You're not going to like it," Perez replied. "It's not operational. According to Cosgrove, the system malfunctioned. Special parts are on order."

"Did you get any specifics about the system failure?"

Perez shrugged. "Just what I told you. Cosgrove was vague about it. Do you think it's too coincidental?"

"I'll talk to Cosgrove."

"I put a BOLO out on the victims' vehicle," Perez added.

At the front desk, the general manager was still processing free lodging vouchers for frustrated guests. Clayton asked for Cosgrove.

"He went home," the manager replied. "Said he'd cleared it with you."

"Do you know what kind of vehicle he drives?"

The man shook his head.

The young deputy guarding the front entrance confirmed Cosgrove's departure.

Clayton stifled an impulse to give the kid a well-deserved butt-chewing. Instead, he leaned close and said, "No one leaves these premises unless permission comes directly to you from a senior officer. Is that understood?"

Deputy Eddie Paxton's face flushed red. "Yes, sir."

Clayton called Perez on his cell phone and asked if he had Cosgrove's home address.

"Affirmative. What's up?"

"He lied that he'd been cleared to leave and left."

"Day shift got called in early. I'll have them send a unit to bring him back."

"If he's not home, I want surveillance planted outside."

"Roger that."

"Find out what kind of vehicle he owns."

"Affirmative."

A new text message from Captain Rodney appeared on the screen. Clayton was wanted at the mobile command center ASAP to brief Sheriff Vasquez.

———

The mobile command center was a tricked-out recreational vehicle the size of a commercial bus that contained secure communication systems, uplink computer capacities, video surveillance capability, a gun locker, a bathroom, and a small conference room carved out of space at the rear of the bus. An officer at a computer station was running quick background checks on hotel guests who'd been interviewed by Clayton's small team of detectives and the additional personnel Rodney had called out.

Ramon Vasquez and Frank Rodney sat in the conference room behind a round table, the sheriff paging through a folder, the captain scribbling notes on a yellow pad. Clayton stepped into the room and both men looked up. Neither smiled.

"What's the status?" Rodney asked.

Clayton ran it down. CSI staff was still working the two crime scenes, nothing yet from the MI, and no plausible suspects had been identified. All hotel guests screened so far had come up clean in state and federal crime databases.

"The night manager left without permission," he added. "A unit is en route to his house to detain him if he's there."

"Is he a suspect?" Rodney asked.

"I don't know, but we need to find out."

"How did that happen?" Sheriff Vasquez inquired, gesturing to an empty chair.

Clayton sat. "A rookie mistake by Deputy Paxton. I counseled him."

"Write him up," Rodney ordered.

Clayton glanced at Ramon, who said nothing. "I've admonished him. That should be enough."

"Very well," Rodney grumbled.

Vasquez smiled tightly and handed Clayton the file. "This is what we have so far about the victims, faxed to us from the Eagle Pass, Texas, PD."

Clayton read quickly. Six months ago, using their aliases, James Goggin and Lucy Nautzile had taken a one-year lease on an apartment in town and paid cash for a late-model Ford Explorer at a local used car lot. According to the manager at the apartment complex, they had no jobs, and no known friends or acquaintances. Neither party had any contact with nor were known to local law enforcement agencies. That was all the information available so far, but Eagle Pass PD would follow up later in the day.

"It's a small, understaffed department in a high-intensity drug-trafficking area," Sheriff Vasquez added. "I've spoken to their acting police chief, and he's agreed to have his criminal division do additional legwork."

"As of now, we know nothing of their whereabouts before they arrived in Eagle Pass," Rodney said. "Once we wrap up here, we'll have to dig into that."

"Affirmative," Clayton replied.

Rodney leaned forward in his chair. "I spoke to the special agent in charge of the DEA El Paso Division and asked about Eagle Pass. It borders Piedras Negras, Mexico, across the Rio Grande. It's a busy international crossing used by the cartels to smuggle drugs, contraband, and illegals into the country. I put in a request to ICE for any intelligence they might have on our victims—frequent border crossings, extended stays in Mexico, any vehicle inspections."

"If the killings were tied to the drug cartels or human trafficking, we may have a possible motive," Clayton replied.

"There's a casino on the Texas side of the border, operated by the Kickapoo Tribe, which might also figure into the mix," Rodney added.

"Even more interesting," Clayton replied.

"But hypothetical," Vasquez injected. "All we know right now is the victims pissed off somebody, big-time. What do you know about the Kickapoos?"

Clayton shrugged. "Not much, really. As a child I heard stories that back in the day they were fierce warriors and hated enemies of the Apache people."

Vasquez leaned back in his chair and looked at Rodney. "Get started intelligence-gathering. I want to know more about the Kickapoos, Eagle Pass, the casino, and what law enforcement is up to down there, on both sides of the border."

"The cartels own the Mexican police," Clayton remarked, "and they employ their own assassins."

Vasquez nodded. "The sicarios." He glanced at Rodney. "Query the Mexican Feds. Ask them if they have anything on a sicario who likes to scalp his victims. Check with Interpol as well."

Rodney scratched a note to himself. "Right away."

Clayton's phone rang. It was the patrol deputy at Cosgrove's residence. There was no answer at the front door, the place was locked up and secure, and his vehicle was not anywhere inside the trailer park or nearby.

"Stay put, I'm on my way." Clayton stood and looked at Vasquez. "Cosgrove was rattled by the murders. He could be planning to harm himself. Forced entry at his residence to check on his welfare might be necessary. Ten-four?"

"Go ahead," Sheriff Vasquez replied.

Rodney nodded in terse agreement

———

The trailer park was in a working-class neighborhood not far from downtown off a heavily traveled city street. Clayton joined Deputy Leon Duran in his unit at the far end of the compound, parked next to an older single-wide on concrete blocks with a sagging aluminum screen door.

Duran, an eighteen-year veteran of the department, told him the front and rear doors were locked and the shades were drawn on all the windows.

"Cosgrove drives a ten-year-old Toyota Corolla," he added. "I cruised the trailer park coming in. It's not here. Didn't see it on any side streets, either. Spoke to his next-door neighbors. Nobody heard him arrive."

Duran touched the onboard computer keypad and read off the license plate number for the Corolla. "No lien, everything current, including insurance, no moving violations on his driving record. A BOLO has been issued."

"Cover the back door," Clayton said. "I'll go in the front."

The front door had a keyed lock but no dead bolt. Clayton jimmied it open, announced he was the police, drew his weapon, and went in low. A single table lamp illuminated the semidarkness. The combination living-kitchen area appeared neat and tidy, although the furnishings verged on thrift-store shabby.

He flipped on the light switch and called out again as he approached the bedroom. Dresser drawers were open, and clothes were piled haphazardly on the unmade bed. The room had a stale, sweaty smell to it, similar to the odor that serious drunks gave off when they were drying out.

The medicine chest above the sink in the adjoining bathroom had been swept clean of toiletries. A copy of the Alcoholics Anonymous Serenity Prayer was thumbtacked to the wall above the commode. Damp towels filled the bottom of the tub.

Had Cosgrove returned home directly from the hotel, showered, packed, and left in a hurry? Or had it been staged to look that way? Everything about the case felt decidedly weird.

Clayton shook off conjecture and cleared the rest of the trailer. In a room used as a home office, a past-due notice from a loan company had been crumpled up and thrown in a wastebasket next to a small desk. In a desk drawer, he found a form letter denying Cosgrove's application for veteran's medical benefits, based on his dishonorable discharge from the Navy. He'd served during Operation Desert Shield and separated from the service in 1993.

Outside, Clayton asked Deputy Duran to stand by until he spoke to the trailer park manager.

Tom Pearce, the manager, was a short man in his sixties with a sunken chest and a bad cough. His double-wide at the entrance of the two-acre trailer park also served as the office and rental center. Pearce told him Cosgrove rented his trailer three years ago and lived alone. He dug into a file cabinet and retrieved Cosgrove's rental application and signed lease agreement. It showed his previous employment history, his prior residences, his local bank, and his monthly income at the time of his application.

If the information was accurate, Cosgrove had lived in Las Cruces for at least nine years and had prior experience as a front-desk clerk or maintenance engineer at three different area hotels.

"Was this information verified?"

"Not by me. I just take the information and send copies to the company that owns the park. They've never turned anyone down in the five years I've been here."

At Clayton's request, Pearce made him a copy of the lease application.

"Does Cosgrove have any frequent visitors?" he asked.

"Not that I know of. Keeps to himself. A quiet boozer, I'd say. He drinks a lot of beer and puts the empty cans in our communal recycle bin for pickup."

"Have any strangers been around lately asking for him?"

"Just you."

"Did you see him drive in earlier? Or leave?"

"Nope, sure didn't."

"How about any unfamiliar vehicles last night or this morning?"

"Haven't seen any."

"A late-model Ford Explorer with Texas plates, perhaps."

Pearce laughed and shook his head. "I'd have noticed that. Most people living here drive old clunkers, including me."

"Do you know where he worked recently, before he started his job at the new hotel south of town?"

"He hadn't been working, as far as I could tell. At least not regular for six months. Did odd jobs here and there. I hired him a couple times to clean up litter around the property, and he did day labor for a landscape company."

Clayton thanked Pearce for his time and returned to Deputy Duran outside Cosgrove's trailer. He had him put out a missing person bulletin on Cosgrove and to stay put until a detective arrived to relieve him.

"Is this a crime scene?" Duran asked.

"I'm not sure. It needs a closer look before we call out the techs."

"No problem."

Clayton returned to the hotel, where satellite TV news trucks now lined the access road. The hotel parking lot was almost empty, signaling guests had been cleared and allowed to depart. A CLOSED FOR THE DAY sign was taped to the hotel's automatic front doors.

Clayton had hoped to avoid Captain Rodney by bypassing the mobile command center, only to find him in one of the large conference rooms being debriefed by an investigative team of eight detectives, a CSI supervisor, and Sergeant Perez. Sheriff Vasquez was absent.

Rodney glanced in Clayton's direction as he slid into an unoccupied chair. He'd arrived in time to learn that guest interviews had wrapped up with no viable suspects identified, the MI had declared the victims dead, mostly likely by having their throats cut, and CSI was still harvesting evidence at the crime scenes.

Clayton's interest jumped a notch when the CSI supervisor reported that several critical components to the CCTV system may have been deliberately damaged.

Rodney called on Clayton last for an update. He reported that Cosgrove had apparently disappeared and gave a quick summary of what he'd discovered at the trailer park. He suggested the possibility Cosgrove had been an accomplice in the homicides.

Rodney didn't challenge the notion. Instead, he announced that he was assuming command of the investigation.

"Nobody's being admonished here," he added with a glance at Clayton. "You've all been doing your jobs. Sheriff Vasquez wants that to be perfectly clear."

Clayton wasn't dismayed by the decision. It was a major case that necessitated top brass oversight and coordination. He wasn't being bounced off the case, just relieved as the primary. Now he'd get to see what kind of chops his new boss had.

Rodney directed Clayton to focus on the embezzlement at the Mescalero casino and find out about any recent contact the victims might have had with former coworkers and people on the rez.

"Get me a motive and a suspect soon," he demanded from everyone before ending the meeting.

Clayton left a message for his wife, Grace, before wheeling out of the hotel parking lot. He was on the road to Mescalero and would check back later. To hurry along the hundred-mile journey, he'd run a silent code three as soon as he reached the highway.

———

No matter the circumstances, Clayton always found returning to Mescalero lifted his heart. Born and raised in the high-forested ancestral mountains of the Apaches, his ties to home were strong and persistent.

The reservation, a big, splendid slice of mountains, valleys, streams, and rivers, still only lightly touched by the hand of man, overlooked the vast, imposing Tularosa Basin to the west and the edge of the wind-blown Staked Plains to the east.

He'd often wondered what Mescalero would have become if the White Eyes had kept it as their own. The trashy sprawl on the fringes of the 720-square-mile Apache homeland suggested it would be something less than glorious.

Lucy Nautzile's girls, Angie and Jennie, lived with their grandmother, Blossom Magoosh, in her small house on the outskirts of the Mescalero village, away from the major highway that cut east and west through the rez in the Sacramento Mountains.

Off a paved secondary road, the house was sheltered by a pine tree grove nestled between two shallow arroyos. It had snowed overnight, a good three inches, and only Angie's and Jennie's boot tracks showed in the long driveway. Blossom's snow-covered old pale green Datsun pickup truck was parked next to the enclosed front porch. Smoke drifted from the rooftop chimney.

Clayton was glad the girls were at school. He had no desire to tell them that their mother was finished. Better to have Blossom carry the news and alert family to begin the preparations for the rituals and ceremonies to come.

Blossom answered Clayton's knock at the front door and ushered him inside to the tiny front room warmed by a woodstove.

Searching his face, she said, "Clayton Istee, why do you wish to see this old woman?"

No more than five feet tall, her face carved with wrinkles, Blossom was a traditional Apache healer, frequently sought for her remedies to cure sicknesses of mind and body.

"I have come to speak of your daughter who once was," Clayton replied respectfully. It was taboo to say aloud the name of a newly dead.

"Ah," Blossom said, her expression unchanged. "She is finished?"

"Yes."

"And the man?"

"Also finished."

Blossom gestured at an armless side chair. "Sit."

Perched on the edge of the chair, Clayton asked if Blossom had recently seen or heard from her daughter.

Blossom slowly sat down on a small sofa. "Two days ago she came here with the man. She gave me a thousand dollars for the girls and said she'd soon have much more to fix my roof and buy a new kitchen stove."

"Did she say where she got the money?"

"No, only that once she had settled, she would come for the girls and they would live with her."

"Did she see the girls?"

"Yes, but only for a few minutes. The man waited outside and kept beeping the horn to make her hurry up."

Clayton asked about the man and the car. Blossom confirmed the man had been James Goggin but could only recall that the vehicle had been black in color and not a truck. She didn't remember seeing a license plate.

"When did you last see her before this visit?"

"The day she ran away with that man and left the girls with me. Once in a while, she'd send money for them, or call to talk. But she never said where she was living or what she was doing."

Clayton asked about postmarks on the envelopes. Some had come from Texas, others from Mexico, but Blossom couldn't say where. The notes came with money. The girls had tacked them to a bulletin board in their shared bedroom. Most simply read, "Mommy loves and misses you."

In the front room, Blossom reached for her coat hung on a wall rack near the door. "I must go now and get the girls from school."

He helped her with her coat, put his business card on the lamp table next to the chair, and asked her to call if she remembered anything else.

Blossom nodded. "When will her body come home?"

To keep the living cleansed and any possible death sickness away, Apaches dealt with death swiftly. "I'll ask to have it brought here as soon as possible."

"Thank you."

He followed Blossom outside and watched her rattle her way down the driveway in the old Datsun before calling his mother. His family was related to Blossom's family, cousins going back generations. Arranging for the journey She Who Could Not Be Named must soon make from The Shadow World to The Real World would require prompt action on the part of many.

"I'm at Blossom's house," he said when Isabel answered. "There's bad news. Her daughter is finished. Blossom has gone to bring the girls home from school."

"What happened?"

"It's been on the TV."

"The hotel killings?"

Clayton didn't respond.

Isabel sighed. "How terrible. I'll come right over. I wish you'd taken the tribal conservation job."

"The offer came too late. You know that."

"I do."

"We'll talk again soon," Clayton said. He disconnected and checked the time on his phone. His cousin Selena Kazhe, a senior executive with the tribal casino enterprise, would be his next stop. From her he hoped to get more details about the embezzlement Lucy and Goggin had pulled off. Maybe it had some connection to their gruesome deaths.

CHAPTER 2

Long before the resort and casino existed, there had been no
lake or golf course, just a beautiful high-country valley watered by a
perennial stream tucked away in an old-growth pine forest. In the summer, Apache families camped with their livestock until fall when the
cattle and horses were gathered and sold, often to ranchers off the reservation. Now the valley embraced a four-star resort in its second itera-
tion. It was a year-round destination for high rollers, outdoor enthusiasts,
sportsmen, and well-heeled vacationers. The only livestock remaining
were the horses that guests rented for an hour-long guided trail ride
around the man-made lake, weather permitting.

Selena Kazhe was on the telephone when Clayton knocked on the
open door to her office. She blew him a kiss, waved at an empty chair,
and kept on talking. Clayton settled in and caught snatches of the one-
sided conversation, which had to do with problems recruiting qualified indigenous applicants for several mid-level management positions.

Above average in height and full-bodied, Selena had an infectious
laugh, a natural ability to show genuine interest in everyone she met,

and a tough negotiator's attitude when it came to tribal business. The few personal items that adorned her office included an arrangement of three old Apache baskets on the sideboard, a large, framed reproduction of the original map of the Mescalero Reservation on the wall, and a silver presentation bowl on her desk from the Mescalero Apache Cattle Growers, which she kept filled with candy.

She finished the call, dropped the handset in the cradle, settled back in her chair, and smiled. "You're not here to brighten my day, are you, cousin?"

"Why do you say that?"

"You have a serious look on your face."

"I'm not a fun-loving guy by nature."

Selena laughed. "Liar. So, are you here on official business?"

Clayton nodded. "Two years ago Lucy Nautzile and James Goggin embezzled a lot of money from the casino and then disappeared. Tell me what you know about it."

Selena leaned forward. "It wasn't casino money they took. The rumor around the rez that we hushed it up is totally false. The money belonged to a guest, who came regularly twice a year to gamble. She always deposited a large amount of cash to cover her expenses and table gaming losses. She liked poker and roulette. Whatever was in the account when she departed went with her."

"But why didn't you report it?"

"She adamantly refused to let us report it to the police."

"Was that legal?"

"On our part, yes. I told her that the entire amount would be reported to regulatory and tax agencies as a personal gaming loss. She was all right with that."

"Has she been back since then?"

"No."

Clayton's eyes widened. "She took a personal two-hundred-thousand-dollar hit? Why?"

Selena straightened and gave Clayton a serious look. "Why do you need to know about this?"

"Hours ago, Goggin and Nautzile were murdered in a Las Cruces hotel. Scalped with their throats cut."

Selena shook her head disbelievingly. "That's terrible."

"The woman's name?"

"The name she used was Celine Shepard."

"Why do you say 'used'?"

"A government agent said it was a phony name."

"What kind of government agent?"

"A DEA special agent paid us a visit after we reported her gaming losses to the IRS and state gaming commission. He ordered us to keep everything confidential."

"Did you learn the woman's real identity?"

Selena shook her head.

"Did you document what happened?"

"Yes, our security chief at the time kept a file on everything pertaining to the situation."

"I need to see it."

Selena rose and headed for the door. "Of course. Wait here."

She soon returned unsmiling and empty-handed. "The file has been misplaced. I don't know how that can be. I have staff looking for it."

"What about the business office invoice records of the woman's previous stays at the resort?"

She went to her desk and reached for the phone. "I'm sure we have them."

Her quick call resulted in another strike. Apparently the invoices of

Celine Shepard's resort charges were unavailable. A computer system crash had wiped out a number of billing records.

Selena gave the telephone a dirty look and hung up. "I don't know what's happening. This isn't right."

"No, it's not," Clayton agreed. "Was the computer crash recent?"

"Six months ago. And the report by the security chief was kept in a locked filing cabinet accessed only by authorized personnel."

"What about CCTV digital footage of Celine Shepard?"

Selena shook her head. "From two years ago? Unless there's a reason, we don't archive what happens on the floor."

"Will you ask anyway?"

She stepped to the door. "I'll check with personnel in the security booth. Give me a minute."

Clayton stared at the old map of Mescalero. He had no jurisdiction on the rez. Only Selena's willingness to cooperate had gotten him this far. Was it a stretch to think everything had been deliberately wiped clean in advance of the double homicide, here and at the Las Cruces hotel?

As expected, there was no video of Celine Shepard. With Selena's permission, Clayton spent the next two hours talking with resort and casino employees who'd had direct dealings with the woman. He came away with very little other than a physical description of Shepard: five-five, slender, well toned, maybe approaching her mid-thirties, brown hair and brown eyes, light complexion, no visible birthmarks or tattoos, no accent. As one employee in the resort spa put it, "A total trophy babe without the title-holder present."

There was no evidence of late-night trysts with men or women in the Presidential Suite where she always stayed, and nothing suggesting heavy drug or alcohol use. She kept to herself, arrived in a different rental car each time, gambled like a pro, had meals in her suite, took full advantage of the resort gym, and made occasional daytime shopping trips to nearby Ruidoso. Win or lose, she was a big tipper. In her suite she was often found by maids or room service at her laptop or on her smartphone.

In spite of an exhaustive record search, none of the missing or erased documents could be found or retrieved. No one could remember the name of the DEA agent who'd appeared to put a lid on the case.

With Selena observing, Clayton interviewed the accounting manager who'd supervised Lucy and James Goggin. Although policies had since changed, it had been simple for them to issue a chit for the money in Shepard's account. The one bit of good information was that the manager had entered into his daily journal the name of the DEA special agent who'd met with him, Bernard Harjo. That gave Clayton his first glimpse at a worthwhile lead. Finding Harjo was critical.

He finished up in the human resources office, entering basic information on his tablet from Goggin's and Nautzile's personnel files.

In the casino parking lot, he pulled up the phone number for the El Paso DEA Division on his smartphone, called, and asked to have Special Agent Bernard Harjo located. Advised that there was no such agent in the district, Clayton made a polite, persistent request that Harjo be found wherever he was stationed, since he had information possibly vital to a double homicide investigation. The agent who took the call promised to get back with contact information ASAP.

Clayton left the parking lot headed for the office and the paperwork that awaited him. He told dispatch he was mobile and checked the time. With luck, he might get off-duty in just under fourteen hours. It made him yearn for a job more conducive to family life. But what kind of work would that be?

His radio crackled. Captain Rodney asked for his ETA and said he'd meet him at headquarters. Clayton responded he was about two hours out if he pushed it a little. As he accelerated, he kissed the idea of a fourteen-hour workday goodbye.

———

Frank Rodney was waiting outside, smoking a cigarette, when Clayton pulled to a stop in the secure SO parking lot behind the building.

"Have you got anything?" he asked as Clayton approached.

Clayton told him about Celine Shepard, how her two hundred K had been stolen by Goggin and Nautzile, why the money was never reported as a crime, and the DEA agent who'd shown up soon after.

Rodney grunted. "So that's why Samantha Hodges wants me to call her. She's the special agent in charge of the DEA El Paso Division."

"Whatever Agent Harjo knows about the casino job and Celine Shepard, we also need to know," Clayton said.

Rodney snorted as he ground out his cigarette and put the butt in the designated container by the door. "If only the Feds cooperated that way. Don't worry, I'll push it."

Rodney's office was still half moved into, with several books on a mostly empty bookshelf that displayed a few of the awards he'd won in his career, and some unpacked boxes on the floor next to a brand-new filing cabinet. He settled in his desk chair and told Clayton that Cosgrove and his vehicle remained missing and nothing of significance had been found during the search at his single-wide trailer, nor at the homicide crime scenes. Deep computer background checks on all hotel guests and staff had turned up several DUI convictions, some unpaid parking fines, but nothing that would flag a potential murder suspect.

"What did you learn about the victims?" Rodney asked.

Clayton summarized from his notes. Goggin had been forty-eight, never married, and worked in two casinos in Oklahoma prior to getting his job as a senior account specialist at Mescalero. He'd had no wants or warrants and a clean slate at his former jobs. Nautzile, thirty-six, a tribal member and widowed mother of two young girls, had been with the casino for eight years, earning several promotions in the accounting department. She'd never been arrested or charged with a crime. NCIC background checks were under way.

"So far, nothing about either of them jumps out as being ingenious crooks," Clayton concluded. "I think their mistake was picking the wrong person to rob."

"That's your working motive for the murders?"

"As yet, I don't have a better one."

"There might be one," Rodney countered. "Drugs."

He went on to explain the detectives assigned to intelligence-gathering had harvested some interesting tidbits. ICE reported Nautzile and Goggin made frequent crossings from Eagle Pass into Piedras Negras. So many that upon their return from Mexico their vehicle had been occasionally inspected for contraband and drugs. Nothing had been found.

Due to their frequent cross-border travels, the special agent in charge of the DEA Resident Office in Eagle Pass had them on a watch list. A reliable confidential informant had reported both were drug users who'd been dealing cocaine and speed on the side to customers at the casino.

Rodney handed Clayton an email from the casino stating the victims were regulars at the blackjack tables, small-time gamblers who never bet more than a couple hundred dollars each visit. Furthermore, management had no knowledge of illegal drug sales on the premises by any person or persons.

Clayton rolled his eyes at the disclaimer.

"Yeah, tell me about it," Rodney agreed. "It's gotta be the only drug-free casino in the country."

Clayton laughed, surprised the captain had a sense of humor.

Rodney pushed back from his desk and stood. "Do your reports and go home. You need sleep."

Clayton left thinking maybe Rodney wasn't all bad as a boss. At his desk, he called Grace and let her know he would be home after he finished his paperwork.

"I'm making meat loaf sandwiches and potato salad for dinner," she replied. "Will that be enough?"

"Sounds great."

"Your mother called and told me who was murdered at the hotel."

"I knew she would."

"Is there anything you need me to do?"

It was her way of asking if he was all right. "Just be there when I get home," he replied.

"Always, my love."

He finished up and read through everything again, making sure he'd sequenced events correctly, proofing for typos and misspellings, and ensuring all the salient points in his supplementals had been covered.

Before logging off, he couldn't resist taking a quick run through the reports filed by other personnel working the case. Rodney had given him the pertinent details. Yet in spite of the plodding, solid investigative work, Clayton somehow felt the case was stuck in suspended animation. Aside from finding out who in the hell Celine Shepard really was and what role she might have played in the murders, Cosgrove's disappearance nagged him. It seemed so untidy compared to everything Clayton had seen at the hotel.

He was convinced Cosgrove had been complicit in the crime. Paid to disable the CCTV system, falsify the hotel registration, perhaps even delay the 911 report of the homicides. If so, he was a loose end any professional hit man wouldn't leave dangling. Not for long, anyway.

Where was Cosgrove? On his way to some remote Mexican village to live off the money the killer had paid him for his services? The BOLO should have stopped him at a border crossing. Supposedly he hadn't returned home after leaving the hotel, although there was evidence of a hasty departure. Where did he go in such a hurry?

The hotel was part of a cluster of mid-price inns intermingled with family-style chain restaurants, gas stations, and convenience stores on the edge of the city. The uniformed division logs didn't show any patrols made searching for Cosgrove's vehicle at the nearby commercial properties. Was it sloppy shift reporting or an actual oversight?

He skimmed the reports entered by the investigators. There were no notations that a canvass for Cosgrove or his vehicle had been made in the immediate area. Clayton decided to take a look for himself.

———

In the fast-fading light of a nippy March evening, the spires of the Organ Mountains tinged gold from the sun low on the western horizon, Clayton slowly cruised the area. He circled buildings, checked all the parking lots, and eyeballed the curbside vehicles. On the periphery of the commercial zone, early dinner take-out business had picked up at a franchise fried chicken joint. At the rear of the property, Clayton found Cosgrove's Toyota Corolla parked inconspicuously next to a large trash dumpster, partially hidden from view.

He turned on the unit's emergency flashers and lit up the Toyota with the driver-side spotlight. He could see Cosgrove behind the steering wheel, head bowed against his chest. He drew his sidearm and approached cautiously. The sight of dried blood covering the front of Cosgrove's lightweight jacket told him the man was dead.

He cleared the exterior of the vehicle, put on disposable gloves, and tugged at the door handles. All four doors were locked. He used his flashlight to get a better look inside. It was impossible to tell how Cosgrove had died. Clayton guessed his throat had been cut, but he hadn't been scalped.

He called it in from his unit. With his phone he took photos of the car and several more of Cosgrove's upper body through the windshield, before smashing a rear door window with a safety hammer. Carefully he unlocked and opened the driver-side door and gently lifted Cosgrove's head. His mouth was twisted in agony, his throat cleanly cut.

The inside of the car was a trash pit. Old fast-food containers, plastic coffee cups, soft-drink cans, newspapers, and junk mail littered the floorboards and seats. A suitcase tucked behind the driver's bucket seat caught Clayton's eye. He pulled it out. Inside was one set of clean clothes, and a valid U.S. passport and current Texas driver's license made out for one John Chandler, with Cosgrove's photograph. High-quality forgeries.

An envelope with the return address of a bank in Juárez, Mexico, yielded a two-day-old deposit slip. A hundred thousand dollars had been credited to a John Chandler's new checking account.

Clayton figured the money in the Mexican bank was probably as bogus as the fake surname. Cosgrove had been reeled in on the promise of starting a new life.

Clayton put the suitcase on the hood of the Toyota. An unmarked vehicle with emergency lights flashing punched through a line of startled drivers waiting for their orders at the drive-up window.

"Who is it?" Rodney demanded as he dismounted his unit.

"John Cosgrove," Clayton replied. "Killed with the same MO, minus being scalped."

"Who tipped you to this?"

"Not who but what," Clayton replied. "Nobody thought to canvass the surrounding neighborhood for Cosgrove's car. I decided to take a look."

Rodney's jaw tightened. The responsibility for the screwup fell on him. He waited for a snide look or comment. Clayton said nothing.

"That was smart thinking," Rodney noted. "What else did you find?"

Clayton showed him the contents of Cosgrove's suitcase.

Rodney waved the deposit slip in the air. "Promised a hundred grand and a new identity? Unbelievable."

"He was never going to live to collect the money."

"I don't believe this case has anything to do with the Mescalero casino job," Rodney speculated.

"Not the theft," Clayton agreed. "It's all about the woman, Celine Shepard. Either they didn't know who she was, were too stupid to find out, or didn't care."

"Well, who in the hell is she?"

"I'm hoping Special Agent Harjo can answer that question."

Rodney shook his head. "I spoke to Samantha Hodges at the El Paso Division. She put the kibosh on your request. Harjo's out of the area on a high-priority undercover assignment."

"Surely he's got time to make a phone call," Clayton groused.

"I'll ask again."

"One more thing, Captain. The hotel registration for Nautzile and Goggin listed a black Explorer with Texas plates. That tallies with the vehicle Eagle Pass PD reported the couple drove. Yet Cosgrove said he couldn't definitely ID the vehicle. Neither could Blossom Magoosh when I asked her about Lucy's visit to the rez. Perhaps the Explorer was never here in the first place."

Rodney nodded. "I'll have the detective on duty start checking car rental agencies from here to Eagle Pass."

Patrol units, CSI vehicles, and two unmarked vehicles had converged at the scene. Several civilians had left their vehicles in the drive-up window queue to watch the excitement. Two burly deputies held them back. It was going to be a miserable night for the fast-food chicken franchise.

"Am I done here?" Clayton asked, his stomach grumbling. He couldn't remember the last time he'd eaten.

"Yeah, you're done." Rodney paused. "I like the way you used your head, Detective."

Clayton smiled. "That's kind of you to say. If you can find a way to get me in touch with Agent Harjo, I'd appreciate it."

"I'll work on it."

"Thanks."

Clayton drove home and parked in the driveway. He typed a quick supplemental report on his onboard computer about finding Cosgrove's body and sent it off. As he got out of his unit, Grace appeared at the front door, arms crossed.

"I've put our dinner on the table," she called out to him.

Slender, with tawny, flawless skin and thick eyebrows above dark eyes, his beautiful Grace always made him smile. "Coming."

———

It was just the two of them for dinner. Their daughter, Hannah, a student at New Mexico State University, was researching a term paper at the library on campus, and their son, Wendell, was living in Albuquerque, enrolled in medical school.

The thick meat loaf sandwich and chunky potato salad were plentiful and satisfying. Clayton ate without saying much while Grace studied him, a small smile on her face.

"What?" he asked, between bites.

"You look tired."

"I should be, but I'm not. More wired than tired. It's been quite a day."

"Is it over?"

"I'm not going back to work, if that was your question."

"Good."

"But I may do a little computer research."

Grace's smile faded. "That's working."

"Not for long, promise." Clayton stood to clear his plate.

"Don't make me come and get you at bedtime," Grace warned.

He stepped to her side of the table and kissed her. "You can come get me anytime."

Grace's smile returned at full wattage.

After they cleaned up the dinner dishes, Clayton sat with his laptop at the dining table. He recalled as a child hearing stories from Great-Uncle Percy, then in his late nineties, about a tribe of Kickapoos from Mexico, and fierce battles they fought with the Apaches in the long-ago times. He found it interesting that Goggin and Nautzile had gravitated from one tribal casino to another. He wondered if there was a connection.

He accessed the intelligence reports posted on the department's site and learned that the Kickapoos originally were from ancestral lands in the Great Lakes. Forced westward during the growing influx of European immigrants, they became ferocious enemies of the White Eyes and of other Indian nations, including the Apaches.

Although they'd been granted tribal lands in Mexico, Kansas, and Oklahoma, it wasn't until the 1980s that a reservation was established at Eagle Pass for a migrant band of Mexican Kickapoos that seasonally camped in a shantytown under the international bridge. Many accepted U.S. citizenship, others did not.

It was interesting stuff, but hardly germane, as far as he could see. Was there a connection or not? He scanned Internet web pages, looking for any news stories that connected the Eagle Pass or Mexican Kickapoos to drug dealing, human trafficking, money laundering, or any other criminal undertaking. He looked for reports of Eagle Pass

Casino mismanagement on several national gaming and regulatory compliance sites. Nothing popped up.

He shut down the laptop and checked the time. Ordinarily, it was way too early to go to bed, but he was beginning to feel sleepy. He could hear the low sound of the TV in the family room and decided to join Grace for a while and watch the early news. His phone buzzed, showing an unknown out-of-state number.

He answered and a male voice asked, "Are you really Apache?"

"Who is this?"

"Answer the question."

"Give me a reason to."

"You wanted to talk to me, not the other way around."

"Agent Harjo?"

"One more time; are you Apache?"

"I am."

"Speak the language?"

"Yeah, plus Spanish."

"Okay, here's the deal. There's a direct American Airlines flight from El Paso to L.A. leaving tomorrow midmorning. A ticket in your name will be at the check-in counter. With it will be instructions on where you are to go and how to get there. Follow them exactly. Take public transportation only to your destination. No taxis, no rental cars, nothing except the bus and your own two feet."

"Wait a minute, slow down."

"I'm not finished. Wear the scruffiest clothes you got—what you do yard work in will be just fine. Don't shave. Bring no weapon or police ID. Tell no one about this. That includes your wife."

"I have to get approval."

"That's been taken care of. Show up late and I'm gone. Show up early and a big Cherokee bouncer will give you a bruising you won't soon forget."

"What is this place?"

"You'll find out. I understand you did some undercover assignments in the past, so this should be a no-brainer. Don't look for me, I'll find you."

"Is this going to be worth my time?" Clayton snapped. "Do you know who I'm looking for?"

"We wouldn't be having this conversation otherwise, Istee."

The phone went dead. The text icon at the bottom of the screen showed a new message that read: "Special duty assignment to Los Angeles next date approved by SO-1. Report upon return. Rodney."

Clayton powered off the phone. In the family room, Grace was thumbing through a magazine, half watching a PBS period drama about rich English aristocrats.

He sank down next to her on the couch.

"Who called?"

"Work. Nothing important, except I don't have to get an early start in the morning."

Grace smooched his cheek. "Good. Get some sleep."

"That's the plan."

Smooched again by Grace, Clayton wearily climbed the stairs, his thoughts churning. Everything about Harjo's phone call told him the man was undercover, probably working narcotics. He wouldn't risk blowing his cover on something trivial, so Celine Shepard must be a big deal. But was she a big deal to the DEA, or just to Harjo?

Clayton got into bed. Tomorrow, he'd be walking blind into a situation outside of his control, to a place he knew nothing about, in a city where he was a complete stranger. Not a reassuring exercise in confidence-building.

He could bail on taking the risk and make another attempt to connect with Harjo through official channels. The idea wasn't appealing. He doubted—just from Harjo's tone—that he'd go for it.

More likely, the agent would turn silent and become permanently unavailable.

There was something happening that went way beyond the Mescalero casino caper, Celine Shepard, the double homicide, Cosgrove's murder, and a nameless, faceless killer. Clayton wanted to know what it was. Special Agent Bernard Harjo was the key.

He fell asleep with a promise to himself not to die in L.A.

CHAPTER 3

Following the instructions that came with his airline ticket,
Clayton left LAX on a Metro bus, got off in downtown, walked to a
light rail station, and took the train to a stop in East L.A. He left the
station and walked along the empty sidewalk next to the roar and blur
of never-ending traffic, wondering if there was any place in the city
where stillness and silence existed. He doubted it.

The nature of the cityscape, unfriendly to pedestrians, further
soured his already unhappy mood. He'd obeyed Harjo's demand not
to tell Grace where he was going or why. By doing so, he'd broken
a family pact they'd made years ago to always know how to find one
another. Here he was, with Grace unaware of his whereabouts, undercover without a cell phone or police ID, in a strange city with no
backup, about to meet a DEA agent he knew nothing about.

His decision not to say anything sat heavy on his mind. He should
have told her.

Careful along the way to stay alert for any tails or signs of surveillance, he remained watchful as he neared his destination. He walked

past sprawling windowless industrial warehouses, large metal-clad complexes home to major manufacturing companies, and long-haul trucking outfits with cavernous loading bays that backed up to a noisy nearby freeway. With mountains hazy to the east and the ocean invisible to the west, paradise did seem paved-over.

A forlorn side street with a block of run-down buildings, mostly shuttered storefronts, interrupted the dreary commercial architecture. Clayton paused outside the Legends Lounge and took a last, long look around. Except for two old men sitting on a curb sharing a bottle in front of a vacant shoe repair shop and a shuffling old woman pushing a shopping cart filled with her possessions, the sidewalks were empty.

He was right on time.

The Legends Lounge's broken neon sign tilted precariously above the entrance, and the front windows were covered with faded advertising posters of popular brands of whiskey and beer. He pushed his way inside with an elbow to avoid the crusted, filthy door handle and paused to let his eyes adjust to the dark. The place was long, narrow, and stank with the smell of booze sweated out by generations of serious alcoholics.

Six men perched on barstools faced a large grimy mirror advertising a Mexican beer and a big-screen television that hung above a shelf of half-empty whiskey bottles. On the TV, a show relived the greatest touchdown moments in Super Bowl history. The man closest to the door, a muscular, surly-looking Indian with shoulder-length dark hair, eyed Clayton suspiciously. Probably the Cherokee bouncer Agent Harjo had warned him about.

At a row of booths against the opposite wall, a snoring drunk sat slumped over, his head resting on the table with an empty shot glass near his limp hand. Clayton glanced at the bartender, who jerked his head in the direction of a man alone at a back table, his face hidden beneath the brim of a cowboy hat.

The man said nothing when Clayton approached, eyeing his ragged blue jeans, faded long-sleeve work shirt, and scuffed boots.

"You don't look much like an Indian," he finally noted in Spanish.

"Just what does an Indian look like to you?" Clayton shot back. "Are you Harjo?"

Harjo nodded. "I am. Sit down."

Clayton slid onto a chair. "Why the cloak-and-dagger?" Underneath the cowboy hat, Harjo had high cheekbones, a wide nose, and deep-set eyes. His hair was tied in a long braid that fell midway down his back.

"I usually don't meet people at my office," Harjo replied, switching to English. "You're an exception. Don't ask for more of an explanation."

"It never entered my mind. What have you got for me?"

"Slow down, Istee," Harjo replied. "First, I want the specifics on your killer's MO."

Clayton laid it out. The ear-to-ear surgically sliced necks, the scalping of both victims, the clean crime scene with no—as yet—helpful trace evidence, and the after-the-fact murder of the killer's accomplice, a helpful, clueless hotel night manager.

With a slight smile on his lips, Harjo shook his head in appreciative disbelief throughout Clayton's rendition.

"You know this guy?" Clayton asked when he finished.

"I know of him," Harjo replied. "But this the first I heard that he did wet work north of the border."

"Does he have a name?"

"That, I don't know. He's a freelance sicario, not tied to any of the drug cartels. They call him El Jefe, because he's the baddest Mexican assassin of them all. Commands top dollar and hand-picks his jobs."

"Indigenous? Mestizo? Hispanic?"

Harjo shrugged. "I don't know if he's an Indian, mixed-blood, or a blond, blue-eyed descendant of the Spanish conquistadores."

"How does he tie in with Celine Shepard and the two hundred thousand James Goggin and Lucy Nautzile ripped off from her at the casino?"

Harjo pushed back his chair and crossed his legs. The Cherokee near the front door relaxed. "I don't know that he does."

"You don't know a lot of stuff," Clayton observed.

Harjo laughed, pointed at the bartender, and held up two fingers.

"Why did you bring me here?"

"Celine Shepard is really Carmella Schuster, a German-Mexican whose great-grandfather immigrated from the Fatherland after World War II and landed in Piedras Negras. Probably a Nazi. At least a sympathizer. He married a local Mexican girl and settled down. To make a long story short, Carmella is the lover of Sammy Shen, a Chinese-Mexican from the same town. He's pure Asian, no mixed blood. Chinese are particular that way. They grew up together and pissed both families off by falling in love. I want Sammy."

"Why?"

"He's a third-generation Chinese gangster who, among other enterprises, specializes in laundering large amounts of Mexican drug cartel money. He filters it through different venues, but particularly likes to use casinos as a conduit. Much easier and safer than banks or front organizations, especially if you have key people on the inside."

"Were Goggin and Nautzile his people at Mescalero?"

"Hell, no," Harjo huffed. "They took Carmella's money all on their own, with no knowledge of who she was. I'm surprised they stayed alive as long as they did."

"Why did you hush up the theft?"

"Carmella does front work for Sammy, casing casinos as possible places to move large sums of money. If it looks promising, Sammy either bribes an existing key employee or recruits someone to get on the inside. At the time, our guy at the Mescalero casino was the chief of security. He was close to sealing a deal with Sammy through Carmella when your victims walked out with the two hundred K and blew it sky-high."

"You still haven't told me why you cleaned up for Carmella."

"In the hopes Sammy would try again. So far, it's a no-go."

"Why am I here?"

Harjo paused to let the bartender deliver two bottles of beer.

"Goggin and Nautzile got dead because they showed up at the Eagle Pass Casino, which is on the doorstep of Sammy's home ground and exactly the wrong place to be. I'm betting Sammy found out where they were and contracted El Jefe to kill them. Find the sicario and just maybe we can lasso Sammy and Carmella."

"Is it that hard to do?" Clayton asked, taking a beer from Harjo's outstretched hand.

Harjo nodded. "He runs his organization like a miniature CIA. He's got properties and homes around the globe that he uses once and then sells. He's got a network of agents and analysts that have outsmarted us for years. We'll plug up one of his money streams and he'll open five more on different continents. Now we've got intelligence that Sammy's planning to open his own string of casinos on the Mexican side of the border. If and when he does that, the illicit millions pouring into the United States will be almost immeasurable. He'll use shadow companies to buy up high-end commercial and residential properties, just like the Russian mobsters have been doing for years. Hell, he'll probably buy control of a few state-chartered banks and some small real estate companies to make it all look legit."

"This is all very interesting, but none of my concern."

"Exactly," Harjo replied. "Sammy won't be looking over his shoulder for you. Nor will he care if you're hunting El Jefe. He'll figure the chief can handle anything we throw at him."

"Are you trying to set me up?" Clayton asked.

Harjo sighed and took a long pull on his brew. "As a gesture of agency cooperation, I'm offering you a chance to use our resources. You get El Jefe with our help. We in turn get a shot at Sammy Shen and his girlfriend."

"As I understand it, Mexico has yet to fully legalize casino gaming," Clayton said.

Harjo leaned forward in his chair. "I'm impressed you're so well informed. Sammy's close to buying up enough Mexican politicians to get that law changed. If that doesn't work, he'll find another way. "

"Just how close can you get me to El Jefe?"

"A confidential informant working with our Eagle Pass agent is willing to trade El Jefe's location in exchange for dropped charges on a low-level marijuana bust. El Jefe supposedly lives somewhere in Sammy's neighborhood, on a godforsaken part of the Bolsón de Mapimí in Northern Mexico."

Clayton sipped his beer. "This CI knows where El Jefe is?"

"That's what he says, and he's been reliable in the past. As he tells it, our target has a large ranchero out in the middle of nowhere."

"I want to see his dossier."

"Of course. It will be waiting for you at your office."

"Why do you want to give this to me?"

"Because El Jefe doesn't know you, and I'm too well known to the Mexican federal police and local cops owned by the cartels. They'd sell me out in a heartbeat."

"Your cover's blown south of the border," Clayton rephrased.

"Pretty much."

"No way I'd go in alone without police powers, ironclad authorization, and backup. Besides, my bosses will never go for it."

Harjo drained his beer. "Don't bet on it. If you take this on, you'd go undercover with a DEA agent commission in your pocket, official sanction, and backup in the person of Special Agent Danny Fallon. He's a former Navajo police officer and highly decorated Iraq combat vet with three tours under his belt. Speaks fluent Navajo, Spanish, some Chinese, and a smattering of Arabic, in case you encounter any Iraqis."

"How come the Mexican police don't know Fallon?"

"Another good question. Danny's out of the Vancouver, British Columbia, resident office, specializing in drug-money laundering investigations involving Chinese nationals. He's never been assigned south of the border, thus he's an unknown quantity, like you. Plus, he's former Special Forces."

Clayton smiled. "Hell, you don't need me. Just send in your guy."

"You're not interested?"

"Interested, yes. Willing, no."

"You're skeptical and need corroboration." Harjo held out a USB flash drive. "I understand. Take it."

Clayton hesitated. "What is it?"

"Five case studies by the Mexican Centro Nacional de Intelligencia of assassination MOs identical to your double homicides. The victims were two corrupt high-ranking federal police officials, a district court judge who refused to be bribed, an Army colonel on the payroll of a major cartel, and a human trafficking smuggler who kidnapped the wrong girl. None of the criminal investigations were released to the public."

"I'll take a look."

"Good." Harjo put the flash drive in Clayton's outstretched hand.

"But it doesn't mean I'll play ball."

Harjo stood. "I know you'll want my bona fides. You'll find a file on your desk when you get home."

Clayton got to his feet. "Maybe there's another way to get to El Jefe and your pal Sammy Shen."

Harjo smiled and nodded in the direction of the bar door. "If you think of it, let me know and I'll go to work for you. Don't take too long deciding."

"I won't."

"This meeting never happened. Understood?"

Clayton nodded. "It was your party."

The Cherokee was at the door waiting to usher Clayton out. Busy watching the video replay of an end zone catch in a decades-old Super Bowl, the customers at the bar paid no attention as he passed by.

Clayton paused on the sidewalk. The two old men sitting at the curb had moved to the shade of a recessed entrance of a boarded-up store across the street. The homeless woman was nowhere to be seen. An idling Chevy van halfway down the street raised his concern for a moment until a man came out of a small package liquor store carrying a case of beer and quickly drove away.

A second set of instructions enclosed with Clayton's plane ticket directed him to take a different route back to the airport from the Legends Lounge. Smart thinking, but was it necessary? What exactly did Agent Harjo want to keep secret? His L.A. operation, whatever that was? Or his involvement in hunting for El Jefe?

Clayton didn't doubt Harjo's word that the sicario had assassinated Goggin and Nautzile. But he'd feel easier about it if he had some additional confirmation.

He walked past another complex of flat-roofed, rectangular, windowless buildings to a bus stop where a group of eight males, all older Mexicans and smokers, patiently waited for the next Metro local to arrive.

He stood a safe distance away from the cloud of tobacco smoke that hung over the men, figuring if there were no traffic tie-ups or airport delays, he'd arrive back in Las Cruces in time to stop by the office and review Harjo's credentials.

Before Harjo, Clayton's most recent experience involving a DEA agent hadn't gone well, resulting in an explosive gunfight with four people dead, including a New Mexico State Police officer who'd been a friend. And although Harjo's proposal intrigued him, he wasn't interested in becoming bait to snare a big-time Chinese-Mexican gangster. But he did want to learn more about Harjo and the CI willing to lead the way to El Jefe. What were their agendas, really?

Did it matter? If after dinner he told Grace where he'd been today and why, it would make it almost impossible to go undercover in Mexico without risking his family. He could either be honest with Grace or respect the confidentiality of his meeting with Harjo.

Clayton decided to hold off deciding anything until he'd done his research and considered all the options.

———

Delayed on the flight out of L.A., Clayton arrived in El Paso late in the afternoon. From his unmarked unit in the airport parking lot, he left a voice message for Grace asking her not to hold dinner for him. Driving north on 1-10, he broke protocol and didn't inform dispatch he'd returned to duty. He wanted time without interruption to read through the files Harjo said would be on his desk.

Except for the rugged and starkly beautiful Franklin Mountains that filled the eastern horizon, there wasn't much to admire on the short drive to Las Cruces, and the heavy long-haul truck traffic on I-10 kept Clayton's attention on the road. By the time he arrived at the office, Sheriff Vasquez and Captain Rodney had radioed that they were home and off-duty. All the better. He'd rather brief them in the morning, when he knew more about the players in Harjo's scheme.

Swing shift was out on the streets and only Vasquez's administrative assistant and gatekeeper Charlene Romero was still at her desk at the reception area outside the sheriff's office.

Thankfully, no detectives were loitering after-hours in the Investigations Division, and the area was quiet. Settled at his desk, Clayton quickly entered a summary of his meeting with Harjo into the case file before turning to the folders in his in-basket.

He started with Harjo's confidential informant, Juan Jose Garza, the man who allegedly knew how to find the nameless El Jefe. A native-born U.S. citizen with extended family in Piedras Negras, Garza was thirty-two years old and had a history of substance abuse. He'd been arrested and convicted of petty crimes including shoplifting and disturbing the peace, had a more serious DUI offense, and pled out to one breaking-and-entering charge that put him on probation for a year.

Busted a year ago for possession of marijuana with intent to sell—a felony that could have cost him hard time in a Texas prison—Garza had cut a deal with the DEA to report on conversations with his uncle, a high-ranking commander in the Piedras Negras Municipal Police Department who was, according to an intelligence report, the local drug lord.

Juan Garza's earlier reports had given the DEA good information on key members of the cartel who'd gunned down rival gang members in a shoot-out in front of a Mexican drug treatment center. The information had been turned over to the Mexican authorities, but how it had been used was absent from the file. Furthermore, there was nothing to suggest Garza had personal knowledge of El Jefe or actually knew his whereabouts.

Clayton put the file aside and opened Harjo's dossier. In his mid-forties, he'd been with the DEA for seventeen years, recruited out of the Tucson PD, where he'd worked undercover for three years. He graduated valedictorian in his DEA training class and returned to Tucson, where he continued undercover until his reassignment to the U.S. Consulate General Office in Guadalajara, Mexico.

After the Guadalajara duty tour, Harjo was assigned to the El Paso Division. His duty stations after El Paso had been redacted from his file. Citations for his various departmental honors and awards were also missing. It made Clayton suspicious. Such a big black hole in a dossier with so many commendations meant Harjo was a special asset.

Doing what? Clayton wondered. *Something dirty? Something wet?*

Appended to Harjo's file was Special Agent Danny Fallon's résumé. He was all Harjo claimed him to be; a highly decorated Army Special Forces combat veteran fluent in Navajo, Spanish, and English, with some Chinese and Arabic. He was a certified wilderness survival and combat arms instructor who'd been visiting faculty at the FBI Academy and DEA Training Academy in Quantico.

Fallon had received a DEA Superior Performance Award for identifying and confiscating over thirty million dollars in laundered drug money funneled into British Columbia by a Chinese export company. He was thirty-five years old, divorced, with no children.

Clayton locked the files in his desk drawer and looked up to see Sheriff Vasquez coming through the door.

"Charlene snitched on me that I was back, didn't she?" Clayton said with a smile.

A cop first and politician only as an afterthought, Vasquez nodded and pulled up a chair. "Of course, that's her job. How did it go with Harjo?"

"You read the files he sent?"

Vasquez nodded.

"Then you know he wants me to partner with a kick-ass ex–Special Forces DEA agent and a Mexican-American CI former drug user who can allegedly guide us to our supposed killer, the mysterious El Jefe, living somewhere in the wilds of Northern Mexico. What a plan."

Vasquez flashed an easy grin. Along with his smarts, his sincerity and calm personality had won him a solid victory in his race for sheriff. "You're not convinced?"

"I told Harjo I want to first look for El Jefe my way."

Vasquez crossed his arms and leaned back in the chair. "And which way is that?"

Clayton smiled sheepishly. "I'm thinking about it."

Vasquez laughed.

"I'll rewind the investigation from scratch," Clayton proposed. "There's a clue out there I've missed."

"You've got three days," Vasquez said.

"What?"

"Three days," he repeated. "By then, if you're still spinning your wheels, we'll do as Harjo asks."

"Why?"

Vasquez sighed. "Because DEA convinced the Department of Justice to increase our federal grant to fund body cams, drones, upgraded communication systems, new onboard vehicle computers, and state-of-the-art surveillance cameras—all stuff we badly need. But authorization is predicated on our playing ball with Harjo."

Clayton grunted. "Great."

"But I did get you three days." Vasquez put a three-ring binder on the desk. "That's the intelligence report on current High-Intensity Drug Trafficking Operations in the Eagle Pass–Piedras Negras sector that Rodney put together, along with some demographic facts and interesting information about the Kickapoo Indians. Happy reading."

Clayton laid his hand on the binder. "Exactly what happens in three days?"

"That has yet to be made clear. Agent Harjo will be in touch. This is highly confidential. Not a word to anyone."

"I'm not happy about this, Ramon."

"I want this case solved, Clayton. There's a lieutenant's slot opening soon. Keep that in mind."

Clayton smiled at the maybe promotion offer. He'd lost his lieutenant rank once to politics and once to his own stupidity. "Do you think the third time would be the charm, amigo?"

Vasquez shrugged and grinned. "In your case, who knows?"

Clayton's expression turned serious. "If I do this, I want protection twenty-four/seven for my family, and that includes Hannah at NMSU and Wendell in Albuquerque."

"I can swing that."

"Promise."

"You have my word. If and when this is a go, you can tell them you're on a special assignment, but that's it."

Clayton powered down his computer and pushed back from the desk.

"Understood."

"Good. Buy you a drink?"

Clayton smiled. "Let's go."

———

For most of her married life, Grace had lived with the daily uncertainty that comes from being a cop's wife. There were times when it took all her willpower to say nothing about her fears. When Clayton was late coming home for dinner, she'd sit in her favorite living room chair and read, listening for the sound of his police car in the driveway.

Tonight, she struggled to concentrate on a historical novel set in Elizabethan England. Rather than any undue concern for Clayton's lateness—he'd called to say he was having a drink with Ramon Vasquez—it was the endless melodrama of the novel that kept pulling her out of the story.

She put the book aside, resolved to do a better job of selecting titles on her next library visit.

It wasn't like Clayton to stop for a drink after work. In fact, Grace couldn't remember the last time it had happened. What was this about? Nothing bad, she hoped. After all, Clayton and Ramon had been friends for years. Still, Ramon was sheriff and ultimately Clayton's boss.

The tuna casserole she'd made warmed in the oven. If he wasn't home in thirty minutes, she'd go ahead and eat without him. Their daughter, Hannah, a NMSU cross-country runner, had eaten early and left for a team meeting.

Sometimes, alone in the house, with Wendell in Albuquerque and Hannah busy at school, she missed the closeness of her family in Mescalero. On the weekend, she would go home to participate in the burial rituals for She Who Could Not Be Named and to offer comfort to Blossom and the girls. She expected Clayton to go with her. In fact, she yearned for the day when they could permanently return.

The sound of an arriving car brought Grace to her feet. She retreated to the kitchen to remove dinner from the oven. She turned as Clayton entered and almost dropped the casserole dish. He was unshaven, wearing his most ragged shirt and a pair of paint-splattered blue jeans suitable only for house chores. On the job, he'd never dress so shabbily unless he was undercover. Something he'd promised not to do ever again.

"What's this?" she demanded crossly.

"I haven't been demoted to janitor, promise," Clayton replied with an unconvincing smile.

She placed the casserole on the counter. "Tell me."

"There's nothing to tell."

She glared at him.

"Don't get steamed. I had a meeting today with an undercover federal agent." He tugged at his shirtfront. "For his protection, this is how he asked me to dress."

Grace pulled off the oven mitts. "Is that all you're going to say?"

"It was about a lead in the double homicide. For now, that's all I can say."

Grace bit her lip.

"Okay?" Clayton asked.

She reached for the dinner plates. "Fine."

But it wasn't, and they both knew it.

CHAPTER 4

In the morning before breakfast, Clayton checked his email and found photographs of Sammy Shen and Carmella Schuster, aka Celine Shepard, sent by Special Agent Harjo. A good headshot of the woman captured her innocent-looking brown eyes and symmetrical features accentuated by a slightly prominent chin that suggested a toughness about her.

Sammy Shen's image was a rather grainy telephoto shot. Lean, with angular features and wide-set eyes under thick brows, Sammy wore a finely tailored expensive suit and had a slight smirk on his face.

Over toast, bacon, and coffee, Clayton and Grace sat with Hannah, who was excited about an upcoming college track-and-field invitational to be held in Austin. She'd been training hard to surpass her personal best in the five-thousand-meter race and hoped to return home with a win. Her infectious enthusiasm for the competition allowed Clayton and Grace to avoid renewing the previous night's mild squabble.

He left home an hour before his shift started, informed dispatch he was traveling to Mescalero, and pushed back the memory of Grace's tight-lipped smile after he'd kissed her goodbye. As he approached the summit of the San Augustin Pass with the stunning view of the wide Tularosa Basin stretching to the distant Sacramento Mountains, his police radio crackled with static.

Unsure if dispatch was trying to contact him, Clayton responded. Captain Rodney replied, asking why he was going to Mescalero.

He explained that he now had photographs of Sammy Shen and Carmella Schuster. "I'm going to show them around and see what shakes loose."

"It's worth a shot," Rodney replied agreeably. "Check in with me when you get back."

At the casino, Selena Kazhe granted Clayton permission to conduct additional staff interviews. He concentrated on workers most likely to have had repeated contact with Celine Shepard, especially parking attendants, housekeepers, salon beauticians, and servers at the upscale resort restaurant.

Nothing new emerged until he spoke to Truman Balatche, a valet parking supervisor working the day shift for a sick friend. Clayton had gone to high school with Truman's mother. A former Marine sniper, Truman had returned from Afghanistan with a Combat Action Ribbon, a Purple Heart, and a severely mangled foot that made him limp badly. Several surgeries at a VA hospital hadn't corrected it, but Truman kept going anyhow.

He smiled and nodded at the photograph of Sammy Shen. "Man, I remember him and his ride. Top-of-the-line, sweet Audi Q8. Had to cost over a hundred K. He always tipped a twenty, even if he only stayed for ten minutes."

"When did you last see him?"

"Couple years ago. He wasn't a guest. He'd just come to pick up his lady friend."

"Celine Shepard?" Clayton showed Truman her photograph.

"Yeah, that's her. Some hot number."

"Did you record the Audi's license plate?"

Truman shook his head. "No need. He was just here to pick her up and drop her off. But it was a Mexican plate."

"Remember the state that issued it?" Clayton asked.

"No, but I think it was one of the frontier plates Mexicans have if they live along the U.S.-Mexican border."

Clayton held up Sammy's photo again. "Are you sure this man drove the Audi?"

"Absolutely."

"Do you recall anything else?"

"The lady liked to shop at this one store in town, High Country Boots on Sudderth. They sell handmade cowboy boots and custom hats that are way beyond my pay grade. Sometimes she'd come back loaded down with three or four shoeboxes."

"What about her personal vehicle?"

"Always a car with Texas plates."

"Any chance you'd have a record of it?"

Truman shook his head. "Not from so long ago. Check with reception."

"A computer crash wiped out the records," Clayton replied.

Truman nodded. "Something is always going wrong around here. Last week our internal phone system went down in the morning for an hour. Pissed off a lot of guests who couldn't get room service."

Clayton smiled. "Not good for business. Thanks for your time, Truman."

"No problem. You might want to talk to people at the airport. Most of our big-money guests fly in on private jets and keep a spare car there. Must be nice to live the good life."

"Must be," Clayton echoed. "Say hi to your mom for me."

Truman turned to greet an arriving vehicle. "Will do."

———

Clayton drove a canyon road to the village of Ruidoso, where a large, illuminated sign on Sudderth Drive directed motorists from town to the casino. Ruidoso was strung along gullies, gaps, and ravines with a noisy, narrow river running through its heart. The high mountains of the surrounding national forest gave the village most of its charm.

High Country Boots fronted the two-lane street through town in a retail area that drew the majority of the tourist business. It was too early for the stores to open, and in the chilly March air only a few pedestrians wandered the sidewalks. A CLOSED sign in the window of the boot store prompted Clayton to continue on to the Sierra Blanca Regional Airport.

Although the name of the airport suggested something grand and it had a postcard view of Sierra Blanca, there were no commercial flights. Dozens of corporate jets and small private airplanes were either tied down in neat rows, parked under sunshades, or stored in individual hangars.

At the administration building, Clayton spoke to the airport manager, Wilson Gramm, a round-faced, friendly man with a full head of white hair. He nodded in recognition at the photograph of Sammy Shen.

"He stopped flying here a couple of years ago," Gramm said. "Haven't seen him since. Owned a Gulfstream. Kept a car here, too, a nice Audi. In fact, it sat untouched for over a year. A private trucking company came, loaded it on a flatbed, and hauled it away."

"I need all the information you've got on the aircraft, the car, and the trucking company that fetched it," Clayton said.

Gramm gestured in the direction of his office. "Sure, that's not a problem."

Within a few minutes, Clayton had copies of paperwork that

included airport invoices to park and refuel the Gulfstream, store the Audi, and allow the trucking company to remove and transport the car. All the bills had been paid by a company named China Dolls, a Mexican limited partnership located in Piedras Negras.

Clayton left pleased with the information but unsure exactly how it would help. Knowing more about Sammy Shen was interesting, but he still wasn't convinced Harjo's target was relevant to his investigation.

His stop at High Country Boots added nothing to his growing storehouse of curious but unconnected facts. The ownership had changed and the new proprietor, a West Texas gal with blond highlights in her long, brown hair, didn't recognize Carmella Schuster's photo and had no knowledge of her as a customer. Clayton left his business card behind on the off chance Carmella's—aka Celine Shepard's—cowboy-boot-buying fetish might soon bring her back to Ruidoso and the store.

With nothing substantial to grab on to, he was starting to believe in the possibilities of improbable coincidences. He laughed at the idea. People get murdered for a reason, rational or not. Stealing two hundred grand from a gangster's lover may have been cause enough, but what if that wasn't the only motive?

Harjo had thrown a ghostly assassin Clayton's way as the key to solving the crimes, but what about the victims? In homicides without a known perp or primary suspect, Clayton knew to always look to the dead for answers. He decided to put Harjo's El Jefe on hold and take a closer look at Goggin and Nautzile.

He made a U-turn on Sudderth and headed back to the office.

———

His first day on the job at the Doña Ana County Sheriff's Office, Frank Rodney showed up with his own personal office chair, an expensive ergonomic model in teal-gray that provided a multitude of adjustments designed for comfort, support, and improved posture. It got the unit detectives speculating, some with dismay, that their new boss was going to be a bureaucratic desk jockey. It didn't take long for the dire prediction to circulate back to Rodney. He made no attempt to dispel it.

What his troops didn't know was that years ago, as a uniform patrol sergeant, Frank had ruined his back assisting fire department personnel move a six-hundred-pound male who had suffered a heart attack from a second-floor bedroom. It had nearly forced him into early retirement. Because it wasn't a heroic in-the-line-of-duty injury, Rodney never spoke of it. In fact, it embarrassed him. But it had almost crippled him and taken months of intensive rehabilitation before he'd been allowed to return to work. Soon after, he'd been promoted to detective lieutenant.

His ergonomic chair and a daily early morning exercise regimen kept him upright, physically mobile, and capable of doing the job. Now, if he could only stop smoking.

He was thinking of stepping outside for a cigarette when Detective Istee knocked on his open office door.

"Got a minute?" Clayton asked.

Rodney nodded at an empty chair and tamped down his urge for a smoke. "Take a load off."

Clayton pulled a chair up to Rodney's desk. "Harjo's information on Sammy Shen and Carmella Schuster checks out. I was able to ID both as being at the casino. However, that doesn't mean El Jefe is our killer."

"Have you got anything that tells us otherwise?"

"Not yet," Clayton replied. He quickly summarized his futile attempts to unearth anything useful from Goggin and Nautzile's former work associates at the casino. "It appears that stealing the two hundred K was a one-off lark that surprised everyone. And nobody knows anything about Nautzile's soon-to-be-rich story she told her mother. I'm waiting on the New Mexico Gaming Commission to fax me their pre-employment background investigation reports on Goggin and Nautzile."

"In the hopes of?" Rodney queried.

"God only knows," Clayton answered. "Anything I may have missed."

"You've got two days before you rendezvous with Special Agent Fallon," Rodney noted.

"Put Harjo and his pals off for a couple more days."

"Why should we do that?"

"Because I don't want him pulling all the strings. If he's on the up-and-up, he'll be flexible. If not, what's the rush?"

"You don't trust him."

Clayton stood. "If I have to go in, I want to be fully prepared. If I can break this case without going, all the better."

"Understood. I'll speak to the sheriff."

"Thanks." Clayton glanced at the still mostly empty bookcase and pile of boxes stacked in a corner. He shook his head disapprovingly and cracked a grin. "You really should finish unpacking and settle in, Cap. That's if you're planning to stay here for the long haul."

Rodney repressed a smile. "I'll think about it, Detective. Thanks for the interior decorating advice."

"Anytime."

Clayton left and Rodney sat back, surprised and delighted by the brief, friendly exchange. It had been the first bit of amicable banter he'd had with anybody on his staff since day one. Maybe he was starting to make some inroads with his people. Maybe he was starting to like this guy Istee. Maybe it was time to lighten up.

He rose, cut open the shipping tape on a packing box with his pocketknife, and filled a shelf with framed family snapshots and a few of his more prestigious awards and service recognition plaques from his old job back East.

On a lower shelf he arranged his important criminal investigation and law enforcement reference books, and a stack of FBI research bulletins he frequently consulted on matters of forensic and scientific methodologies and techniques.

Pleased with himself, he stepped back and looked around. Putting stuff out did make the office look better. After he grabbed a smoke, he'd return and finish unpacking. Maybe he was here for the long haul.

———

At his desk, Clayton found an additional research report on the Kickapoo Indians Captain Rodney had asked staff to compile. He put it aside in favor of the state gaming commission background investigations on Goggin and Nautzile that had just arrived as an email attachment. Both contained customary information about the applicant's education, prior employment, credit history, criminal records check, motor vehicle reports, and personal references. Everything appeared to be in order.

What caught Clayton's eye in Lucy's dossier was a summary of an interview conducted by the investigator with Houzinnie Yuzos, a registered nurse at the Gallup Indian Medical Center. He should have remembered her. Basketball teammates in high school, best friends since childhood, Lucy and Houzinnie had been selected to the all-state team their senior year, the first Mescalero Apache girls to be so recognized. Their achievement had been written up in the area newspapers and they'd been feted during a special ceremony at a tribal council meeting, which made them instant celebrities on the rez.

If Lucy had confided in anyone about her get-rich plans it just might have been Houzinnie. Although their lives had gone in completely different directions, hopefully the two old friends had stayed in touch. He called Houzinnie's home telephone number listed in the report and got an automated message saying the number was no longer in service. He tried the medical center, asked for the human resources department, and was told the office had closed for the day. He identified himself as a police officer and asked if Yuzos was on duty, only to be told that for security reasons that information could not be released over the phone.

Clayton had moved his family from the rez to Las Cruces almost twelve years ago. It was only a two-hour drive back home and they returned to visit frequently, but with nearly four thousand tribal members living on the 463,000-acre homeland, it was impossible to know everyone. Clayton had no idea who in Houzinnie's family still lived there. Isabel, his mother, a tribal elder and former council member, just might.

He called, got her voice mail, left a message, tucked the Kickapoo report under his arm, and started for home.

———

The house was empty when Clayton arrived home. On the refrigerator was a note from Grace saying she and Hannah had left to be with Blossom, the girls, and other family members who'd assembled on the rez for the arrival of Lucy's body. They'd be gone overnight.

Clayton understood. In the critical time between the passage from one world to the next, those who are newly dead must gather tracks and revisit places and people important during their lifetime. A proper ritual was required to make sure the dead transitioned from The Shadow World to The Land of Ever Summer.

His absence would be noted. He felt a stab of guilt for not being there.

There was a voice message on the landline phone from Isabel saying she, too, would be with Blossom and the family. She added that last year Houzinnie's mother, Betty, had suffered a broken hip from a bad fall and now lived in Gallup with her daughter. She'd ask Elmer

Yuzos, Houzinnie's brother, to call Clayton with information on how to contact her.

On his own for dinner, Clayton warmed up some leftover black bean soup, threw together a salad, sat at the kitchen table, and started in on the Kickapoo report. His cell phone buzzed before he finished reading page one.

"Are you bailing out on me?" Special Agent Bernard Harjo demanded.

"What's your rush?" Clayton countered. "Is El Jefe going to vanish within the next two days?"

"That's possible."

"If you can't chill while I do my job, I'm not the right guy for you."

Harjo sighed. "Tomorrow's Friday. How about Tuesday? Will that do?"

"Yeah."

"Why the pushback?"

"You have to ask?" Clayton replied.

"I'm not trying to set you up," Harjo answered.

"That's good to hear."

"I'll have details for you on Monday."

Harjo disconnected before Clayton could reply. He put the phone down and returned to the Kickapoo report.

———

Bernard Harjo plugged his phone into the charger at the base of a table lamp and settled into one of the two off-white leather easy chairs positioned in front of the picture window of the five-star, high-rise suite. Far below, the greater Los Angeles Basin sprawled, crisscrossed with clogged freeways, residential neighborhoods chopped up by major arterial streets and ringed by strip malls, and drought-thirsty brown hills that looked ready to burst into flame. In the hazy distance, a thin ribbon of blue hinted at the ocean.

At the top of the DEA pay scale, Harjo earned a six-figure annual income augmented by a twenty-five percent special duty differential, and a generous expense account. With no dependents or ex-wives to support, he enjoyed an occasional indulgence, and today was one of those days. Especially rewarding, as it had been some time since he'd crawled out of the L.A. slums.

He glanced at Agent Danny Fallon, who was busy cracking open an expensive bottle of single-malt scotch. "Istee thinks he's bait."

"Well, isn't he?" Fallon replied. He poured two neat shots into whiskey glasses. "Ice?"

"It doesn't have to work that way," Harjo replied. "One cube, please."

Using tongs, Fallon plucked a cube out of the ice bucket, dropped it in Harjo's glass, and handed it to him. He poured himself a water chaser, eased into the adjacent empty leather chair, and raised his glass. "Here's to you."

"And to you," Harjo replied, looking out the window. "Even from up here L.A. sucks."

"Explain yourself," Fallon said.

Harjo shot him a confused look. "About L.A.?"

Fallon laughed. "No, about not playing Istee for a patsy."

Harjo smiled. "I'm still trying to work that out." He'd been Danny's rabbi ever since he graduated from the academy. Over the last five years, Fallon had become Bernard's best friend.

Fallon was tall for a Navajo, with a wide forehead, thick black hair, dark leathery skin, and deep-set eyes. He seemed to live inside himself better than anyone else on the planet Harjo had ever met, other than maybe an ancient Tibetan monk or two.

Watching Harjo sip his scotch, Fallon stayed silent. He knew Harjo's target wasn't Sammy Shen, at least not this time. It was Juan Jose Garza's uncle, the corrupt police commander and narco-trafficker in Piedras Negras. His name was Luis Lopez Lorenz, and he'd hired El Jefe to kill James Goggin and Lucy Nautzile. Not because they'd stolen Carmella Schuster's gambling money from the Apache casino. But because they'd found and taken a million dollars of Lorenz's money.

Over a period of several weeks, Lorenz had moved several truck-loads of his drug profits to an abandoned ranch house outside of Eagle Pass. With no close neighbors and facing a straight stretch of pavement, it was off a rural, seldom-traveled road. No overhead power lines crossed the highway, there were no bends or curves, no brush or trees bordering close to the shoulders, and only the slightest rise in elevation. A perfect landing strip for a Pilatus PC-24. With great range and speed, it was perfect for rugged takeoffs and landings.

The money had been guarded day and night until the plane arrived. In a hurry to get it loaded and airborne quickly, one cash bundle of a million dollars had been inadvertently left behind by Lorenz's men. At least that's what Luis had been told after-the-fact. It hadn't been missed until the middleman in Houston, an international commodity broker, called the following day to report the shortage to Sammy Shen. By then it was gone. But a remote battery-operated CCTV system Lorenz had installed caught Goggin and Nautzile exploring the old ranch house, finding the money, loading it in their vehicle, and driving away. The license plate on the SUV had been enough to ID them.

After the men who'd botched the shipment had been brutally murdered in a safe house and disposed of, the ranch house was burned to the ground. Only then did Lorenz hire El Jefe to find and kill Goggin and Nautzile. He agreed to pay an extra bonus to have them scalped north of the border so that everyone in Piedras Negras and the state of Coahuila knew never to take anything that belonged to him upon penalty of death.

However, one of the gang members Lorenz had killed for screwing up the money shipment had been Mark Villalobos, a young DEA undercover agent who'd infiltrated the cartel. He was also Harjo's nephew, his sister's oldest son.

"If Istee doesn't cooperate, I may go with you," Harjo said, studying the remaining scotch in his glass. He stood to get another drink. "Shit, I am going with you."

Fallon held his tongue as Harjo refreshed his scotch and laid out the plan.

———

Clayton's phone rang. He had finished reading that the Mexican government in the nineteenth century had given the Kickapoos a remote reservation in the state of Coahuila.

Clayton answered.

"You need to talk to my sister?" Elmer Yuzos asked.

"I do," Clayton replied. "But while I've got you on the phone, did you recently see or talk to Blossom Magoosh's daughter?"

"No, but I heard she was seen driving around the Old Ladies Village with her boyfriend."

The Old Ladies Village, a century-old failed attempt by the government to separate the generations, now housed extended families, but the label persisted. "When was that?" Clayton asked.

"Just before she got finished," Elmer responded flatly. He gave Clayton Houzinnie's phone number and hung up.

Houzinnie answered Clayton's call on the second ring.

"Elmer said you needed to talk to me," she said.

"I do," Clayton replied. "Was Blossom's daughter in touch with you recently?"

"All the time. I think I was her only friend. She'd call from Eagle Pass where they were living. I don't think she was that happy there with James."

"When was the last time?"

"Two days before she got finished. She knew I'd moved my mother here to live with me and she wanted to know if I'd rented her house. I told her no, there were too many things wrong with it that had to be fixed first, and I didn't have the money."

"Did she want to rent it?"

"I think so, but she didn't say."

"What did she say?"

"That she was homesick and wanted to have her girls with her again. Since no charges had been brought against her for stealing the money from the casino, she wondered if she could return and start over again."

"With Goggin?"

"She didn't say, but I assumed so."

"What did you think of the idea?" Clayton asked.

Houzinnie paused. "Ever since we were little girls, she always thought she could fix things, no matter how bad she messed up. By the time we graduated from high school, basketball was the only thing we had in common."

"Did she mention anything about money?"

"No. Except she did say something about making things right with the casino."

"Thanks," Clayton said. "I may need to talk to you again."

"Anytime," Houzinnie said. "Call my cell phone. That's the best way to reach me."

She gave him the number.

Clayton thanked her again, disconnected, and reached again for the Kickapoo report. He'd only just read that in the middle to late twentieth century some tribal members had lived under the international bridge separating Piedras Negras from Eagle Pass. They were mostly migrant workers living in squalor, dependent on wages earned on North American farms for their subsistence. There had been no Eagle Pass reservation with a Kickapoo casino back then. And when offered the chance to become U.S. citizens, not all of them took the federal government's offer. Many chose dual citizenship, some turned it down flatly.

Clayton found their independent spirit admirable. It was akin to the Apache way of keeping their traditions and culture separate from the world of the White Eyes.

When he had the time, he promised himself to learn more about the Kickapoos, which meant in their language something akin to those "who move about." They seemed to be much like the Apaches of old who'd ranged from the Rocky Mountains to the Great Plains and deep into the interior of Mexico.

He left the report on the desk and readied for bed. It was much too quiet in the house. Wendell's lively presence was now mostly gone for good, only occasionally rekindled when he came home on his short visits from medical school. And when Hannah finished college and left, taking her beautiful, fierce warrior spirit into the world, what would he and Grace do?

The bed was never warm enough without Grace in it, and he missed her. He fell asleep still feeling guilty for not being with her and Hannah to lend his support to Blossom Magoosh and the girls.

CHAPTER 5

Maria Guadalupe Sedillo, resident DEA agent in Eagle Pass, always enjoyed the forty-mile drive to Carizzo Springs in neighboring Dimmit County in spite of the flat, dusty ranchland that bordered both sides of the highway. Although she missed the mountains of West Texas, the quiet drive through the rural landscape was a nice break from her routine.

Before Eagle Pass, she'd worked quite happily at the El Paso DEA Division until her career took a nosedive. All because she'd volunteered at her church to help provide food, clothing, and shelter to the growing numbers of Central American women and their young children seeking asylum. Illegal immigrants, they'd been processed and dumped on the streets by the Border Patrol when all the temporary area holding facilities had reached capacity.

Agents in the office who heard about her volunteer work began calling her Sister Mary. But it was no joke. Soon, the more macho men began openly saying she was more social worker than cop. Not a good thing for the tough-on-drugs image the DEA wanted their special

agents to project to the public. After a local TV news program broad-
cast a segment about her charity work with illegals, she began receiving
supposedly friendly backchannel advice from district superiors to find
a less politically charged charitable cause.

Sedillo didn't take their advice. It was both a matter of faith and
a way to honor the memory of her mother, Arella, who'd died of
heart failure on the floor of a tool manufacturing shipping department,
working at minimum wage—at one of her three jobs.

As a young teenager from a small fishing village close to the Honduras border, Arella had been raped by a local police officer who threatened to kill her family if she said anything. The second time he raped
her, she ran away. Alone, pregnant, on foot, and with little money,
seeking help where she could find it, she walked over sixteen hundred
miles to Juárez, and crossed the Rio Grande into El Paso seeking asylum. It was granted. She was one of the lucky ones.

Sedillo marveled at her mother's bravery to make that perilous
journey at such a young age, to live among strangers in a new country,
forever apart from her family. She was proud of her mother's persistence to learn a new language and make a home for the two of them
on very little money.

Arella had died young, never to see her daughter graduate from
high school or receive her college diploma with honors. Sedillo never
stopped missing her.

Six months after her first unofficial warning, Sedillo was abruptly
transferred to Eagle Pass. That settled the bureaucratic dilemma of
what to do with a devoted churchgoing Latina special agent who had
a sterling performance record but refused to take a hint.

Because the transfer came with a small raise and a ten percent special duty pay differential, they called it a promotion. Most of the salary bump got eaten by a subsequent increase in her monthly employee
pension contribution. Whoopee.

In Eagle Pass she had little time for anything but work. Her predecessor, marking time until retirement, had watched from the sidelines as drug money and narco-trafficking poured in unchecked. Starting out, Sedillo had spent most of her energies getting to know her small staff, including intelligence research specialists, diversion investigators, a forensics team, and office personnel. Working with area immigration and customs personnel, she slowly built up a small network of supposedly reliable informants across the border, only to have them provide basically old or useless information.

As she approached the town of Carrizo Springs, the appearance of palm trees swaying in the wind rose up. There were rows of them in Piedras Negras as well, marching along the thoroughfares. But even after a year, the palm trees felt out of place to Sedillo. So did she.

Eagle Pass was a forlorn town in spite of the flashy neon signs along the roadways, the constant traffic to and from Mexico, and the recent spurt of franchise hotels along the main highway corridor. Harsh and unfinished, the dismal downtown lacked a true core. Recent growth had been kick-started by the success of the nearby Kickapoo tribal casino. It had become the area's major attraction, pulling in visitors from San Antonio and surrounding towns in a two-hundred-mile radius.

The 125-acre Kickapoo Reservation on the banks of the Rio Grande outside of town gleamed in stark contrast to the mishmash surrounding it. Anchored by the six-story casino and hotel, the reservation had dozens of modern new homes, a health center, a community center, and a tribal government building. Paved roads, new infrastructure, and a modern water system were already in place for continued planned growth. Since the reservation's creation in the 1980s, the population had doubled, most of the growth coming from the Kansas and Oklahoma Kickapoo Tribes. The community was thriving.

Sedillo turned her attention to the task at hand as she drove the dismal main drag of Carrizo Springs—another small town with a hard edge—and parked behind the Oasis Surf and Turf Restaurant. It was a low-slung, stick-built watering hole painted bright red that served more hard liquor and beer than beef and fish.

With the recent expansion of immigration detention facilities in town and the subsequent creation of jobs, business was booming at all the local watering holes.

Ten minutes early, she sat back with the AC on and waited for Juan Garza, her CI, to arrive. If all went as planned over the next week, he would be her ticket out of purgatory.

But it would have to be an express ticket. A recent onset of blinding headaches had forced her to see a Houston neurologist. After tests and consultations with other specialists, the prognosis wasn't good. She had an inoperable brain tumor, stage four. On the outside, with treatment, she had maybe a year to live. Without it, half of that.

Sedillo had yet to decide what to do. Quit the job and take the treatment option? Work while her quality of life was still reasonably good? What would an extra six months give her? Happiness? Love? New friends?

Doubtful.

There was nobody to hold her hand. Nobody to lean on. Doing the job well was all she had left, and she was tilting in that direction. So far, no one at DEA knew. If they did, she'd be yanked. Much as the idea of getting out of Eagle Pass appealed to her, that wasn't the way she wanted it to happen. She wanted to go out with a win.

Her CI, Juan Garza, the nephew of Luis Lopes Lorenz, drug lord of Piedras Negras, had been busted by an Eagle Pass undercover officer working with Sedillo. The threat of felony charges for possession of a controlled substance with intent to sell or distribute was enough to encourage him to become a cooperating individual—the polite term for a snitch.

To avoid time in a Texas prison, never a pleasant prospect, Juan was willing to pass on whatever tidbits he learned about his uncle's drug-trafficking operations.

Because of his family ties to Lorenz and her suspicions of his possible motives to cooperate, Maria had dug deeply into Juan's past and personal history before going operational.

His parents, Gilberto and Carmen Garza, were apparently devout Catholics who donated generously to church charities. They dined annually with the local archbishop and were good friends with their parish priest. Gilberto, a member of the Knights of Columbus, owned a popular indoor mercado in an old converted Piedras Negras warehouse, and rented out retail space to farmers, food vendors, craftsmen, and artists. He also operated the largest and most profitable grocery store in the city and was part owner of a twenty-four-hour stop-and-rob convenience store in Eagle Pass.

All three of the Garza children, Lourdes, Hector, and Juan—the youngest—had been born in Texas. Lourdes was a professor of Latin American studies at a midwestern college. Hector, an executive chef and partner in a four-star restaurant, lived in San Francisco. Only Juan, age thirty-two, had stayed in Piedras Negras.

He'd flunked out of the University of Texas in Austin after a drug-fueled freshman year. When sober, off drugs, and cleaned up, he worked for his father, mostly as a handyman. However, more often than not he was stoned, high, or drunk. Whenever Maria met with Juan he was—at least—always slightly buzzed.

Every intelligence report from federal agencies and the Mexican authorities confirmed that Gilberto and his younger half-brother Luis had been estranged for many years. Dozens of personal affidavits from prominent citizens, established business owners, government officials, and civic leaders on both sides of the Rio Grande testified to Gilberto's moral and law-abiding ways, and his long-standing, irreconcilable falling-out with Luis. Years of satellite surveillance and sporadic undercover operations in Piedras Negras showed no contact between the brothers or their immediate family members.

With the exception of Juan, the black sheep of the family. He could always count on a handout from his uncle, crash at one of the cartel safe houses, or get a free meal at one of the many Piedras Negras eateries that paid monthly protection to Lorenz's henchmen to stay in business. Some said Lorenz, who had never married or had children, favored Juan as a surrogate son.

Dismissed as a worthless leech by cartel underlings, as well as by the cops—corrupt or otherwise—on both sides of the river, Juan had become Sedillo's best source of information regarding Lorenz's operation.

Through him, she'd learned that Lorenz had recently sent a large shipment of money to Houston to be laundered and afterward had executed four of his men who'd handled the assignment. Juan didn't know why the men had been killed, just that something had gone wrong.

He'd also reported that Sammy Shen had recently met with Lorenz at a Chinese restaurant in Piedras Negras owned by Shen's family. The two men had then traveled together to the Kickapoo village, followed by four of Lorenz's assassins in a black SUV. There was some talk among his henchmen that a pact was to be made with the Kickapoos, but nobody knew what it was about.

At the Houston DEA Division, that information had caused some excitement. Intel had confirmed reports that the Mexican Kickapoos were in discussions with the Coahuila government to establish a new reservation close to the Rio Grande. Rumors were that it would either be located near the old abandoned Kickapoo campgrounds that had existed under the international bridge for years, or directly opposite the Eagle Pass, Texas, reservation.

Based on Sammy Shen's involvement, DEA analysts figured it could be a first move to get a casino up and running in Piedras Negras. Why

Shen and Lorenz thought they needed to hire El Jefe to move the plan along was anyone's guess. Exactly who needed to be assassinated? The top-level Coahuila officials were petitioning the Mexican federal government to permit casino gaming along the border states. Who might be standing in the way?

Sedillo lowered the sun visor and checked her lipstick in the vanity mirror. She had a long jawline and square chin. Plain-looking described her best, especially given her stocky frame, inherited from the Zapotec ancestors of the man who had raped her mother. Men weren't drawn to her like moths to a flame.

She chuckled at the ridiculous thought of being anything but herself as Juan Garza ground his truck to a stop next to her vehicle. A woman didn't need allure or feminine charm to be dangerous, and Sedillo was feeling less constrained to go by the DEA playbook. The shock of her impending mortality felt somehow liberating.

Juan got in her car. His sleepy-looking eyes were bloodshot and he smelled of marijuana. The remnants of his good looks had gone to seed long before Maria had met him. Ten-year-old photographs in his dossier showed a once-handsome young man with an infectious smile. Drugs aged a person fast.

"You buying me lunch?" Juan asked half jokingly, nodding in the direction of the closed restaurant's back door. He was always looking for a handout or money.

Sedillo shook her head. "That's not happening. Tell me what you've got."

Juan leaned back. "Okay. In three days we meet Jose Hernandez in the Kickapoo village. He says only three people can come with me, otherwise he won't do it. Bring ten thousand dollars."

"What for?"

"Hernandez is our guide to El Jefe. Twenty-five hundred is his fee per person."

"How long will it take us to reach El Jefe's location?"

Juan shrugged. "I don't know, but there aren't any accommodations en route. He says there will be some rough going, and there's no guarantee El Jefe will be there. He comes and goes."

"Where do we meet you?" Sedillo asked.

"I'll let you know the day before. Colonia de los Kickapoo isn't like the rest of Mexico or like any other Indian reservation anywhere. Figure you'll be entering a foreign country that you know nothing about."

Juan grinned and reached for the door latch. "This is gonna be an expedition, so come prepared."

Sedillo nodded. "This better work. Don't fuck with me, Juan."

Her language made him pause. His grin faded. "Not happening," he replied.

———

American by birth but purely Mexican in his heart, Juan Garza always smiled at the sight of the huge Mexican flag atop the towering staff sitting prominently on the Piedras Negras riverbank across the Rio Grande—the Rio Bravo to true Mexicans. It was impossible to miss the national coat of arms: a golden eagle perched on a prickly pear cactus gripping a snake in its beak and talons. A signal that Mexico was far different from the United States.

Juan thought a Jolly Roger should be run up under it to warn all ill-informed tourists that they entered at their own peril. Mexico was a very foreign and dangerous place. Always was, always would be.

He drove across the bridge remembering the days of his childhood. There had been no tall black border fence that cut through the heart of Eagle Pass. The narrow streets of Piedras Negras had been dirty, and the brightly painted businesses in the core of town had masked badly needed repairs. But back in the day, citizens had filled the streets after hours and at nighttime for conversation, music, and companionship.

No more. Vendors still hawked their goods to day-tripping Americans in town to shop, fill their prescriptions at the cut-rate drugstores, or have extensive dental work done at bargain prices. But after dusk when the tourists were gone, the vendors went home to their houses, protected by security fences and window bars. Like everyone else, they stayed put for the night.

In Piedras Negras, the rich and the poor spent what was necessary to keep the criminals, addicts, and gang members out of their homes and on the streets. Border agents staffed a checkpoint in the middle of the international footbridge where once people freely passed back and forth. Over one hundred sixty thousand people lived in Piedras Negras, the city spreading out east, west, and south. There were wide boulevards, modern manufacturing facilities, contemporary office buildings, new schools, parks, and residential subdivisions. An attractive esplanade along the riverbank served as a viewing station where the curious could watch the newest group of immigrants attempting to swim to Texas, only to be pulled from the water by the Border Patrol and returned to Mexico.

Those who couldn't swim and had enough money huddled under the bridge waiting for traffickers to smuggle them across where the wall ended.

The sounds of the city had also changed. The constant roar of commercial eighteen-wheel traffic, the aircraft flying to and from the airport, the wailing sirens of emergency vehicles on both sides of the river, the clatter of the trains crossing the railroad bridge above the river, the sporadic semiautomatic gunfire, all served to shatter any illusion of a sleepy Mexican town.

That image had died some years ago after a massive prison break resulted in six months of armed clashes between civilians and the military. The federal government finally stepped in and supposedly cleaned everything up, especially the police department. Not surprisingly, the comandante, Uncle Luis, wasn't touched.

So much change that changed nothing, Juan thought sarcastically as he pulled to a stop in front of the safe house where he'd been staying for the past month. In a neighborhood that had become a failed public works project to provide affordable housing, it was indistinguishable from the rows of two-story block buildings on small lots up and down both sides of the street. Secured by fences, security gates, and window barriers, different only in cost, height, and design. Like the city, it was a barrio under siege.

Underneath the fresh face of the city nothing was truly different. Along the border you could still easily bribe a cop, buy drugs or a woman cheap, get randomly robbed, mysteriously disappear, or be slaughtered at a nightclub during a spontaneous gunfight by rival gangs. Drugs flowed north, money and weapons flowed south, hundreds of millions got laundered courtesy of American corporations, and crime flourished. All was in equilibrium.

The two men in the front room of the safe house looked up from the television and nodded as Juan waved and went downstairs to the basement. He entered a tunnel behind a corner door, hit the light switch, and started walking. High enough for a man over six feet tall to pass without butting his head, the tunnel had been carved out years ago by mine workers when it became clear the Americans were using satellites to spy on Uncle Luis, trying to penetrate his drug-trafficking enterprises. It was one of two that had been built leading to a secret meeting room under a long-established Chinese restaurant on a nearby main street owned by Sammy Shen's family.

When the tunnels were completed, the miners who had built them disappeared.

The tunnels ran for three blocks under buildings, sidewalks, and streets to the secret room. There, conversations were guaranteed to be private. But to be sure, sweeps for listening devices were conducted before every meeting.

The dark tunnel walls, cut through thin veins of coal, absorbed the overhead glare of the electric lights. In English, Piedras Negras means "black stones." So named because of its rude beginning as a center for coal mining, the city commemorated its past with a seal of an eagle, wings spread, on top of a coal pile.

Or was it a shit heap with an eagle on top? Amused by the notion, Juan pushed open the door to the basement of Shen's Famous Chinese Restaurant. It was a comfortable room, with six leather easy chairs arranged in a circle with a large round coffee table in the middle. A well-stocked wet bar filled one wall and a small bathroom was opposite the stairs to the dining rooms and kitchen above.

Sammy Shen and Uncle Luis were sitting in two of the leather easy chairs. Sammy's father, Longwei, stood in front of a large wall-mounted split-screen CCTV monitor watching as the last of the luncheon customers lingered at their tables and the kitchen staff finished the cleanup and began the dinner prep.

A man with a mop of unruly hair, his head lowered, entered through the restaurant's front door.

Longwei turned away from the screen and sat with Sammy and Luis. "He's here."

Juan settled into one of the remaining chairs.

"What did you learn?" Luis asked.

"Shouldn't we wait?" Juan replied.

Lorenz glared at him.

"Either Agent Sedillo knows nothing or she's smarter than I thought," Juan began.

"She's dying of a stage four brain tumor," Sammy said.

Juan shrugged. He'd long stopped marveling at Sammy's sources of information. "Okay, so she's dying. She still didn't tell me anything new."

He switched his attention back to Uncle Luis. "She asked nothing about the DEA agent you had killed. I think she doesn't know about it. All I do know is that three cops are coming here to track down El Jefe for the Las Cruces killings. I'm just the local contact to introduce them to their Kickapoo guide. The plan and the schedule haven't changed."

"But are they coming to kill or capture me?" El Jefe asked from the bottom of the basement stairs. Thick through the chest, with a wide nose under a broad forehead and wildly tangled hair, Estavio Trevino—El Jefe—joined the group. "Perhaps I'm not the only target."

Lorenz laughed. "In our business, distrust is a virtue. But we have no evidence to suggest otherwise."

"If El Jefe is right, we should wipe them out before they can do anything to anybody," Juan suggested.

Lorenz shook his head in displeasure. "Brilliant." All his people, including Juan, were trigger-happy murderers of one sort or another. And although he liked it that way, at times controlling his attack dogs tried his patience.

"That would surely not go unnoticed in Washington," he added. "Such stupidity would make doing business much more difficult for us. We are scrutinized more closely now than ever before because of all the asylum-seekers crowding the border."

Juan shrugged again. Sometimes Uncle Luis sucked all the fun out of life.

Lorenz turned to Trevino. "Every contact we have within DEA tells us this is solely an extraction operation. Juan takes them to their Kickapoo guide, who in turn leads them to you. The capture of El Jefe, the notorious Mexican assassin, will make heroes of them all and bring much praise to the Washington administration."

Sammy looked at Lorenz. "Has there been any talk at DEA about Villalobos, the undercover agent you had killed?"

Lorenz shook his head. "Nothing."

"That troubles me," Longwei said. "Surely there should be a price on your head."

"Which again raises the possibility that they have multiple targets," Sammy speculated. "All of us in this room, perhaps."

"Kill them when they cross," Juan proposed again.

"Expeditious," Trevino replied, "and not without merit, but as your uncle suggested, stupid nonetheless."

"Propose an alternative," Longwei prompted.

"If we knew their identities it would be easier to sort out their motives, other than simply capturing me," Trevino said. "What if we take them prisoner and demand ransoms of five million dollars each? The same amount the DEA pays for the capture of a cartel drug lord."

"Bold," Longwei replied, impressed.

"Their people would come at us hard and fast," Lorenz conjectured. "I am sorry to have brought this upon us. But all must know they cannot steal what is mine."

"I wanted Goggin and Nautzile dead as much as you did," Sammy said.

"Swindlers and thieves," Longwei pronounced.

"I was paid generously by you for a specific service," Trevino replied to Lorenz. He paused and looked at each man. "I will dispose of this threat myself."

"If you kill them here in Mexico while they hunt for you, it won't solve anything," Juan noted. "At the river or in the country, it would be all the same."

Lorenz cocked an eyebrow at his nephew. "Sometimes I still have great hopes for you."

Juan suppressed a smile.

Sammy leaned forward. "It's a good point. I say we lead them into a trap as El Jefe suggests and demand a ransom for each."

"The woman Sedillo as well?" Juan asked.

Sammy nodded. "Why not?"

Juan glanced at Estavio Trevino. "I told Sedillo I would be coming along."

Trevino's eyes narrowed. "Only to the colonia. If I allowed you into the Bolsón, you wouldn't return."

Trevino survived untouched because he had never been found in the vast forbidding Bolsón de Mapimí that stretched over parts of four Mexican states, where he allegedly lived in a remote, fortress-like hacienda. Those who tried had died.

Juan swallowed hard, clamped his jaw tight, and looked away.

Lorenz stared hard at Trevino, who met his look unflinchingly. "I'm still waiting for you to recover my money. A million dollars isn't petty cash."

"I agreed only to try," Trevino snapped. "I have someone looking for it."

"That's not good enough."

"It will have to do."

Longwei held up a hand to stop any further contentiousness. "For many years our families and our friends have prospered because we've cooperated and been smart. Let us not be petty."

Lorenz nodded glumly. "Yes, of course you're right."

Trevino shrugged in agreement. "As you wish."

"Good," Longwei said. "As for the Americans, perhaps we should do nothing. Let them come, look, and leave empty-handed."

"They are coming for me," Trevino emphasized. "If I have to kill them, I will."

"Completely understandable," Longwei granted. Lorenz and Sammy nodded their concurrence.

"I must leave." Trevino rose and looked at Juan. "Bring them to the village as agreed. I will take over from there."

"Jose Hernandez has been promised a fee to guide them to you," Juan protested.

"He knows better than to do that. As quickly as possible, I must learn who these men are and what they truly want to accomplish. At the village, you will introduce me as Vicente Ruiz. The money is Jose's to keep."

"Will you release them if the ransoms get paid?" Sammy asked.

For the first time during the meeting, Trevino smiled. "I will send you their scalps as gifts. The ransom money will be mine."

"Planning to retire?" Lorenz inquired, eyebrow raised. Twenty million would be a sizable amount even for Estavio. Perhaps his biggest payday ever. He wondered if Trevino had recovered his stolen million dollars and decided to keep it. Not an unreasonable possibility.

"Something like that." With a goodbye nod, Trevino departed.

Sammy waited for the click of the electronic latch that secured the basement door. "I'll find out who the DEA is sending to visit us," he said.

"You'll let Trevino know?" Lorenz inquired.

"Of course. He would be displeased otherwise."

"Should Don Gilberto be informed?" Longwei asked Lorenz.

Lorenz shook his head. "My brother needn't be bothered."

CHAPTER 6

The official street address of the Eagle Pass DEA offices listed it on U.S. Highway 277, which is actually Main Street, just outside of town. It was housed in a compound of newer buildings, nicely land-scaped on the street side but unmarked except for the numbers. The average motorist passed by without realizing its importance in the bor-derland war on drugs.

Behind it, the local campus of a junior college—a grouping of slightly more than a half dozen buildings—drew most of the attention and traffic. Virtually next door on the same side of the street stood a national-franchise chain hotel, convenient for the visiting bosses from the Houston Division and DEA personnel in town on temporary assignment.

Born and raised in Eagle Pass, Wanda Cantu, assistant to the admin-istrator, had been with the department long before the office had moved into the new facility. She'd been hired right out of junior college to help expand drug abuse prevention services to schools in the surrounding area. It had served as a stepping-stone to her current position.

The job had been a perfect fit, allowing her to look after her retired, aging parents, Rodolfo and Yolanda Cantu, who owned a small ranch-style house in an older neighborhood of town near the Rio Grande.

By circumstance, the responsibility of caring for her parents had fallen to Wanda. A social worker had told her that almost always it was a daughter who became the caretaker because women were more nurturing. For Wanda, it had been taxing, exhausting, and not in the least bit rewarding. But there was nobody else to do it. All her parents' relatives lived in Monterrey, Mexico. Her older brother worked on an oil platform in the Gulf of Mexico and returned home rarely. Her sister, younger by a year, was married to a career Army sergeant and living with her family on a military post in Germany.

Wanda made do, traveling daily from her apartment where she lived with her three cats to her parents' home to check on their welfare and fix them a meal. But when a major storm dumped over sixteen inches of rain in less than twenty-four hours, the river and nearby creeks overflowed, flooding out Rodolfo and Yolanda.

With no insurance, Wanda was forced to move them in with her. She took out a large bank loan to pay for the necessary home repairs required before the city would approve reoccupancy.

Halfway through the renovation, Wanda's mother, Yolanda, had a stroke that left her permanently wheelchair-bound. Wanda hired a part-time aide to look after both her parents while she was at work, which put a strain on her financially. A week before they were scheduled to move back in the house, Rodolfo fell, broke his hip, and suffered a severe concussion, leaving Wanda with a major crisis to manage.

After many tests and consultations, the clinic doctors told Wanda that both parents could no longer live independently. They strongly advised nursing home care.

All the area assisted living facilities were at capacity, and Wanda's parents had assets that disqualified them from government programs.

She had burned up all her leave time trying to find an alternative, when one of the clinic doctors suggested applying for help through a new foundation funded by an anonymous donor. Within a week, her written request for financial assistance was approved, legal papers were signed, and Rodolfo and Yolanda were moved into a nice San Antonio assisted living facility, a hundred and forty miles away, that cost thousands of dollars a month. It had been a true miracle.

Six weeks later Wanda met the anonymous donor and discovered that some miracles came with strings attached. If she failed to act as Sammy Shen's agent on matters of importance to him, he'd expose her to the DEA as a paid informant. Sammy Shen owned her.

Wanda returned to her childhood home after her parents died with her cats and an occasional live-in boyfriend who came and went as he pleased. It was a short walk to the Catholic church where she'd been confirmed and had worshipped all her life, an easy drive to work, and not far from the casino where she sometimes liked to go with girlfriends to play the slots.

Wanda was content with her life and her job. Only Sammy's rare phone calls jolted her back to reality. Because her position with the department required a security clearance, each of his requests for information was a smack in the face, reminding her of her disloyalty, her treachery. Each time she did as he asked, the fear of discovery overwhelmed her, made her tremble.

On a cool Saturday evening, Wanda was in the backyard pruning some shrubs that bordered the rear lot line when the new cell phone Sammy had sent to her by courier rang. She hesitated, thinking to let it go to voice mail, but decided not to. She hurried inside, stripped off her gardening gloves, and answered.

"You have three important people arriving from out of town early next week," Sammy said without preamble. "Who are they?"

"I don't have that information."

"Don't be difficult, Wanda."

"I really don't know."

"What do you know?"

"The resident agent is handling everything personally."

"I want their names, when they're due to arrive, and where they'll be staying, tonight."

Wanda almost choked with fear. "Tonight?"

"Yes. I'll call you back in an hour."

The connection went dead.

Stunned, Wanda sank down on the living room couch. Sammy had never asked her to take such a big risk before. Her electronic key card would log her in and out of the building after hours. If asked, what valid reason could she give for going into the office on a weekend night?

She ran a list of possible reasons through her mind and decided that searching for her misplaced checkbook would do. That was it. She'd sat down at home to pay some bills, looked high and low, and couldn't find it. Perhaps she'd left it in her desk, so she'd decided to go and look. Surely that would be seen as innocent and reasonable behavior by anyone who asked.

She grabbed her purse, locked the house, and made the short drive to the office. In the secure parking lot, she took a deep breath and walked quickly to the employee entrance, looking straight ahead so that there would be no mistaking her identity on the CCTV. Everything she did had to appear normal.

The building was empty. She passed by the communication room, the small, secure armory, the conference room, and accessed the administrative suite that housed the offices of the resident agent and the administrator. Wanda's small, windowless office in a corner of the suite was tucked next to a walk-in supply closet. With her door open she could sit at her desk and see everybody who entered and left the reception area. That was the way she liked it, so as not to feel too claustrophobic.

There were no surveillance cameras in the administrative area, but still Wanda hesitated before deciding to leave her office door open. *Everything normal,* she reminded herself.

She settled behind her desk, powered up the desktop computer, entered her high-security passcode, which gave her clearance for all current and pending operations, and within minutes had the information Sammy Shen wanted. Rather than print it out, she wrote it down and slipped the paper into her purse.

Terrified that the hour had run out, Wanda checked the time on the cell phone. She was under the deadline and would be back home before Sammy's next call. She took another deep breath, shut down the computer, killed the lights to the suite, locked up, and left.

She never, never wanted to do anything for Sammy Shen again. But how could she stop?

———

Wanda drove home mulling ideas of how to break Sammy's grip on her. She was qualified for administrative and support jobs at her GS rating or higher in other federal agencies. If she left DEA and moved out of law enforcement entirely, he'd have no more use for her. Even if she had to relocate to San Antonio or another town to take the job, it would be worth it. She'd rent out the house and make a little additional income on the side. Move back when she could take her retirement.

She arrived home calmed by her scheme, determined to get started on it right away. She unlocked the door and flipped on the light switch. Special Agent Maria Sedillo stared at her from the easy chair that faced the front window. One of the cats, Honey, was in her lap, purring.

Wanda's knees started to buckle.

"Sit down, Wanda," Sedillo ordered, nodding at the couch. "Before you fall and hurt yourself."

She stumbled to the couch and sank down like a leaden lump. "How?" she asked, her voice strangled.

"We'll get to that later. When Sammy Shen calls, you'll tell him exactly what you learned. If he wants more information, you'll agree to provide it. Understood?"

Dumbstruck, Wanda nodded and waited for Agent Sedillo to say more. Instead, she sat silently, petting Honey, a preoccupied, detached look about her.

The ringtone to the cell phone made Wanda jump. She retrieved the paper from her purse and answered nervously.

"What have you got?" Shen asked.

"The men are Special Agent Bernard Harjo, Special Agent Danny Fallon, and Doña Ana Sheriff's Detective Clayton Istee. Agent Fallon is assigned to the Vancouver Consulate General's Office, Agent Harjo is on special assignment in Los Angeles, and Detective Istee is stationed in Las Cruces, New Mexico. They arrive in two days and are booked into the hotel adjacent to the office. The resident agent will accompany them."

"Well done, Wanda," Sammy replied, his tone softening. "Find out when they plan to cross into Piedras Negras and if they've asked the Mexican federal police to meet and accompany them."

"I'll do my best."

"Of course you will. Remember, destroy the phone immediately. You'll get a new one delivered tomorrow."

The disconnect icon flashed. Wanda dropped the phone on the cushion.

Special Agent Sedillo stared intently at Wanda. "Tell me exactly what he said."

"He wants to know when they plan to enter Mexico and if the

Mexican Feds will be assisting. I'm to destroy the phone right now. A new one will come tomorrow. That's always the way we do it."

Not wanting to disturb the cat on her lap, Sedillo held out her hand.

Wanda brought her the phone and retreated to the couch. "How did you find out about me?"

"You queried one of my Houston neurologists, allegedly on my behalf, requesting a copy of my test results be sent to the office. They complied, but only after calling me to confirm that the request was legitimate, as I'd asked of all my doctors. I went along with it to see what you would do. Did Shen put you up to it?"

Wanda nodded. "I've been giving him your schedule when he asks for it. He wanted to know why you were taking annual leave to go to Houston."

"How did you know it was for medical reasons?"

"Several of the doctors' offices called to change appointment times. I took the messages for you."

"So you did." Maria smiled. "Who have you told about my brain tumor?"

"Only Sammy Shen."

"Keep it that way. Tell me, how did Shen recruit you?"

Wanda explained it all: her crippled mother, her father's bad fall and concussion, and the expensive nursing home bills paid by an anonymous donor who turned out to be Sammy Shen.

"How sad that you got sucked in," Maria said sympathetically.

"What's going to happen to me?"

"For now, we'll play it as if nothing is different," Sedillo answered. "But understand this: You've been flipped. Everything you do for Sammy will be under my direct supervision."

"Yes, yes, of course." Relieved, Wanda smiled weakly. "I'm so sorry about your condition."

Sedillo's laugh was harsh and short. She stood, brushed cat hair off her slacks, and put the cell phone in a pocket. "Don't be. I'd rather be dead than be you."

The words hit Wanda like a body blow. She didn't stand up until the sound of Sedillo's car faded away. All three cats were at her feet, calling to be fed. She'd forgotten their dinner.

In the kitchen, she prepared an expensive meal of the cat food she bought online by the case for special occasions. They were chattering with delight as she put the dishes on the floor. Milling around, they swatted at each other, growling as they went for the food.

She stepped around them, went to the small desk in the living room, opened her laptop, and started typing out her confession, trying hard not to forget anything. It had to be complete. She began with what had happened to her parents and how Sammy Shen had recruited her. After several attempts to justify her dishonorable behavior, she deleted the passage. It read like a sob story. She deserved no sympathy. Instead she concentrated on facts, listing everything she'd done for Sammy, adding the dates as she recalled them, approximations when she couldn't.

She read it through several times, corrected typos, added bits of information, formatted the text. Finished, all that was needed was her apology. She worded it carefully, taking full responsibility, avoiding any rationalizations.

She closed the file, wrote two short email notes to her sister in Germany and her brother on the Gulf oil platform, and clicked send. She returned to the confession. The apology would never be enough, but there was no more to say. She sent it to Agent Sedillo's official email, closed the laptop, opened the desk drawer, and picked up her father's old Smith & Wesson .38 Special.

She'd read somewhere that it didn't really hurt if you did it the right way. She stuck the barrel in her mouth and pulled the trigger.

———

In the office on her computer, Resident Agent Sedillo finished a quick intelligence report of her conversation with Wanda Cantu, leaving out only the particulars pertaining to her medical condition. She was about to shut down the desktop and go home when notification of a new message from Wanda popped up. She opened the file and read it quickly.

"Oh, shit," she snapped, heading for the door.

CHAPTER 7

Without anything other than a shadowy Mexican assassin as a suspect, Detective Clayton Istee returned his focus to the victims. Something they did got them killed. What was it? He needed somebody Goggin and Lucy had known to help him kick-start the investigation. But who?

He worked every avenue, talking to everyone he could locate who had known or worked with the victims. He contacted Lucy's old high school classmates and teachers still living on the rez. Reached out by phone to Goggin's out-of-state relatives and Lucy's ex-friends who'd moved away. Talked to her former basketball coach. Followed up with every personal reference they'd provided on their gaming commission employment applications.

Using the gaming commission database, he identified six individuals currently employed at other casinos around the state who'd worked with Goggin and Nautzile. He did a twenty-four-hour road trip to personally interview every one of them. He finished up—zero for six—at the new, modernistic casino and resort that sat on Tesuque tribal land immediately adjacent to the grounds of the Santa Fe Opera. It stood like a poke in the eye to the high-society opera buffs, who'd complained that the new casino spoiled the spectacular views and the oh-so-perfect ambience of the iconic classical music venue.

Personally, Clayton appreciated the smarts of the pueblo people who converted a piece of their land formerly used as a weekend flea market into a business venture to enrich the tribal treasury.

Before starting the brief drive to Santa Fe, he called his father, Kevin Kerney, at his ranch southeast of the city.

"I know it's short notice, but can you meet me in town for coffee in an hour?" he asked when Kerney picked up.

"You bet," Kerney replied. "You know the diner on Cerrillos Road by the mall?"

"Perfect, I'll see you there," Clayton said. Owned by a local family, the diner was close to the Santa Fe Police Department, his last stop. It drew a sizable breakfast and lunch crowd from the local cop shop and the nearby New Mexico State Police Headquarters

Before Mescalero, Goggin had lived in Santa Fe for a time and had been involved in a civil dispute with his landlord that had escalated into assault charges against the property owner, which were eventually dropped. Clayton wanted a look at the police department file, hoping to find someone with a strong enough grudge to hire Goggin and Nautzile's killer. He was down to scratching for the tiniest shard to grab on to.

Again, he came away with nada. The property owner had been an eighty-year-old man with dementia. Clayton had nothing to show for his twenty-four-hour marathon except continued disappointment. Maybe Kerney, with his years of experience in law enforcement, could help him shake loose a new idea.

The walls of the diner, a favorite because of its Northern New Mexico cuisine, were plastered with sports memorabilia from the area high schools, along with photographs of some of the better-known, homegrown star athletes. Kerney was sitting in a booth with a line of sight to the front door when Clayton entered. He smiled and waved as Clayton approached.

"You look glum," Kerney said as Clayton slid into the booth.

"Floundering is more like it."

"The scalping murders?"

Clayton nodded. "I've got nil."

"It's tough when there's no trail to follow."

"Oh, supposedly there's a trail," Clayton replied. "I've just been trying to avoid it."

Kerney raised his eyebrows. "Now you've got my attention. What's up with that?"

"I've got a motive, an MO, and a suspect in Mexico given to me on a platter by an undercover DEA agent," Clayton explained. "All he wants me to do is find and extract him with the help of another agent I haven't met."

"In Mexico?"

"Affirmative. And my sheriff is keen on the idea, to the point of mentioning a possible promotion. I'd go in with federal credentials and government authorization."

"Which won't mean crap to the Mexicans," Kerney noted. "Especially now that they're not feeling very neighborly with all the bullying coming out of Washington."

"I've thought about that."

Kerney gestured to a server. "Are you going to do it?"

Clayton deferred answering until the server took their orders for coffee and scooted away. "Probably. But I can't tell Grace, and that will break my word to her."

Kerney leaned back and nodded. Telling Grace about a risky undercover operation could put her and their kids in jeopardy. It went against protocol. "When Sara was active-duty, I didn't know—couldn't know—where she was all the time. And there were things I did that I've never talked to her about."

"I get that part." Clayton paused for the arrival of their coffee. "But I've left some stuff out which might help you get a better picture. The killer is a sicario, allegedly the best in Mexico. His alleged client is a narco-trafficker and police commander in a border state city. And a Chinese-Mexican gangster and his girlfriend are most likely involved."

Kerney shook his head. "Quite a cast of characters. Is this all from DEA intelligence?"

"I've confirmed the Chinese-Mexican player and the woman, and the intel on the assassin checks out."

"Is there an operation in place?"

"I'm to learn the specifics when we meet at the staging location."

"Which is where?"

"I don't know yet."

"Sounds like a dicey proposition," Kerney noted.

"I'm not happy about it."

"But you're going to do it."

"How can you tell?"

Kerney held back for a minute, composing his thoughts. "I think you're still feeling humiliated—no, that's not the right word—embarrassed, because you were forced to resign from the state police."

"No need to sugarcoat it. I don't like being labeled as unreliable or incompetent at what I do. It's not an honorable position to be in."

Kerney reached out and squeezed Clayton's shoulder. "A hell of a lot of people know that isn't true. It will pass."

"It will pass a lot faster if I can produce a righteous arrest, and soon." Clayton smiled. "You'd do the same. Maybe for different reasons, but you'd do it."

"You're right, but not alone or with strangers I don't know or trust. Promise me you'll bail out at the first sign something is fishy."

Clayton nodded.

"And promise you'll stay in touch with me, at least once every second day. A text message, voice mail, landline call—whatever."

"If it's possible, I promise," Clayton replied

"Fair enough." Kerney took the check from the server and paid the bill. "Should we invite Grace and Hannah to the ranch for a visit while you're gone?"

"It's a nice idea, but unnecessary. Grace, Hannah, and Wendell in Albuquerque will have protection. Besides, Hannah has classes and Grace will be working."

Kerney nodded. "Good planning. Never underestimate your enemy. You know, next week is spring break for the Santa Fe schools. Maybe I can talk Sara and Patrick into a road trip south."

"You don't have to do that."

Kerney brushed Clayton's protest off with a wave of his hand. "Good time to visit before it gets too hot. I'd like to show them Aguirre Springs, and I bet Sara can use her pull with the Army to get permission from White Sands Missile Range to take us on a guided tour of Pat Garrett's old ranch. I think Patrick would get a kick out of seeing where the man who gunned down Billy the Kid lived. There's lots to do down there."

"You've got a ranch to run," Clayton objected.

"And a crackerjack hired hand to gratefully do it without my fuddy-duddy old-man interference." Kerney held out his hand. "Let's shake on it."

"What if Sara disagrees with your road-trip idea?"

"She won't, once I tell her you'll be on a special assignment soon after our visit."

"Figures." Clayton smiled and shook his father's hand. "I don't want you doing anything more than just having fun and visiting. Don't try to go Rambo on me."

Kerney grinned. "Wouldn't think of it."

Clayton put some money on the table to add to the tip. "Good." He stood and slapped Kerney on the back. "Take care of yourself."

"Stay safe," Kerney replied.

They walked out together. Kerney would be turning seventy soon. Sara had called about a surprise birthday party in his honor, rounding up family, old friends, and colleagues from his cop days to attend. She'd booked a rooftop patio venue at a downtown Santa Fe hotel. Clayton had reserved rooms for his family there.

They parted company at Kerney's truck, dusty and mud-streaked from the rutted, washboard dirt road that led to the ranch. Clayton watched him drive away. He'd lost some hair, now wore glasses almost full-time, and had grown a bit of a paunch, but otherwise he looked healthy and fit. Clayton expected him to stay that way for many years.

He climbed into his unmarked unit, followed Cerrillos Road to the interstate, and started out on the long, straight shot to Las Cruces, 280 miles away, cruise control set at eighty.

———

Clayton contacted dispatch as he crossed into Doña Ana County, fifty miles north of Las Cruces. There were six messages waiting for him, all from people in Mescalero, including one from Selena Kazhe and one from Truman Balatche, the parking valet supervisor at the casino. He pulled onto the shoulder of the interstate and asked the dispatcher to relay them by back channel. All were about a suspicious male subject who identified himself as a federal law enforcement officer. He was driving a black Chevy SUV and asking questions about how to contact Lucy Nautzile's family and friends. He'd been spotted in several residential areas, where strangers rarely venture.

No one had told the man anything, which was to be expected when outsiders suddenly approached and questioned Apache people. It showed ignorance and bad manners. Truman's message included a detailed description of the vehicle right down to the license plate. It was likely a rental out of El Paso, he'd added.

Selena's call contained information about the man. Possibly Anglo, in his early thirties, six feet, eyes brown set wide apart, with a noticeable scar on his left hand between the thumb and forefinger. He had a slight accent Selena couldn't place.

Clayton wondered if it was the DEA agent he was supposed to team up with, but that made no sense. He decided to forgo a stop at the office and head straight to the rez.

———

Fernando Olguin knew he was looking for a stolen million dollars, El Jefe had made that very clear. He had also told Fernando, if he found it, not to harm anyone if possible. If he had no success after a reasonable amount of time searching, Fernando was to return home. No criticism would result because of his failure.

He had no reason to doubt his father. From the time of his earliest memory, El Jefe had raised him as a son. Until Fernando was three, he'd never uttered a word, and when he did begin to speak it was in his father's native language, the Algonquian tongue of the Kickapoos. As he grew, he learned Spanish and English and spoke both fluently. Yet a look in the mirror every morning told Fernando he was neither Kickapoo nor Mexican. Eastern European most likely, he thought. Father would neither confirm nor deny his origins.

Nor would he tell Fernando how he came to be under his protection at such a tender age. It was, as he put it, inconsequential, not part of who Fernando was. He'd also given Fernando both his names, Mexican and Kickapoo. And although it had been unnecessary, he'd hunted and killed four deer in order to bestow Fernando with a tribal name. A great honor, he later learned from the Kickapoo elders.

He had every desire to find the money and bring it safely to his father. Until now, in each task he'd been given, he had succeeded. But his efforts so far, and especially today in Mescalero, had been dismal.

He'd retraced the couple's travels from Eagle Pass to Las Cruces, searching each location for a possible hiding place of the money. The only place he hadn't looked was Blossom Magoosh's home. It had taken most of the day to discover where she lived. When he drove by, a row of vehicles was parked at the foot of her driveway. With his binoculars he could see the shadowy movement of people inside the house through the front window. But they were partially veiled by the screening on the enclosed porch.

Fernando decided not to raise suspicions. He drove to the nearby village center adjacent to the major east-west highway that traversed the reservation and parked in front of the tribal museum.

The weak March sun had already dipped behind the forested mountains and the air was decidedly chilly. He put on his parka, stuck his forged police credentials in a pocket, pulled up the fur-lined hood, and walked quickly away. Past the post office a road took him into the low hills where Magoosh's house was tucked on a rise between two shallow arroyos.

In cover of growing darkness, concealed behind a small grove of young junipers, Fernando watched and waited, occasionally scanning the house with his binoculars. An hour passed before visitors began to leave. Soon only three vehicles remained. He guessed the old truck parked nearest the house belonged to Magoosh. Patiently he continued to wait. Eventually a man and a woman emerged and drove away in a restored early-model Mustang parked at the foot of the driveway. That left only the old pickup truck and a new SUV parked at the top of the driveway.

As the night deepened and turned colder, Fernando decided to leave his cover and see who was inside.

Avoiding the driveway, he cautiously made his way up the arroyo that angled toward the rear of the house. His footsteps crunched loudly on the frozen snow, breaking the silence of the night. Several times, he paused and listened for any reaction before proceeding.

At the rear of the house, he was able to see the kitchen through a small window over the sink. Two women sat at the table. A tiny, elderly woman with her head bowed had a shawl over her shoulders. Fernando figured that was Blossom Magoosh. The other, somewhat younger woman was holding Magoosh's hand, talking animatedly, probably consoling.

Fernando backed away. A side window revealed a small bedroom barely illuminated by a night-light. Two small figures were snuggled under blankets on twin beds. Nautzile's girls, sleeping soundly.

At the front of the house, the screened porch made it hard to see anything clearly through the window. Rather than make more noise and risk detection, Fernando crouched and watched, looking for movement. A long two-minute count convinced him that only the two women and two children were inside.

He could easily contain all of them, secure the girls, interrogate the two women, and do a search if necessary. But what if the women refused to cooperate? Or denied knowledge of the money? He would have to hurt them. How far should he go to get truthful answers? And if that failed, an exhaustive search would take some time. Perhaps too much time.

Night was a good time to strike. But a better time would be when no one was home. When no one need be hurt, as Father suggested. At least, not yet.

He stood just as a vehicle swung up the driveway, catching him in the headlights. He froze momentarily, the high beams blinding him, then bolted down into the arroyo, running, unable to see clearly. His foot caught on a rock, twisted his ankle, and he went down hard, landing on the side of his face. He got up, jaw aching, skin rubbed raw, and hobbled away as fast as he could, listening for pursuit.

———

Clayton barged through Blossom's front door, visually sweeping the room, sidearm drawn. He announced himself and called out to his mother. It was her SUV parked outside.

Isabel answered from the kitchen. Clayton found her backed up in a corner, her arm around Blossom, a carving knife in her free hand.

"The girls!" Isabel exclaimed.

Clayton nodded. "Stay put."

The commotion had woken them. He brought them into the kitchen, wide-eyed and fearful. Blossom gathered her granddaughters in her arms.

"What's going on?" Isabel asked.

"An intruder outside. He ran when I turned up the driveway." Clayton looked at Blossom. "Do you have a weapon in the house?"

"A shotgun on the top shelf of the pantry with a box of shells."

"Good. Get it and load it," he said to Isabel as he retreated from the kitchen to the front room. "Use it if you have to. And call 911. Explain what happened and ask them to send the police immediately."

Isabel opened the pantry door. "Where are you going?"

"There's only one way this guy can be headed, and that's down to the highway. I might be able to intercept him before he gets away."

"Be careful," Isabel called as Clayton turned and ran out of the house.

———

Hampered by his twisted ankle, Fernando Olguin stuck to the arroyo until it petered out some distance behind the village center close to a manufactured home with lights on inside and two vehicles parked near the front door. There was no cover in the open field beyond.

He sank down under a large juniper tree, pain throbbing from his foot to his knee, his face wet with sweat and blood. He wiped his eyes and concentrated on what to do next. Cloud cover under a weak quarter moon made it hard to see. Unfamiliar with the terrain, he wasn't sure of the best way to get to his vehicle without detection.

As his heavy breathing slowed, he listened intently for any sound of a car on nearby dirt roads or the crunch of footfalls on the frozen ground. All was quiet.

Staying put wasn't an option. He'd have to risk it. Gingerly he got to his feet, opened his parka, unholstered his 9mm semiautomatic, stuck it in a front pocket, and set off at the fastest pace he could muster. As he reached the open field, the sound of car tires on a dirt road goaded him forward. He'd barely crossed the open field and found cover in the dark shadow of a building when a vehicle passed and turned onto the paved street behind the village center.

———

Nobody was out hoofing it on any of the roads below Blossom's house, which wasn't surprising given the freezing night. Clayton slowed his unit as he passed behind the tribal grocery store, looking for anyone hiding in the shadows. Seeing no one, he made a complete circle around the village center and began checking the vehicles parked in front of the still-open store. None of them matched the description or license plate information Truman Balatche had provided.

He spotted the car in front of the tribal cultural center and museum, drove across the lot to the post office, killed the engine, and waited. Within a few minutes a figure in a hooded parka hobbled into sight, head lowered, left leg apparently injured. From size and shape, Clayton figured it was a male. Was he a drunk on his way to hitchhike a ride on the highway to Ruidoso? Crossing over to the hospital on the other side? Going to the store for a burrito and soda?

The parka looked the same, but Clayton didn't want to make a mistake based on a fleeting glimpse of the man at Blossom's house.

He stayed put until the man veered in the direction of the car at the tribal cultural center. He cranked the engine. The man stopped, turned, and looked back, his hand reaching into a pocket. Clayton accelerated and braked to a stop ten feet away just as the man dropped prone and opened fire.

Clayton bailed and dug for his sidearm. Bullets shattered the wind-shield, smashed into the open driver's door. He rolled, rounds zinging, splatting the pavement next to his head.

He stopped, steadied, and fired repeatedly until the only sound he heard was the metallic click of an empty magazine. He reloaded quickly and got to his feet, weapon pointed at the motionless figure on the ground. A lifeless hand still clutched a semiautomatic. Clayton kicked it away and looked at the body. Two of his rounds had torn through the man's head, one above the left eye and one below the lower lip. The blood on the pavement spread out like a brown satin pillow.

The gunfight had drawn the customers and staff out of the store. People were shouting, pointing. Sirens wailed.

The dead man was no stalker or voyeur. Only a pro would have dropped so suddenly and surely into a prone firing position.

"Shit!" Clayton said to himself. This was not the way he wanted it to go. He held up his shield to the people who were so eager to witness the bloody aftermath and ordered them to stay back.

CHAPTER 8

Suspicious deaths, fatal shootings, and murders on Indian lands automatically belonged to the FBI. That included all police-involved events. At Mescalero, the officers were Bureau of Indian Affairs federal cops, not appointed by tribal authorities.

Clayton wasn't a big fan of either agency. But since he was on the rez and clearly outside his jurisdiction, he had no control over the situation.

Expecting a long, drawn-out night, he made quick calls to Grace at home and the Doña Ana SO before the BIA cops arrived. He told Grace he'd been in a gunfight on the rez and reassured her that he was unhurt. By radio he gave dispatch a brief summary of the event and requested Captain Rodney be sent to his location ASAP.

Three marked units, tires squealing, screeched to a stop ten feet away. With hands raised, Clayton displayed his shield over his head and yelled he was a cop, which only momentarily kept three nervous, pumped-up BIA officers at bay with their weapons drawn. They boxed him in, ignored his credentials, and secured his sidearm. They put him facedown on the pavement and cuffed his wrists to the back. He remained pressed against the cold, damp concrete, his cheek bleeding from the pebbles ground into his face, until Doña Ana County SO dispatch confirmed that he was a legitimate police officer on official business.

Brought to his feet by the BIA sergeant and roughly uncuffed, he shivered, wiped the bloody crust from his cheek, and silently cursed the man. His wrists ached from the tightly ratcheted cuffs that had pinched hard against bone.

"Can I have my weapon and ID back?" Clayton asked.

"No can do," the sergeant said briskly, turning to the other two officers. He told them to move the crowd to the front of the store and hold them there. As the onlookers shuffled back, they used their smartphones to record the drama, light flashes peppering the night like huge fireflies.

"I want to take a look at the victim and search his vehicle," Clayton said, reining in an impulse to put the overweight cop on the ground and grind a knee on his neck.

The sergeant shook his head. "Can't do it. The FBI agent en route from Roswell wants nothing touched until she gets here."

Clayton took a deep, calming breath. "The dead man may have murdered three people in Las Cruces. I'm the investigating case officer. It's important that I gather whatever evidence I can find."

"You'll have to wait."

"I admire your spirit of professional cooperation," Clayton snapped, tired of playing nice.

The sergeant shrugged and touched Clayton's elbow. "You'll wait in my unit."

Clayton jerked his arm away. "Unless you're charging me with a crime, back off. I'm staying right here."

The sergeant shrugged. "Fine. But if you go near the body or the vehicle, I'll detain you. Got it?"

Clayton stared at the sergeant. With high cheekbones, dark eyes, a broad nose, and brown skin, he was decidedly Indian-looking. His name tag read MACKENZIE CLOUD. "Ute?" he guessed.

"Southern Ute."

Apache enemy. Clayton took one step back. "It figures."

"Stay put," Sergeant Cloud said as he went to peer inside the victim's vehicle.

FBI Special Agent Linda Foster-Nelson, all of five-foot-three and just on the light side of a hundred and ten pounds, was a brash, know-it-all Fed. Without the FBI jacket and the weapon strapped to her belt, she could easily pass for a pleasant-looking kindergarten teacher. However, she suffered from the typical FBI rookie affliction—common to officers newly released into the field on their own—of taking herself too seriously.

It wasn't endearing. She curtly dismissed Clayton's request to search the victim or his vehicle.

He told her not to be stupid, which won him the right to observe the further proceedings locked in the backseat cage of Sergeant Cloud's unit. Frustrated, he watched as the crime scene perimeter was established, photos of the victim were taken, and evidence from the vehicle was gathered, including a tablet computer, two smartphones, and an arsenal of assault weapons, long rifles, shotguns, magazines, and boxes of ammunition. All of it nicely and neatly spread out on tarp on the pavement behind the victim's vehicle.

Foster-Nelson and Sergeant Cloud were bagging and tagging evidence, including the victim's forged law enforcement ID and shield, when Sheriff Vasquez and Captain Rodney arrived.

"You locked my detective in a police cruiser?" Vasquez snapped at Foster-Nelson, towering over her. "Jesus, I'll have your head on a platter."

Foster-Nelson opened her mouth.

"Don't say a fucking word," Vasquez thundered.

Foster-Nelson rallied. "You have no jurisdiction here, Sheriff. I suggest you don't make a scene."

Bright red in the face, Vasquez clamped his mouth shut.

Frank Rodney opened the back door to the unit and looked in. "You okay?"

Clayton climbed out. "Yeah."

"At least you aren't cuffed."

"Not anymore."

Rodney shook his head in dismay. "Why?"

"The victim carried federal police credentials," Clayton answered. "She locked me in the unit waiting on confirmation of his identity."

"You killed a Fed?"

"He was no Fed."

"You're sure of that?"

"I am."

"Tell me what happened."

Clayton made it quick and pertinent. He covered the reports he'd gotten from residents about a man flashing a shield on the rez and asking questions about Lucy Nautzile's family. He summarized the description of the man and his vehicle he'd received from several citizens. Finding the individual outside Blossom's house and chasing him. Finally, the shoot-out.

"Think he's our killer?"

"I have my doubts, but he tried to take me out like a pro."

Rodney grunted. "Let's go cooperate with the FBI."

"I'll let you handle that part."

———

Computer inquiries to national law enforcement data systems soon confirmed that the dead man's Department of Homeland Security police credentials and personal identification documents, including a Texas driver's license and credit cards issued by a Mexican bank, were fake. His handgun was unregistered, and the labels had been removed from all of his clothing. There were no lodging, meal, or gasoline receipts found on the body or in the vehicle. An envelope containing $4,623 was tucked inside a briefcase. Seventy-six dollars was discovered in a wallet carried in the victim's back pocket.

A record check of the victim's purported name, Lawrence Anico, along with his physical description and fingerprints taken at the scene, yielded no match. There were no hits on cross-checked law enforcement personnel databases. This particular Lawrence Anico, now dead, didn't exist. Twice.

Only the car had a traceable history. It had been rented from a national chain at the San Antonio airport. Over fourteen hundred miles had been added to the odometer, more than twice the driving distance from San Antonio to Mescalero. The GPS tracking device on the rental showed that the driver had crisscrossed into Mexico at border towns several times, staying overnight in Fort Stockton, and stopping in Alpine and Presidio before moving on to Van Horn and making a final push to El Paso and Las Cruces. From there it had been local travel, finally arriving at the rez early that afternoon.

By phone, Frank Rodney called two detectives back in to work, gave them the vehicle's GPS information, and ordered a telephone canvass of every hotel, motel, bed-and-breakfast, and Airbnb rental along the vehicle's route. He wanted to know if Nautzile and Goggin had stayed in any of the locations, and if a man posing as a Department of Homeland Security special agent had been asking questions about them.

Chastised but unbowed, Special Agent Foster-Nelson refused the sheriff's request to turn over the collected evidence to his office. By phone, she'd consulted with the special agent in charge of the Albuquerque Division, who concurred. A killing on the rez by anybody, cop or not, meant the Feds owned it, including the evidence.

"That totally sucks," Clayton snapped at Foster-Nelson. "You're impeding my investigation."

Foster-Nelson held her cool. "You have admitted to the fatal shooting of the victim, Detective Istee. Before I can release you, I need to take your statement."

"Let's get it over with," Clayton replied.

Sheriff Vasquez and Captain Rodney drove Clayton to the nearby police department, where they took up sentry duty outside the interrogation room. Facing a television camera and speaking into a table microphone, Clayton spent the next ninety minutes answering Foster-Nelson's questions, explaining the basics of his investigation and finally going over in detail the gunfight outside the tribal grocery store.

When he finished, Foster-Nelson stood and turned off the camera. "That's all for now. I may want to speak with you again to clarify some points."

She returned his credentials and handgun. "We may need your weapon for ballistic testing," she added.

Drained, exhausted, but still completely pissed, Clayton didn't budge from the chair. "I want access to all the information you get about the victim, a complete list of the evidence gathered at the scene, *and* the results of any forensic examinations, tests, or lab work."

Foster-Nelson smiled frostily. "I'm sure we'll be able to accommodate your request in good time."

Slowly, he stood. "You're going to make one great bureaucrat."

Foster-Nelson opened the door. "How kind of you to say."

On the short drive to Clayton's unit, Vasquez told him he'd spoken to Grace and reassured her that everything was okay.

"Did you tell her what happened?"

"Only that you had been attacked without provocation. I want a lid kept on this until we know more."

Clayton held back a sigh. Grace would have her claws out if he tried to sidestep or short-circuit what happened. "I'll call her."

"Are you driving home tonight?" Vasquez asked as he pulled beside Clayton's unmarked vehicle.

Clayton nodded. "I'll check on Blossom and my mother and call Grace from there."

"You're on administrative duty as of now," Vasquez noted. "Get some sleep and call in tomorrow afternoon. Don't come to the office."

"We need to talk about what happens next," Clayton said. "I don't want the operation with Agent Harjo shut down. Not after this."

"Don't worry about it," Rodney said.

"We'll talk," Vasquez added.

The body of the dead man on the pavement had been covered. The crowd had dispersed. Only the BIA cops were there watching over the corpse, waiting for a medical investigator, emergency lights still flashing on all three squad cars.

Clayton reached for the door latch. "This wasn't our killer. He was good, but not that good."

"I hope you're wrong," Vasquez replied.

"Maybe he wasn't here to kill you or anyone else," Rodney suggested.

Clayton stepped out. "Then why the arsenal in the trunk of his car?"

"Self-protection?" Rodney proposed, straight-faced.

Clayton laughed as they drove off.

———

The officer who'd responded to the 911 call at Blossom's house was gone. Isabel answered Clayton's knock at the front door. The girls were snuggled with their grandmother on the couch in the small living room watching a DVD cartoon movie about a boy's search for his lost dog. Clayton asked if everything was okay and got nods and smiles in return.

In the kitchen, Isabel poured him a cup of coffee and they sat together at the table. Clayton didn't have to tell her much about what had happened. In the age of smartphones, breaking news stories—especially anything to do with gun violence, natural disasters, or man-made catastrophes—were uploaded on social media almost instantly.

As soon as the gunfight started, cell phones in Mescalero had begun ringing, photos were downloaded, and videos streamed. Isabel handed him her phone. A text notification scrolled across the screen about a fatal police shooting on a New Mexico Apache reservation. It had gone national on a major web browser news feed.

"Just what I don't need," Clayton commented. At least so far, no names had been given out by the Feds.

"You may have saved our lives," Isabel replied.

"I honestly don't know if that's the case."

"You could have been killed protecting Blossom, the girls, and me."

"That didn't happen."

"I was terrified you'd been shot." Her eyes were moist.

Clayton took her hand. "That didn't happen, either. I'm okay, honestly. Have you talked with Grace?"

Isabel nodded. "Just before you arrived. She's very worried."

"I'll call her before I leave for home. Do you want me to request overnight police protection for Blossom and the girls?"

Isabel shook her head. "Blossom's brother is coming up from Alamogordo. He'll be here soon. I'll stay with them until then."

Clayton finished his coffee and stood. "Okay."

Isabel's expression turned somber. Her jaw was set, her eyes now clear. Years of experience told Clayton that she was ready to launch into a lecture.

He was in no mood. He cut her off with a kiss on the cheek. "Not now."

Isabel sighed. "We'll talk soon."

"Soon," Clayton agreed.

In his unit, he notified dispatch he was off duty, parked out of sight behind the grocery store, and called Grace.

———

Losing all hope, Estavio Trevino logged on one last time to a secure email account routed through La Paz, Bolivia. Once again, there was no message from Fernando. He was hours overdue for his daily check-in, and only some disaster or misfortune would have kept his adopted son from fulfilling his duty.

Fernando was forever loyal and trustworthy in all matters pertaining to family and in the discharge of any tasks given to him by his father. From a very early age, Trevino had trained him well in the art of self-defense, the use of weapons, wilderness survival, and the skills and techniques of an assassin.

But he'd never sent Fernando out on a kill and had no plans to do so. As Fernando had grown into manhood, he'd become a valuable assistant for advance research and scouting, and any necessary follow-up assignments. Using Fernando in this way allowed Trevino to remain almost invisible at the time of the kill, virtually impossible to identify.

Had Fernando asked to be given a target of his own, Trevino would not have denied him. But it was not in his nature. He could kill, but not humans. Trevino believed it had to do with a nightmare memory buried deeply in Fernando's three-year-old mind.

His free-spirited German parents traveling with him on an extended camping journey through Mexico had driven into the remote and isolated Bolsón de Mapimí, far west of the Kickapoo homeland, beyond the lovely, vast ranches ringed by mountains. There, at a campsite surrounded by low naked hills, crumpled mesas, gray and lifeless in a windblown emptiness, they had been set upon, the husband murdered, the wife raped and killed, all their possessions stolen, and the child left unharmed and alive near the smoldering embers of the campfire.

Trevino found him two days later wandering down a dry arroyo almost within shouting distance of his hidden hacienda. He was filthy, hungry, thirsty, and in tears, clinging to him fiercely. Trevino carried the little boy home, knowing that Kitzihiat, the Great Spirit of the Kickapoos, had brought the child to him as a gift.

The boy spoke no Spanish or English. In fact, he spoke not a word at all. After he'd been washed, fed, given fresh milk and a warm bed, Trevino charged his Mexican housekeeper to be gentle with the boy, while he went to solve the mystery.

It took a day to find the murder site and three more days to find the stolen vehicle, a VW camper van, parked in a lot behind a bright yellow house in the town of Múzquiz. He'd waited and watched until two men came out and left in the van. When no one answered his knock at the door, he drove to the town center, walked back, and got in through an unlocked back window.

Inside, he'd found personal items, clothing, and identification documents belonging to the German couple and their boy. A more thorough search convinced him that the two men—brothers in their late thirties—were the only occupants. He gathered up every item in the house that might possibly belong to the victims, put it in garbage bags, and waited. It was night when the men returned, drunk and staggering, carrying take-out food from a taqueria.

He killed them silently and quickly, took the garbage bags to the van, and drove away. Off a dirt road in the foothills above the city, he burned the van and everything in it. Walking toward a distant hilltop, he saw it explode into a fireball when the flames reached the gas tank.

In a brief minute the first emergency siren screamed into the thin air from the town below.

That was the night Trevino became a father.

He closed the laptop, left the library, and walked to the media room, where a large-screen television with access to major satellite and Internet subscription services was mounted to a wall. Trevino surfed the El Paso and Albuquerque television stations for any stories about serious crimes, road accidents, or major mishaps that might have occurred in the region. Except for a motorcycle fatality involving a soldier from Fort Bliss, not much else was making headlines on the late evening news. He switched to the YouTube app and ran through the most recent user uploads. A short video of a police shooting incident on the Mescalero Apache Reservation caught his attention.

A body lay on the parking lot pavement near a car that looked identical to the vehicle Fernando said he'd rented in San Antonio. The video was shaky and the picture too fuzzy. The person talking was hard to understand. Something about a cop gunning down somebody outside the tribal grocery store.

Had Fernando shot someone? Been shot?

Trevino scanned for more YouTube footage. He found two more, three more videos, showing a cop holding up his badge as uniformed officers arrived, announcing himself as a Doña Ana sheriff's detective.

Trevino froze the frame and called Lieutenant Roger Ulibarri of the Texas Department of Public Safety at his home in El Paso. For years, he had bought information from Ulibarri, and paid handsomely for it.

"Find out what happened at Mescalero and call me back within the hour," he said when Ulibarri answered.

"Ten-four," Ulibarri replied.

Trevino dropped the phone on the couch cushion and prowled restlessly through his hacienda and its grounds. It was a modern, low-slung, sprawling house with detached staff quarters, a stable and horse corral, and a five-car garage hidden by a twelve-foot adobe wall that enclosed the entire ten-acre property. Beyond the wall were thousands of acres Trevino owned with only one way in and out, unless, of course, you knew the alternatives.

As he roamed, he prepared for bad news. It was the only way he knew how to live.

CHAPTER 9

A combination of luck and a called-in marker had DEA Special Agent Bernard Harjo in the air to Albuquerque for an emergency meeting with the FBI special agent in charge and Linda Foster-Nelson, the Roswell field agent who'd caught the fatal shooting investigation of a still-unidentified subject at Mescalero.

The DEA had a fleet of about a hundred aircraft, and while most of them were used for surveillance and interdiction, a few corporate-class jets ferried the bosses around on their way to career-enhancing meetings. Harjo's free ride came as a result of scheduled maintenance for the plane at the Fort Worth DEA aviation center. He'd be picked up by the pilot on his return to Los Angeles in a different, freshly serviced aircraft.

That was the lucky part. The marker he'd used was with Ben Shiver, the honcho of the FBI Albuquerque Field Office. Years ago, during a joint operation on Indian land, Shiver had unlawfully restrained and physically assaulted a pushy, arrogant freelance photojournalist, who filed charges against him. Harjo had witnessed the event and swore it never happened. Thus, Shiver's ass was saved. Thus, Foster-Nelson was ordered to Albuquerque ASAP.

Harjo was anxious to land and find out exactly why the man Clayton Istee had shot to death had no confirmed identity, no known history. Behind the faked, professional-grade police credentials and other forged personal identification documents found among the unknown SUB's possessions, a black hole existed. That seemed ludicrous. He had to come from somewhere, be somebody.

Fifty miles out, the plane began a gradual descent into Albuquerque. The city was pressed against the foothills of the striking Sandia Mountains, and as with all large southwestern cities, there were endless, ubiquitous strip malls, traffic-laden surface streets, interstate highways that cut through its core, and a downtown slowly sputtering toward revitalization. Surprisingly, there weren't too many skyscrapers, which gave it a more open scale, and the Rio Grande, with its thick bosque, interrupted a good deal of the man-made ugliness.

The FBI field office consisted of several unimposing buildings in a compound behind an inconspicuous low-security fence. Tucked in among a hodgepodge of industrial and commercial business parks, it bordered an access road that fronted a northbound 1-25 access lane.

Shiver and Foster-Nelson met Harjo at the reception area and took him directly to a conference room adjacent to Shiver's office. Just prior to going undercover several years ago, Harjo had last seen Shiver at a law enforcement conference in Montreal. At six-three with no body fat, Shiver tended to lope rather than walk, and, by nature, talk rather than listen.

Foster-Nelson seemed unassuming and, in Harjo's assessment, a bit unprepossessing.

Evidence collected at the scene of the fatal shooting of the unnamed subject was laid out and neatly labeled on the long table. Seated at the far end, much to Harjo's surprise, was his nominal boss, Samantha Hodges, special agent in charge, El Paso District.

"Hello, Bernie," Hodges said genially.

Harjo hated to be called Bernie. He stifled a grimace, nodded pleasantly, glanced at everything on the table, and said to no one in particular, "Where's the corpse? It would have made a great centerpiece."

Shiver smiled politely and gestured at the contents on the table. "You'll have to make do with the autopsy photographs. Everything's labeled, but I'm sure you'll have questions."

Harjo started with the photos. The man had been in his early thirties, slightly under six feet, brown eyes, muscular, with no tattoos or distinguishing marks.

"No fingerprint matches?" Harjo inquired.

Shiver shook his head. "We ran them again, as you asked."

"We also ran facial recognition software and didn't get a match," Foster-Nelson added, referring to her notepad. "However, Interpol came up with an interesting comparable: Herman Joseph Arensdorf, forty-eight, who is serving a fifteen-year prison term in Germany for voluntary manslaughter. He's never been out of the country and he has no known relatives living abroad."

"Our subject was German?"

"Predominantly German, with some French thrown in," Foster-Nelson replied. "But ancestry analysis isn't always accurate."

"Because there's a chance there might be a family connection, we've asked for the German prisoner's DNA profile," Shiver noted. "His lawyer is blocking our request in hopes of getting his client's sentence reduced. In the meantime, we're running the surname Arensdorf through every federal, state, and local database we can access."

"Great," Harjo grumbled. "What about the tablet and the cell phone?"

"Both the hard drive and the SIM card were erased as soon as the technicians powered on the devices," Foster-Nelson answered. "Wiped clean with the same type of technology the CIA uses. The serial numbers show they were manufactured in China for sale in the EU."

"Is there anything here that's American-made?" Harjo asked, waving a hand over the table.

"Not really," Shiver replied. "The weapons are all foreign-made and were never reported stolen or exported from their country of origin. The subject's clothing had all tags and labels removed, but fiber analysis suggests the apparel was not manufactured in North America. Same for the luggage."

Harjo eyed the top-of-the-line weapons. Glock, SIG Sauer, Beretta, Taurus, all in perfect order. "No latents from anyone other than the victim?"

Shiver shook his head. "ATF is contacting the firearms manufacturers to find out how the weapons could have slipped through customs."

"Personal items?" Harjo inquired.

"Sure, stuff you can pick up at any drug or convenience store," Shiver said. "The money's authentic. Good old American greenbacks that have been in circulation for a while. Not stolen or traceable to any financial institution as far as we know."

"Nothing on the dental work?"

"Nothing out of the ordinary," Foster-Nelson answered. "A few fillings, no major dental work."

Harjo grunted in displeasure.

"Hope dies hard, doesn't it, Bernie?" Samantha Hodges said.

"Did you come here to console me?"

Hodges got to her feet. "No, to pull the plug on your little Mexico expedition. CIA has stepped in and assumed control. They believe this has the look of something beyond a drug cartel operation."

Harjo waved his hand in disbelief. "What? This is too slick, too smooth for dumb Mexicans to pull off? Give me a break. What we know out of the Doña Ana Sheriff's Office is that our dead perp was backtracking on the couple scalped and murdered in Las Cruces and looking for something they'd had in their possession."

"That's true," Hodges agreed.

"Who were assassinated by the best sicario in the business under contract to a major Mexican drug trafficker who also happens to be a corrupt high-ranking cop. This was nothing more than a very high profile contract hit meant to send a message. Not the start of some budding espionage escapade requiring a CIA black ops response."

"Nothing has been said about anything like that happening," Hodges cautioned. "What *is* happening is that Washington has decided there's enough controversy at the border with Central American refugees clamoring for asylum and overwhelming the immigration system. You are not going to punch your way into Mexico in search of a possible suspect and cause a public relations catastrophe for the administration. There's already enough diplomatic tension between the two countries. CIA will assess and determine if any action is appropriate."

"That's it?"

Samantha Hodges nodded. "Special Agent Fallon goes back to his duty station in Vancouver, you go on thirty days' annual leave, and we let the Doña Ana County SO know the operation has been scrubbed."

Harjo turned on his heel to leave.

"Do you understand?" Hodges snapped.

"Yeah, sure," Harjo said on his way out the door.

———

Harjo turned in his rental car at the airport general aviation facility and sat at a table in the nicely appointed empty reception area with a clear view of the runways. With a cup of coffee at his side, he opened his tablet and began entering every last detail he could remember of his meeting at the FBI field office. He wanted his facts and observations to be as comprehensive as possible, right down to his Q&A with Shiver and Foster-Nelson. Additionally, he wanted a record of the comments Hodges had made tanking his operation, passing the buck to the CIA, and ordering him on immediate, involuntary leave. Surely it had all been recorded in real time by Shiver and Hodges.

As he finished a thorough review of his notes, the facilities general manager approached to say his plane was on final approach. Harjo saw the Cessna Citation aircraft smartly touch down.

He paused. Only one question remained about his notes: what to do with them. He'd started the process as an exercise in self-preservation. Hodges hadn't said a word about keeping the substance of the meeting confidential. An oversight on her part?

He accessed email addresses for Danny Fallon and Clayton Istee, attached the document, put "FYI" in the subject line, and sent it. Both had a right to know the game had been changed, especially Istee, who'd likely faced the greatest threat.

Obviously the man he'd killed in self-defense was important to somebody.

Harjo was on the aircraft, strapped in, and ready to depart with no other passengers onboard when the DEA pilot told him he'd been ordered to divert to El Paso and drop him off there.

He smiled and nodded as if it were no big deal. In a way, it wasn't. Ever since his early years with the DEA in El Paso, it had been his home base. He owned a house there in a nice part of town close to shopping, with a view of the Franklin Mountains to the north and the southern Juárez city lights that stretched deep into the night.

He was overdue getting back home. Was it time to start seriously thinking of retirement? Not as long as Luis Lorenz remained unpunished for the murder of Harjo's nephew.

His phone vibrated. A text message from Hodges popped up on the screen. The CIA had classified their meeting as secret. Harjo smiled. He'd wondered where they'd been hiding during the meeting. Too late, spooks. He turned off the phone and stretched out in his seat for a quick nap on the hop to El Paso.

———

Juan Garza entered the basement of Longwei Shen's restaurant through the tunnel door to find only Estavio Trevino present.

"Where is everybody?" he asked, unsettled. He'd never met El Jefe alone before.

"Today it's just the two of us." Trevino gestured at the empty chair.

"Why?"

"At my request. Sit."

Garza did as he was told. "What's up?"

"When you convinced the resident DEA agent you could guarantee how to find me, what exactly did you tell her?"

"What does it matter now?" Juan replied. "The plan has been canceled. Nobody's coming. Everybody's safe. It's all been a waste of time, worrying about nothing."

"It matters."

"What's it got to do with me?"

"You're not listening." Trevino smiled. "Special Agent Sedillo never would have agreed to accept you as a guide to find me simply because you said you could do it."

Juan looked hurt. "I never said I could do it, Jefe. I told her Jose Hernandez could. I explained all this before."

"And you wanted to accompany Jose and the American police to my casa, knowing it is prohibited."

Juan shrugged. "I thought it would be cool to see where you live."

"Why?"

Juan looked away. "Maybe to brag a little. Be suave, que no? I've been to El Jefe's. How cool is that?"

"What did you tell Agent Sedillo to make her believe you knew where I lived?"

"Nothing, honest."

Trevino sighed in frustration. "The woman is not stupid. You told her something."

Juan hesitated, lowered his head, and nodded gloomily. "I bugged Jose a little about your hacienda. Got him to tell me how your ranchero was on the edge of the Bolsón de Mapimí in a valley hidden by rocky hills. How there was only one way in through a cut between two mesas. He said it was many long steps away, whatever that means."

"You gave her something tangible to believe," Trevino noted amiably.

Juan perked up. "Yeah, just playing the role, making it real."

Trevino waved his hand dismissively. "Enough."

"That's it?"

"Sí and thanks."

A relieved Juan left through the tunnel door.

In deep reflection, Estavio Trevino drummed a finger on the arm of his chair. Jose had given Juan too much information. That knowledge now belonged to the Garza brothers, Longwei Shen and his family, and the DEA resident special agent. Jose would have to be punished.

He had other places to live no one knew about, but the ranchero was his favorite. Should he kill them all?

Perhaps not. At least not yet. There was still the Coahuila hunting ranch he had optioned to buy. The closing was in a week. Consisting of five thousand acres close to the international border with live water and wetlands, it had a large and healthy population of deer and wild turkey, as well as porcupines, squirrels, lynxes, rabbits, and armadillos. Complete with a one-bedroom cabin, it would be his legacy to the tribe, which sorely needed abundant game for religious purposes.

Over the years, the Kickapoos had almost wiped out all wildlife in the valleys and mountains surrounding the village. With the addition of the new hunting ranch, no longer would the Mexican and Anglo ranchers who denied them access to their plentiful wildlife be a problem. No longer would Kickapoo men be fined and jailed by the authorities for hunting out of season. No longer would the naming ceremonies for infants be delayed because the tribe lacked the four deer required for the feast.

With the casino, the Eagle Pass reservation had given the Mexican Kickapoos a way out of poverty. The Coahuila hunting ranch would give them a way to maintain and preserve their identity and heritage.

First, he'd deal with the ranch. It would take all of his cash to buy it outright, but he had other assets he could access if needed. He would also speak with Jose Hernandez to learn how much damage to his privacy had been done. If no major adjustments were necessary, he'd deal with Jose, and then learn all he could about the half-Apache deputy sheriff who had murdered Fernando.

Once ready, he'd capture and slowly kill Detective Clayton Istee.

CHAPTER 10

Clayton endured two days of administrative leave and a day of restricted desk duty before he was cleared to return to work. He used his desk duty time to catch up on paperwork and do some additional online research about El Jefe, even though the Mexican extraction scheme hatched by Special Agent Harjo had been torpedoed.

Relieved and disappointed by the decision, Clayton struggled to put his ambivalence to rest. On the upside, he didn't have to lie to Grace about participating in a highly questionable undercover mission. But the downside was that this left him no closer to solving the triple homicide case. In fact, it made it even more difficult. As new assignments came in, the case would turn cold. He didn't like that at all.

Sheriff Vasquez and Captain Rodney were more sanguine about it, and for good reason. When the mission got scrubbed, DEA wasn't willing to cough up all the goodies originally promised to the department. However, to show appreciation for such excellent interagency cooperation, a multiyear DEA grant was awarded to fund drug prevention officers at several high schools near the international border.

It was a gold star for the Doña Ana SO. It was front-page news, including editorials that rained praise. TV interviews ensued. Meanwhile, there had been no more mention of lieutenant bars in Clayton's future. He didn't care. The aftershock of taking a life pressed hard upon his mind. Counseling was offered. He declined. However, he did allow himself the privilege of clocking out of work on time. Nobody raised an eyebrow.

At home he found relief in the company of Kerney, Sara, and Patrick, who were visiting from Santa Fe on spring break and staying at a lovely B&B near downtown. During the weekdays while Grace and Clayton were at work and Hannah was in class, Kerney played tour guide with his family, taking them to the New Mexico Farm & Ranch Heritage Museum, Dripping Springs at the base of the Organ Mountains, White Sands National Monument on the Tularosa Basin, the railroad museum at the train station, and other local attractions, including his alma mater, the New Mexico State University campus.

In the evenings, when everyone had assembled, they either cooked out in the backyard or had dinner at one of the many family-style restaurants in the city. It was good medicine for Clayton's head.

On the last night of their visit, with Grace and Sara chatting in the house and Hannah and Patrick off to see the newest superhero action flick, Clayton and Kerney had some time alone.

Over a brew in the backyard with a warming fire crackling in the outdoor firepit, Kerney asked Clayton if he was ready to return home to Mescalero permanently.

"Not yet," Clayton answered. "I've got some time to put in to max out my pension. Besides, Hannah's thinking about applying to graduate school here at State."

Kerney nodded understandingly. "And you're okay at the job?"

"Sure."

"That sounds pretty wishy-washy."

Clayton laughed. "I'm not happy thinking my investigation is turning cold and nobody except me gives a hoot."

"You can't solve them all."

Clayton's expression hardened. "I can't give up on it. You wouldn't."

"True, but I'm very glad you won't be traipsing around Mexico hunting for this primo assassin."

"You make it sound like such fun," Clayton said lightheartedly. "I'll do it by long distance, if I have to. I've put out some inquiries based on what I know and think I know about this El Jefe. If there's an honest cop or prosecutor in Mexico, maybe I'll get somewhere with it."

"If you need help getting some high-ranking muckety-muck's ear, let me know. I still have some juice."

"Thanks for that. Now, can we talk about something else?"

Kerney raised his empty glass. "Only if I can have another beer."

———

Eagle Pass Resident DEA Agent Maria Sedillo returned from a ceremony in Houston with a commendation in her personal jacket from the special agent in charge. The citation letter noted her outstanding performance in exposing DEA employee Wanda Cantu as an informant to the notorious Piedras Negras Chinese-Mexican gang.

Sedillo didn't feel all that good about it. Had she done her job better, Wanda would still be alive providing valuable information. DEA Houston knew that. But the fact that the Eagle Pass resident office had been compromised for such a long time made it desirable to bestow the honor and hide incompetence. No need to jeopardize every senior supervising agent's career in the Houston office. Instead, all the shiny badges remained untarnished. Long live the bureaucracy.

Sedillo sat in her office unimpressed with the recognition. She needed to do more in the time she had remaining. She'd been unable to get her head completely around the idea that Luis Lorenz's half-brother, Gilberto Garza, was the devout, virtuous, law-abiding citizen that years of department surveillance and deep background probes made him out to be.

Her doubts about the man had floated around in her head for a number of reasons. On an elementary level, the facts made it simply hard to believe the two brothers could be that dissimilar. Although they had different fathers, both had been raised from an early age by their mother, a single woman who'd worked as a food vendor to support her family. The boys had gone to church and school together, shared a bedroom, played soccer on the same team, and had been good but lazy students.

That much Sedillo had learned in the early intelligence reports. Then it went dark. What she didn't find in the records was anything that spoke to the reason for their total estrangement. Surely there was more to *that* story. But it wasn't in the archives.

Instead, in the subsequent report addendums, the falling-out between the brothers was treated as a given, confirmed over and over again by citizens of Piedras Negras who spoke glowingly of Gilberto and hesitantly about Luis. Over the years, nothing had changed the narrative.

Additionally, satellite, communication, and street surveillance supported the assumption. Not once in decades had Luis and Gilberto been seen together, talked on the phone, communicated via email, or exchanged snail mail.

What if it was all smoke and mirrors? If it was a charade, there had to be a way to see through it.

With the El Jefe extraction plan now kaput, Sedillo needed to mount one more scheme to put into play before the time came to meet her maker. It was either that or tread water until the cancer in her head became too unbearable and she had to resign.

She'd promised herself a win. If it wasn't going to be El Jefe, how about Gilberto Garza?

She'd have to come up with a foolproof idea to unmask him and move on it fast. She had an entry point thorough Gilbert's son, Juan. How to use him was the puzzle she needed to solve.

———

Harjo spent his first three days home without once going outside. All he wanted to do was sleep, eat, and ponder what the hell he'd do next. An involuntary leave wasn't a vacation, so he wasn't about to let go of putting a big hurt on Lorenz and his organization.

The front doorbell rang while he was in his pajamas eating a bowl of cold cereal standing over the kitchen sink. He opened up to find his neighbor, Henry Saenz, staring at him with a worried look on his face. The incessant roar of the Interstate 10 traffic flowed up from the valley below.

Short and round in the middle, Henry and his wife Fiona had been Harjo's neighbors since the day he'd moved in. They looked after the house when he was away and wouldn't take a dime to do it. Best neighbors he'd ever had.

"Usually you call to let us know when you are back home," he said. "I was worried."

Harjo smiled sheepishly and stepped aside for Henry to enter. "Sorry, I've been mostly sleeping since I got here. I apologize."

Henry's concerned look cleared. "No need. I've got a boxful of mail at the house for you."

"I'll come get it later. Coffee?"

"I could use a cup."

Harjo brewed a pot. At the kitchen table, Henry caught him up on neighborhood news. A new family had moved into a house on the cul-de-sac one street over. He was astounded how much they'd paid for it. Tim and Judy Ellison, three houses down, had a new grandson, their second. The city had renovated the nearby public park with new benches, playground equipment, trees, sod, and a perimeter fence that was locked at night. The homeless living there had been relocated. The used syringes found there daily were a thing of the past.

"Life goes on," Harjo said. "Anyone looking for me?"

Henry shook his head and got up. "Thanks for the cup."

"Anytime. I'll be over for my mail in an hour."

Henry smiled. "Good to have you back."

"Good to be back."

A shower, shave, and a look in his clothes closet convinced Harjo he needed a trim and some new duds. He dressed in jeans, a long-sleeve T-shirt, and went to get his mail.

El Paso sat squarely on the northern reaches of the Chihuahuan Desert, which meant it would likely be dry and windy no matter the temperature. Windblown dust peppered him as usual as he jogged over to Henry and Fiona's.

Fiona opened the door before he could knock and greeted him with a big hug. A southern girl who had bailed out of a sour marriage to a career Army officer, she'd met and married Henry over twenty years ago.

She was warm, charming, and easy to like. So of course he had to sit down so they could catch up. And yes, he'd enjoy a refreshment along with a piece of lemon pound cake she knew that he loved, made especially for him last night.

Harjo enjoyed every minute of the hour-long visit, as did Henry, who always sat back and marveled at the enchanting woman good luck had sent his way. Being in their company always made Harjo feel almost normal.

Back home, he dumped the box of mail Henry had collected and sorted through it. Most was junk. The house was paid off, as was his personal vehicle. All the routine monthly bills went directly to a CPA who paid them out of a special account. Harjo personally paid his incidental charges in cash or when due.

An envelope addressed in his sister's handwriting and postmarked less than a week ago caught his eye. He placed his palm over the letter, hesitant to open it. Eloisa and Cruz Villalobos only had one child, Mark. After finishing college and against his parents' wishes, Mark had entered training to become a DEA special agent. As valedictorian of his academy class he got to choose his assignment and elected to go undercover. The department sent him to penetrate the Lorenz drug cartel.

As far as Eloisa and Cruz knew, he'd gone missing on a routine assignment in Mexico. That was all they might ever know.

Mark was dead. Harjo believed it and DEA Intelligence concurred, but without corroboration he remained MIA. According to a prosecutor in Coahuila—a semi-reliable source—he'd been one of four Lorenz foot soldiers killed for inadvertently leaving a million dollars behind in a remote Texas farmhouse. After they'd been brutally murdered, their bodies had been burned and their ashes scattered.

Harjo's sister and brother-in-law now existed in no-man's-land between paralyzing anguish and cautious optimism. It had to end. They deserved resolution.

He read Eloisa's letter. They'd heard nothing new from the department and had been given the usual assurances that everything was being done to locate Mark. They'd asked their congresswoman to request more information from the Department of Justice and she'd received basically the same bureaucratic mumbo-jumbo. Was there some higher-up he personally knew who could give them a clearer picture of the investigation? They needed to know something, anything.

Realizing his voice might betray any lies he might tell a sister who knew him too well, Harjo didn't want to chance a reply by phone.

Instead he composed an email to Eloisa telling her he would go to Washington and personally meet with the chief of DEA Intelligence and get back to her soon after. He thought about adding some reassuring BS about Mark being okay and it would all work out and decided against it. Instead, he closed with love and clicked the send tab.

The wind had abated when Harjo left the house for a quick clothes-buying trip, a trim at the walk-in hair salon, and a swing by the drug-store to pick up some travel-size toiletries.

He'd be traveling, but not to Washington. He was booked on an afternoon flight to San Antonio, where he'd pick up a rental and drive to Eagle Pass. There, he'd settle into a suite at a discreet, privately owned hacienda on the outskirts of town where no one would be looking for him. Once he was reacquainted with the area and had his bearings, he'd flush out a cartel underling and encourage him to disclose a way to reach Lorenz without getting caught.

Harjo smiled. It had been a long time since he'd taken a real, relaxing vacation. If everything clicked, this would be the best of them all.

———

Among the Kickapoos, Estavio Trevino was more than what his nickname El Jefe indicated. When it was necessary to harvest deer for important tribal ceremonies, he was always chosen chief of the hunt. In his native language his name was Wind Stands with Bear Among the Wallows. A great hunter's name that he wore proudly.

Men of the tribe who'd hunted with him told stories of his prowess. He could sit alone and unmoving for hours on a mountain where no deer had been seen for years and, before the sun had dipped below the horizon, kill the necessary number needed for a naming feast or an adoption fiesta.

Every year in March for several weeks, the village and its surrounding seventeen thousand acres were closed to outsiders. During this time of religious rites and tribal ceremonies, secure among his people and removed from all outside influences, Trevino enjoyed his homeland the most. But not this year. The death of his son, Fernando, known among the people as Whistling Bear Paints with Clay, soured the season.

In the past, Trevino had purchased only information from Lieutenant Roger Ulibarri. This time he'd required more from the Texas cop. He was to secure Fernando's body and deliver it to him at the town of Múzquiz on a specific date.

He didn't care how Ulibarri did it, but made it clear his life depended upon it. He also promised a substantial reward.

Ulibarri showed up on schedule on a dirt road outside of town with a tale of how Fernando's body had been released by the FBI and taken to a Las Cruces mortuary for cremation, a customary practice for unknown deceased or those with no living relatives. He'd gotten there just in time to stop the cremation. He paid for embalming services, bought a plain casket, and gave the funeral director a big bribe to secure his cooperation and silence. With the casket hidden in the bed of his pickup truck under a hundred dollars' worth of used furniture he'd purchased at an El Paso thrift store, he'd had no trouble crossing into Mexico.

With Ulibarri's help, Trevino transferred the casket and the junky furniture to his truck and paid the cop in hundred-dollar bills.

Ulibarri pocketed the roll of Benjamin Franklins and made a sour face. "I don't want to do anything like this again."

"You'll do what I ask," Trevino replied flatly.

"Let's just keep it to the information you need to know." Stocky, red in the face, and a bit gone to seed, Ulibarri was still out of breath from the exertion.

Trevino leaned close. "Right now I need to know you're trustworthy, otherwise you won't be going home. No matter what it is, you will do as I ask next time I call. Understood?"

Ulibarri swallowed hard and nodded. "Okay."

Trevino smiled thinly. "Good. Safe journey, amigo."

He waited until the Texas cop was in his truck spewing dust from his tires on the dirt road. Once the truck was out of sight, Trevino turned his pickup onto a faint track that would take him the back way to Colonia de los Kickapoo. His spirits lifted as he carried the body of his son home so that Fernando might properly make his final journey.

CHAPTER II

In the middle of the twentieth century, Trevino's village and a wide surrounding area suffered a severe, long-lasting drought. Growing up after the rains finally returned, he'd witnessed the slow recovery of the land. The river that ran through the village was no longer dry. Springs that were once a trickle gushed water, until the large neighboring rancheros began drilling wells, lowering the water table. Still, water flowed, enough to bathe and wash.

In the valley, grasses and wildflowers carpeted the pastureland, and the high mountains that towered above showed signs that an occasional black bear roamed through the Colonia de los Kickapoo. In his lifetime, Trevino had yet to see one within a hundred miles of the village.

Smaller wild game, hunted to virtual extinction, returned in lesser numbers on the land granted to the tribe by the Mexican government. While out hunting, Trevino rejoiced at the sight of a porcupine hiding in a tree or a squirrel scampering across the trail. The sound of nearby mourning doves cheered him, as did quail startled into flight by his proximity. He'd pause and offer a silent prayer that all the wild creatures would thrive, and bountiful hunting would return as it once had been during the long ago days of the ancestors.

The village was quiet upon Trevino's arrival with his son's corpse. The building of the summerhouses had concluded during his absence. After prayers and a tobacco offering were made, women would gather the saplings needed to complete the thatched roofs.

Trevino drove directly to the graveyard that held the departed members of the Black Bear Clan, unloaded the coffin next to his father's grave, and began to dig. A wet winter and early spring had softened the soil, and his shovel sliced easily into the moist earth.

As he bent to his task in the coolness of the early spring evening, he could hear soft voices floating behind him from the village enclave. People were gathering outside to watch. He paid them no mind. His chief, Caballo Galindo, had granted him permission to bury his son without any help or disturbance. At a later time, Trevino would ask for a ceremony to bring Fernando's soul back to the tribe for one night so that his journey to the spirit world would be unimpeded.

Steadily he dug, standing waist-deep in the now-dry soil, carving out chunks of dirt, flinging them into the ever-growing mound where he would later place a wooden marker to honor his son's memory.

He sang softly to himself as he increased the pace, a breeze whisking the sweat away from his face. His body began to ache, a sign that Fernando's spirit hovered nearby, urging him on. He was glad to feel his son's presence.

Trevino finished at moonrise, climbed out under a star-filled sky, opened the casket, and stopped singing. Fernando's naked body had been cut open and crudely stitched back together. The sight saddened him. He got an old blanket from his truck, tucked it gently around Fernando's torso, and, as custom dictated, put a pinch of tobacco in each of his hands to accompany him on his journey to the spirit land.

He then placed a small carved-wood figurine of the Virgin of Guadalupe next to his head.

His aged Mexican housekeeper, Consuelo, had asked Trevino to do it as a favor. She'd loved Fernando like a grandson. He had no reason not to. Kitzihiat, the Great Spirit, was no different than Consuelo's god, except that he gave Kickapoos certain knowledge others did not have. Slowly, he closed the lid, wondering how to safely jockey the casket into the grave without tipping it over.

Approaching footsteps caused him to turn. Galindo stood a few yards away, a camp lantern in one hand, a shovel in the other.

"Perhaps you need my help, Estavio," he said. Galindo was a tall man still in his prime, and his strength was legendary.

"It would be most welcome," Trevino replied.

Together, they moved the casket to the edge of the grave and slowly lowered it, careful to keep it level. Silently they finished the burial together, sculpting a mound of dirt over the grave site.

"He was a good son to you," Galindo said, careful to avoid the mention of Fernando's Kickapoo name.

"Yes."

Galindo shouldered his shovel and led the way back to the village with his lantern. "Who will you choose to retire his spirit?"

Trevino joined alongside. "Jose Hernandez has a young son, three years old."

"He is of your clan, which is good. I'm sure Jose will be honored by the adoption. But, of his three children, the boy is his only son." Galindo's unspoken next question hung in the air.

Trevino nodded. "I wish the boy to live with me."

"It is permitted, although Jose may not be pleased."

"I will speak to him," Trevino replied. It would be a simple choice, give up his son or die for his carelessness. He thought it was more than fair. Jose would also.

"You must wait until the next new year for the ceremony," Galindo cautioned.

"That is perfect," Trevino replied. "I have much work to do for now. Many jobs."

Galindo paused. "You will be leaving?"

"First to my hacienda, and then I must travel."

"You have done much for our people."

"I hope to do more."

"What will you do with the old furniture you brought?"

"It is for the village. Firewood, perhaps?"

Galindo laughed. "Always welcomed. It is a long trip into the mountains to fetch more. You must be careful out in the White Eyes world. I'll need you back soon to lead the next naming hunt."

"I'll be here," Trevino said.

"Tonight, stay in my house."

"Thank you."

There were nods from tribal members as they passed by, but no one spoke. In the hills above the village a coyote sang. It was not an omen of bad luck, but Trevino willed it into silence anyway.

———

Jose Hernandez stood hat in hand when Trevino emerged from Chief Galindo's house in the early morning hours. He was not surprised to see him. Many years ago, Jose had been a glue-sniffing kid living under the Eagle Pass International Bridge, stealing groceries from convenience stores and begging money from strangers. He'd turned his life around and now made his living employed by the tribe. He repaired and maintained the village fences, transported supplies from town, kept snakes away from dwellings, and ensured visiting outsiders did not violate tribal customs or taboos.

Sturdy and thick through the chest, he had a wide, crooked nose suffered as a young man during a beating by some American White Eye soldiers in a Piedras Negras bar.

"You wish to have my son bid yours farewell?" Jose asked tentatively.

"Yes."

"Of course, he will do so with honor."

The little boy was known as Jose Junior. Inquisitive and fearless. Trevino used his Kickapoo name. "After the fiesta Little Bear Den Near Cattails will live with me. Be my son."

"Jefe," Jose protested.

"I do this generously so that your wife and children will not be without a husband and father," Trevino noted pointedly.

Jose dropped his gaze. "I said too much to Juan Garza about where you could be found. The money he offered made me stupid."

"Yes, it did. If Garza asks again how to find me, let me know immediately."

Jose nodded. "And if you are gone?"

"Kill him, if you think you can get away with it."

Jose blinked rapidly at the daunting thought of it.

Trevino laughed. "Do nothing. Tell me upon my return."

Jose smiled with relief as he watched El Jefe drive away in his truck.

———

From the day of his birth, Estavio Trevino was different, unlike any other Kickapoo baby. He babbled sounds endlessly, crawled and scampered on his hands and knees through dust and dirt to study everything and anything that caught his eye. He drew pictures in the sand by the river of all the animals he encountered, detailed and accurate for one so young. He perfectly imitated the cries of animals and the songs of birds and could whistle better than the most accomplished adults.

As he grew, he mastered language easily. Kickapoo and Spanish to begin with, learned at home, quickly followed by English that he absorbed listening to White Eye visitors at the village or following American tourists in town. At four years old he was reading, struggling to understand the books in the library of an anthropologist who lived in Múzquiz, where his parents frequently visited.

Lured by the man's gifts and money, they were among the many tribal members who spent hours talking to him about the customs and history of the tribe, answering only some of his probing questions, certainly not all. His unsuccessful attempt to unravel and completely understand the Kickapoo people went on for years. After he finally left, there was talk that he had published a book about the tribe.

Each time Estavio went with his parents when they were interviewed, he sneaked a book to read and return during the next visit. It didn't matter if it was in English or Spanish. Nor was the subject matter of the book of any importance. At home, he'd hide the book from his parents and read it in one of the more faraway village fields where he couldn't be seen.

In the tribe, learning the ways of the White Eyes was frowned upon, their system of education rejected and scorned. Estavio had no desire to be a contrarian, but he could not help himself. He had an insatiable desire to know everything.

As he grew up, he put aside books for a time and returned to his love of nature. With his father's guidance, he learned the ways of the hunter and tracker. From his mother came his knowledge of plants and medicine. Through the elders he mastered the stories, prayers, and rituals needed to call the wild animals to him.

In his youth, he'd disappear alone into the high mountains without notice and be gone for days, sometimes weeks, returning with game not seen on the land for many years. It was decided by the elders that he had a powerful spirit; whether it be for good or evil was yet to be revealed.

At the age of seventeen, he left abruptly for six years, making no contact with anyone in the village during that time. Many thought him dead. Soon after his departure, his mother died, broken by cancer, weeping for him in her bed. Six months later, a drunk driver killed his father as he walked along the shoulder of the highway outside of Múzquiz.

Upon his return, Trevino said nothing of his years away from the village. But all could see the changes in him. He was taller, stronger, more confident in his manner. A dominant presence, wary and unsocial, he prowled the colonia restless as a panther before vanishing for a month into the mountains.

There on a remote, forested mountaintop he burned the U.S. Army uniform he'd worn at his discharge. Serving under a forged identity, he'd enlisted, become a Special Forces sniper, risen to the rank of sergeant first class, and been decorated for bravery. As a soldier he'd learned the skills needed to be a killer and had experienced the feeling of satisfaction it gave him.

For hundreds of years, Kickapoos had been warriors, hostile and vindictive to those seeking to destroy their way of life. Capable of great savagery against their enemies, they remained fiercely independent. Tribal elders continued to believe in the return of Kickapoo greatness, provided the people stuck to their old ways. Trevino knew it was pure bullshit. They'd never prevail against the White Eyes' path of perpetual death, destruction, and devastation. But perhaps they could survive.

Six years in the world had opened his eyes. The way to restore his tribe was with money. As a soldier, he'd been paid to kill. Why not, on behalf of his people, continue his craft as a civilian? Surely there were those who would pay well for his services.

He came out of the mountains with the carcass of a freshly killed and dressed bear, an event that caused much rejoicing. The elders, who hadn't tasted the delicacy of bear meat for many years, decided Trevino's return heralded good fortune for the tribe. He was made chief of the hunt for as long as he wished. It fit perfectly with what Trevino had in mind for himself.

He'd also returned as the owner of a small ranchero he'd come upon in a hidden pocket valley with a perpetual spring of clear water that bordered the magnificent and dangerous Bolsón de Mapimí. There he'd found Cipriano Morales, a man of some eight decades, semi-crippled, living alone with two old dogs in his dilapidated jacal surrounded by a small herd of goats. Seated under the open ramada in front of his adobe home on chairs crudely fashioned from mesquite wood, Trevino soon learned Cipriano's wife and two sons were long dead and his only daughter, a naturalized American citizen, lived in Iowa with her children and Ecuadoran husband who managed an auto parts store. He hadn't seen her in forty years.

They talked for two days: Cipriano starved for conversation; Trevino captivated by the old man and the possibilities the ranchero presented. Before Trevino left, Cipriano agreed to sell out for a reasonable sum of money, but only after receiving Estavio's solemn vow to inform Cipriano's daughter of her father's death, and to bury him, when the time came, next to his wife and sons in the family plot on the side of the hill.

Trevino wrote out a transfer-of-ownership agreement that Cipriano signed in a shaky hand, and asked if he had any legal papers that showed proof of title. With a smile and nod, the old man disappeared inside his home and returned with an old leather document pouch. In it was a faded but legible original government deed dated 1878 and signed by Porfirio Díaz, the then-president of Mexico. It awarded to Manolito Morales, Cipriano's great-grandfather, twenty-one hundred hectares of land that included the valley, surrounding hills, and a narrow swath of the Bolsón de Mapimí.

They sealed the agreement with a handshake. A hundred-dollar bill that Trevino always carried in his wallet for emergencies served as a down payment. To celebrate, they drank a bottle of mescal that Cipriano kept for special occasions. Until his passing, Trevino would regularly check on his welfare, bring whiskey, food, and supplies to the ranchero, and keep Cipriano's jacal in good repair.

Trevino had found the bulwark he needed to keep the world at bay. It had become a very good day.

———

Trevino returned home to find his housekeeper still upset about Fernando's death. His reassurance that Fernando had been buried properly with the Virgin of Guadalupe figurine placed in his casket somewhat consoled her. But her presence was a distraction. Needing solitude and privacy, he sent her to her quarters for the remainder of the day, settled in his library chair, and powered up his laptop.

Other than the man was half Apache and had a checkered career, he knew nothing about Clayton Istee. Quickly, his searches yielded valuable, basic facts. He was married, with two children. Both were in college. His wife ran a preschool day-care center in Las Cruces. His mother, a retired director of nursing at the Mescalero Public Health Service Hospital, lived on the reservation.

Istee's father, Kevin Kerney, a retired police chief, lived on a ranch outside of Santa Fe. He was married to a retired Army general, and they had one child, Patrick, a teenager. Archived newspaper articles spoke of Kerney's inheriting considerable wealth. Trevino flagged it for further inquiry.

Recent online articles summarized a cold-case murder investigation of the killing of a college girlfriend of Kerney's, with felony murder charges filed against him, subsequently dropped. The initial investigating officer had been Istee, who'd resigned his position from the New Mexico State Police for mishandling the case. That, too, was interesting. Why would a son go after his father in such a situation?

He was intrigued by Kerney's wife. Trevino's experiences in the Army made it relatively easy for him to know the difference between warriors and posers. Brigadier General Sara Brannon's military service looked to be the real deal.

When he came for Istee and snatched him up, who would look for him? Kerney? His wife? Some unknown?

He settled back in his chair. There was much more to absorb before traveling to New Mexico. Once there, he'd spend however much time was needed to comfortably navigate his way around and observe his quarry before striking.

It was not going to be a quick kill. Istee would suffer long and hard before dying.

CHAPTER 12

Harjo started out for Eagle Pass driving a pickup truck with legal plates he'd rented from a San Antonio used-car dealer. His DEA credentials and a sweet extra fifty dollars on top of the daily rate had sealed the deal. Experience had taught him that driving around a strange town in an ordinary rental car was never smart. Anyone with watchful eyes would notice little things such as a license plate holder or decal that advertised the car rental company, a series of indelible numbers on the plate or windshield sticker used for inventory control, or simply that the make and model of the vehicle screamed rental. Such carelessness would get him made in a hurry. He'd had his cover blown once south of the border in Coahuila. He could get very dead if it happened again.

To blend in with the locals, he pulled into a stop-and-rob along the highway, bought some snack food and sodas, and scattered the empty packaging and bottles on the passenger seat and floorboard. Three ten-spots at an auto junkyard got him some damaged wheels, bald tires, and rusty rims to throw into the bed of the truck. A detour on a muddy gravel county road coated the vehicle with splattered dirt and a sheen of dust.

He arrived in Eagle Pass late in the afternoon and kept right on going until he reached one of the largest unincorporated colonias southeast of town, a low-income slum area without basic services. The roads were dirt, and the houses were cobbled together with whatever building materials people could afford or salvage. There was no running water, no sewage system, and few houses had electricity. The land was owned by the residents—at last count some two-thousand-plus Latino citizens.

Parcels sold to them decades ago by developers had been scraped clean with a promise to build a modern subdivision. Instead, the developers had taken the cash and disappeared. State and local politicians apparently weren't bothered by the massive rip-off or the residents' continuing state of squalor.

At the center of the colonia, Harjo stopped at a closed, electronic wrought-iron driveway gate in front of a large single-story adobe house. Surrounded by a high, plastered block wall that partially shielded a grove of mature shade trees, it was an extravagant oasis in the midst of chronic poverty.

Along both sides of the border, before Airbnb existed or B&Bs were popular, places like Gabriela's had sprung up to cater to a special clientele, mostly drug lords, arms dealers, and professional assassins, with an occasional fugitive from justice thrown in.

The underground network of safe havens thrived in unexpected, out-of-the-way places, which was part of the appeal for traveling underworld bosses and their minions. For a substantial fee, you got a comfortable suite, meals, drinks, and secure communication links to the outside world. Once you were vetted, no personal questions were asked, and you got an uninterrupted good night's sleep.

To book a stay required a confidential code, arrival and departure dates, and full payment in advance cleared through the owner's bank account before you showed up at the front door.

Harjo had stayed here several times before. Gabriela took in only one guest at a time and her rates were rather pricey. An additional surcharge was added to the bill if you also required her personal after-hours attention. Harjo had passed on that, although she was quite alluring.

Due to a last-minute cancellation, he'd lucked out. He beeped the horn, smiled at the CCTV camera mounted on the perimeter wall, and the gate swung open. He eased the truck to a stop in the designated guest parking space and grabbed his gear. Adjacent to the house was a garage with an attached apartment. A building against the far back wall appeared to be either a workshop or studio.

He knocked on the front door. A young, attractive woman greeted him with a slight smile. Harjo had not met her before. She wore a short skirt and a white T-shirt that showed off her tiny waist, slim legs, and slender arms.

"You are most welcome, senor," she said. "I am Catherina. Gabriela is not available at the moment."

"Buenos días," Harjo said. "That's okay. I'll see her later."

"Let me show you to your room," the young woman offered.

"No need. I know the way."

She nodded and politely stepped aside.

The living room was wide and long, with comfortable chairs and couches arranged for either a view of the shady patio through the large front windows or the massive see-through fireplace that backed up to the chef's kitchen. Gabriela collected art—most of it mediocre land-scape oils and watercolors—and it filled the walls.

He made his way through a plant-filled sunroom to the attached guest wing, where much to his surprise he found Gabriela and Special Agent Maria Sedillo seated in the living room waiting for him.

"What's this all about?" he asked lightly, wishing he had a nine-millimeter in his hand instead of in the suitcase. Given the circumstances, he didn't feel particularly trusting.

Gabriela smiled thinly. "It seems you are not simply a well-mannered arms dealer, Agent Harjo."

Harjo shot Sedillo a questioning look before responding. "You now know better. I didn't realize you were friends with the DEA resident agent."

"You'll understand later on," Sedillo replied. "Sit down, Agent Harjo."

Harjo sat across from Sedillo. "Are you enjoying your assignment?"

"Forget the small talk. You are officially suspended from duty until further notice."

"What brought that on?"

"By showing up in Eagle Pass while on involuntary leave. It was ordered by headquarters."

"Why am I not surprised?"

"They don't want you going after Lorenz or El Jefe. Be glad it got canceled. It was a setup right from the start."

"Explain that to me."

"You heard about Wanda Cantu, the mole we had in the Eagle Pass office?"

Harjo nodded. News like that was impossible to contain, especially with the added ingredient of the woman's suicide. "Congratulations on the commendation," he replied, letting the sarcasm roll off his tongue.

Sedillo's expression turned steely. "Wanda emailed me a confession before she killed herself. It included a very detailed chronology of all the confidential information she'd passed on to Sammy Shen over the years."

Waiting for more, Harjo switched his attention to Gabriela and stayed silent. She was close to tears.

"You met Catherina?" Sedillo asked.

"A charming young lady."

"My daughter," Gabriela noted.

"Four years ago, when she was a sophomore in high school, Juan Garza raped her," Sedillo said. "Out of shame, she didn't tell Gabriela. But she did tell an Eagle Pass police officer, who did nothing about it, not even filing a report."

"Corrupt cop," Harjo speculated. "You know this how?"

"From Wanda's confession. The officer passed the information of the rape to Juan's uncle, Lorenz, who asked Sammy Shen to find out if DEA knew about it. Wanda reported that we did not."

Sedillo paused, waiting for Harjo to react.

"You haven't lost me so far."

"That officer is currently an undercover detective with the Eagle Pass PD. Garza became my CI by way of a drug bust the cop fabricated. It was a setup designed to establish another channel into the resident office the cartel could use to gather valuable information or spread disinformation."

"You knew this?" Harjo queried.

"I suspected it," Sedillo replied. "But I didn't suspect Wanda was a mole until she made a few mistakes and blew her cover."

"The cartel isn't about to give up El Jefe."

Sedillo nodded in agreement. "It's really more a syndicate than a cartel."

"Why do you say that?" Harjo asked.

She sketched out her theory that the Piedras Negras crime families were deeply intertwined, that El Jefe was a frequent participant in many of the strategy sessions, and that he'd been employed to kill the couple who'd stumbled upon Lorenz's left-behind million dollars.

She explained that Wanda had recorded in her confession how Sammy Shen laundered Lorenz's drug money two different ways. Most of it got washed through Sammy's complex corporate entities. But periodically it would be transported directly by Lorenz to a different intermediary used by Sammy.

"I believe that money goes to Juan's father, Gilberto, who's a silent partner in the cartel," Sedillo noted. "I've done the research. The cash was for him."

Sedillo had been known during her time in the El Paso office as the best intelligence analyst in the district. Harjo wasn't about to dismiss her hypothesis. "What have you got so far?"

"Years ago when Gilberto bought the Mercado, the legal documents show that Lorenz was a full partner, but I imagine he was too busy rising through the ranks at the police department to be of any help in the business. Later, when Lorenz got into drug smuggling big-time, Gilberto bought him out and paid in cash to do it."

Sedillo smiled, warming to her subject. "But Gilberto didn't have any cash of his own. He was scraping by, barely able to pay the bills. The money had to come from Lorenz."

"Plausible," Bernard said. "Anything else?"

Sedillo told Harjo that China Dolls, Sammy Shen's original enterprise, had started out as a company importing low-cost electronics into Mexico. One of his first retail clients was Gilberto Garza.

"Gilberto was also listed as a shareholder in the company, along with Sammy's father, Longwei," Sedillo noted. "When Sammy jumped into the money-laundering game, Gilberto sold his shares at a huge profit, and Longwei's restaurant went from being a mom-and-pop diner to a fine dining establishment. Brand-new and built from the ground up."

"Who have you told about this?" Harjo asked.

"Just you."

Harjo turned back to Gabriela. "How are you involved in this?"

"I want justice for my daughter. Whatever it takes, and I know better than to trust the pendejo cops on either side of the border."

Harjo shook his head in amazement. He wanted Lorenz, Sedillo wanted Gilberto Garza, and Gabriela wanted Juan. Maybe Clayton Istee should come along to go after El Jefe. And what about Sammy and his father Longwei? And the German-Mexican girlfriend? It was starting to feel like a Keystone Cops version of Murder, Inc.

"How do we follow the money trail to prove all this?" he asked.

"No time for that," Sedillo answered. "Juan is the weak link. You bring him to me, and I'll do the rest."

"The rest?"

Sedillo smiled. "I can be convincing,"

Harjo laughed. He liked her spunk. "This could cost you your job."

"I'm planning on it."

Harjo let the remark pass. "How did you know I was staying at Gabriela's?"

"There have been eyes and ears on you since you left El Paso."

"Whose?"

Maria shrugged. "Us. Them. Probably the CIA. That's who yanked the investigation away from you. There are those in Washington who think loyalty trumps everything else."

"That complicates matters."

"I'll bet they'll let whatever we do play out before intervening," Maria replied. "We can't keep them from watching, so why worry? Are you in?"

Harjo weighed his options. If he refused, he could retire in twenty-eight months and be sailing on a good boat with a good woman he'd met in Bermuda. It was a long-standing, tantalizing, open invitation. Or he could sign on to this suicide mission and get killed trying to bring down Lorenz.

"I'm all in," he said.

Sedillo stood up. "We'll meet in an hour. There's much to discuss."

He watched the women leave, wondering about his bullheaded

stupidity. He'd been living on the sharp edge of disaster for most of his adult life. Was it a result of a latent death wish?

That aside, Agent Sedillo, who'd been teased by some in the El Paso office as Little Miss Social Worker, was one helluva smart cop. Go figure.

———

Juan Garza grumbled as he climbed into his truck for an early morning meeting with Agent Sedillo at the Oasis Surf and Turf Restaurant in Carrizo Springs. She'd called late at night, woken him from a deep sleep, and demanded that they meet real early. And it always had to be someplace away from Eagle Pass.

He smirked at her feeble cloak-and-dagger games. If only she knew how easily she'd been played.

Juan didn't see any sense to meeting her. The big DEA plan to sneak agents into Mexico to capture El Jefe had been jettisoned and Sedillo was dying of a brain tumor. He was tired of playing stoolie, and when her replacement arrived, he wanted the gig to be over.

Uncle Lorenz and Longwei Shen didn't see it that way. With Sammy's informant dead, Juan was the only one with a foot in the door. It was vital to learn what Sedillo may have discovered from Wanda Cantu about the Piedras Negras partners. Whatever she asked him to do would surely provide insight into issues of importance to the syndicate.

Big yawn, Juan thought. Snatch the bitch and torture her. Kill her after she talks. He hadn't dared voice his suggestion to his uncle or Longwei, but it would end any questions about what she knew and let him get back to his real job of running the crews responsible for moving product and keeping order within the cartel.

It had drizzled rain on the drive. The air felt stuffy and the dawn sky was heavily overcast. He parked behind the restaurant, rolled down the truck windows, lit a joint, and looked around. Usually Sedillo would be here waiting for him. But there was only one vehicle in the lot, a pickup parked at the back fence with the hood up. Probably some stumble-down drunk left it there until he sobered up and could reclaim it.

He heard footsteps on the gravel and glanced out the driver's window. A hand slammed his face into the steering wheel. He tried pulling away. A blinding pain hammered his skull, and everything went black.

Harjo holstered his nine-millimeter, checked to make sure Jose was out cold, opened the driver's door, and patted him down for weapons. He was clean except for a smartphone in his shirt pocket. Harjo removed the battery, smashed the phone, and threw it in the dumpster behind the restaurant. He disabled the GPS tracking system, yanked Juan out of the truck onto the gravel, dragged him to his vehicle, and hoisted him into its bed.

Breathing hard, he tied Jose's feet and hands, lashed him with rope to the tie-downs, covered him with a blanket, and crawled into the cab feeling decidedly out of shape and old. What the hell was he doing? No backing out now.

———

Juan came out of a deep fog, the back of his head searing in pain, his forehead throbbing. He was strapped to a straight-backed chair and cold to the bone. He looked down. All he had on were his shorts. The room was dark except for a slideshow of sorts on the screen in front of him. He wasn't seeing well enough to make sense of it. Somewhere in the room an air conditioner hummed.

He felt the jab of a needle in his arm.

"What did you give me?" he mumbled at a shadowy figure standing next to the chair.

"Hello, Juan," Sedillo said. "A little chemical cocktail, that's all. I'll leave you alone for a while. Enjoy the show."

Juan recognized her voice. "Bitch."

A door behind him opened, light poured in, and then it closed. In the dark room, he had only the slideshow to look at. He started shivering. An image of a hand inserting the bit of a cordless electric drill into a man's ear popped up on the screen. It made him gag.

Outside, Sedillo locked the door to the large windowless equipment shed at the rear of Gabriela's lot. Deep into the night, Harjo, Gabriela, and Catherina had emptied the shed, cleaned it thoroughly, and converted it to a makeshift interrogation chamber. In addition to the chair, the screen, and the laptop used to run the slideshow, a digital high-definition camcorder on a tripod was positioned in a corner of the room focused on Garza. It would record everything.

Getting a ride from Gabriela, Sedillo had brought Juan's truck from Carrizo Springs and hid it in the garage.

"How long before he cracks?" Harjo asked as Sedillo approached the back patio.

"I honestly don't know," she replied. "After the methamphetamine-LSD cocktail kicks in, I'm counting that the grotesque, gory slides of torture and dismemberment will overload his senses. We're about to alter his brain function, weaken his body with the cold temperature, and burn away his perception of reality. That should do the trick."

"You hope," Harjo added.

Sedillo smiled. "Juan's a bully, so I'm fairly optimistic. The slideshow runs for an hour without repetition. Let's see how he holds up after two viewings."

"He'll be half frozen to death."

Sedillo settled down at the wrought-iron patio table and powered her tablet. "I'll keep my eye on him."

Harjo was impressed. "Are you sure you're not CIA?"

"I applied," she said. "They wouldn't have me."

———

Juan had thrown up last night's dinner. It was a foul-smelling wet pile in his lap dripping between his legs, slowly coagulating. A series of autopsy slides of bodies being dissected had terrified him. He'd couldn't stand the thought of being cut open. It had been a secret fear his entire life.

His heart was pounding in his chest and he could hear the synchronized beat of blood in his ears. He couldn't feel his hands or his feet. His teeth chattered. Images kept methodically exploding in front of him, but he couldn't tell what he was watching. The pictures blended into abstract colors.

Then his vision turned telephotographic. He saw minute details of each slide. The spray of blood from a chain saw cutting through a man's arm. The gooey mess of a punctured eyeball. Why would anyone show him such horrible things?

He looked down at his chest to make sure he hadn't been cut open with his innards exposed. Tied at the wrists to the chair arms, he could see his fingers were still there. He never realized he had twenty of them. They wouldn't move. He counted again. Nineteen. Had a pinkie been sliced off? He shrieked in dismay.

His head felt woozy. He was wired, jumpy, and his mind wouldn't stop working. Shock waves vibrated throughout his body. Every nerve tingled with electricity. He was blowing up, freezing. In a panic, he tried to rip free from the restraints.

"Let me go!" he screamed. "Let me go!"

Outside on the patio, Sedillo looked up from her laptop, impressed that Juan had lasted two full cycles before breaking down.

"What's next?" Harjo asked from over her shoulder.

"We'll slowly warm him up. It will take another couple of hours before he's cogent. Then we interrogate. I'll keep running the slide-show until then."

"Any chance Lorenz will send his men looking for Juan here?"

"Gabriela doubts it, but you never know."

Harjo placed an AK-47 on the patio table. "Keep it close by."

Harjo cradled an AK in his arm, had a Colt 911 holstered on his belt, and had loaded up on extra full clips and magazines. Sedillo smiled. "I'm glad I remembered to raid the arsenal at work."

"Me, too," Harjo said.

———

The screen went dark. Light from behind flooded over him and a blanket floated down over his shoulders.

Juan looked up. "You're dead."

"Not quite yet," Sedillo replied with a friendly smile.

"Can I go now?" he pleaded, his voice high and quivery.

"We have a little more work to do first. Let's get you cleaned up and dressed."

"Okay," Juan replied submissively.

Harjo cut Juan loose from the restraints, took him outside, hosed him down, and had him towel off. Wobbly, he had a hard time dressing. It took several tries before he got his pants on. Harjo marched him inside, where Sedillo waited. The overhead lights were on. The restraint chair had been unbolted from the floor and removed, replaced by two office-style padded chairs staged for an interview with a small table in between them. On it was a legal-size accordion file. The camcorder had been repositioned to film both parties. Harjo shoved Juan in a chair and stepped back.

Sedillo sat opposite Juan and smiled. A cordless power drill sat on the floor next to her out of camera range. A nice reminder of what could happen.

"The man with the gun will kill you if you try to run," Sedillo said. "Nod your head if you understand."

Juan glanced at Harjo and nodded.

"If you lie to me, we'll have to start all over again with the slideshow and all the other inconveniences. Do you understand?"

Juan gulped. "Yes."

"Good. Are you ready to begin?"

Juan nodded.

Harjo switched on the camera.

Sedillo recited the standard interrogator's introduction that established the basics of who she was, the identity of the subject, the reason for the interview, and the date, time, and place. In this case at an undisclosed location.

"Juan, did you voluntarily agree to this interview?" she asked.

"Yes."

"Have you been coerced in any way to meet with me?"

Juan shook his head.

"Please answer verbally."

"No, you haven't done anything to me."

"I have a few basic questions to begin."

She started out conversationally, asking about his date and place of birth, citizenship status, names of parents and siblings. Was Luis Lopez Lorenz his uncle? Had him talk about his year away at college.

He answered without hesitation, comfortable confirming commonly known facts. Sedillo opened the accordion folder and removed a file. "You've been in rehab twice for drug problems."

Juan slouched against the back of his chair. "Yeah."

"Once for twenty-one days. The most recent was for twenty-eight days, two years ago."

"So, I had a problem. I still use, but not like I used to."

Sedillo flipped through the file. "What I found interesting in both cases is that your therapists diagnosed you as a borderline personality with only a mild cannabis dependence."

"Those records are confidential," he sputtered. "You shouldn't have them."

Sedillo smiled. "It says in the file you're not really an addict. More like an impulsive, narcissistic, angry person with authority issues who is prone to violence. And that you're a gifted liar."

Juan laughed harshly. "You must have someone else's record."

"Why would anybody go into a rehabilitation program twice for a medical condition they really didn't have?" Sedillo questioned. "Any ideas?"

"You tell me."

Sedillo put the file away. "We'll come back to that. Four years ago you brutally raped a sixteen-year-old girl. Remember?"

Juan leaned forward. "That's bullshit."

"Did you even know her name?"

"I've never been arrested for anything like that."

"You make an interesting distinction." Sedillo searched for another file and extracted it from the accordion folder. "The report she gave to the police states she was in town at a party when—as a prank—her companions decided to leave her behind. She was waiting for a taxi on the sidewalk to take her home when you stopped and offered her a ride. When she refused, you hit her, pulled her into your vehicle, drove to a remote location, raped her, and threw her into a ditch. Remember that?"

Juan shook his head. "You're making stuff up."

Sedillo put the file on her lap. "The Eagle Pass cop who took her statement several days later recognized you from her description. Charges were never filed because he was dirty, bought and paid for by your uncle. You got lucky because the victim never told her mother or anyone else what had happened until just recently."

"I'd never do anything like that," he blustered.

"The officer did write a report, but never submitted it. He kept it as a get-out-of-jail card to use in case Lorenz decided to retire him permanently."

Juan crossed his legs.

"That same officer set me up to use you as a confidential informant. You remember that, don't you? Did you really think I'd fall for it?"

Juan averted his gaze, drummed his fingers on the arm of the chair.

"I know your father, Gilberto, is your uncle's partner," Sedillo said. "And I'm guessing you are the heir-apparent to run the family business. All the dots connect. Your makeover as a useless, unreliable black sheep was a perfect cover that gave you lots of flexibility. The setup to make me believe you were a dealer willing to trade information to stay out of prison was a fine con. But that was all spoiled by the fact that only you have open, direct access to both brothers. When I uncovered the two money-laundering streams Sammy used to split the profits between Luis and Gilberto, I knew my theory was valid, and I went after the weak link, you."

Sedillo gestured at the accordion folder. "It's all in there."

Juan eyed it warily. "What do you care? You're gonna die soon anyway."

"Once Luis learns about our little chat, your days in the syndicate may be numbered. If you were in your uncle's position, what would you do to a snitch, family or not?"

Juan sneered. "Depends on the circumstances, bitch."

"Remind me how the syndicate works," Sedillo prodded. "Are there any members besides Sammy, Longwei, Luis, Gilberto, and you? I don't think so, but I'd like to be certain. How do Lorenz and your father communicate? That's always mystified me. What's El Jefe's role?"

Juan rubbed his nose. "I'm not going to tell you shit."

"Protecting your family is admirable," Sedillo replied approvingly.

"But we don't want you or your family, just El Jefe. I told you that from the start of our relationship. Remember?"

"Then why ask me all this other stuff?"

"To confirm what we already know. Lie to me and we'll have to begin all over again." Sedillo glanced at the cordless drill at her feet. "Don't make me have to hurt you."

Juan blinked and looked at the ceiling. "Ask your questions again," he replied in a whisper.

Sedillo smiled. "Of course."

He gave it all up. The basement meeting room built when the new Shen's Famous Chinese Restaurant was constructed. The two secret underground tunnels to the meeting room from nearby cartel safe houses. Exact locations. The secure, buried landline for important conversations with Gilberto at his residence. The second line that ran to Lorenz's homes. The brothers' twice-a-year meetings at their private seaside estate in Costa Rica. Lorenz traveling alone from Mexico City, Garza alone from Houston. El Jefe, a Kickapoo also known as Estavio Trevino or the Bear, his place of residence a remote hacienda outside of the tribal lands.

Juan gave a good description of Trevino. Dark long hair, five-nine or -ten, deep-set brown eyes, long in the face, with a wide mouth.

Agent Sedillo stood. "We'll stop here."

Harjo turned off the camcorder.

"What's next?" Juan asked nervously.

"Let's take a break."

Sedillo promised Juan food and something to drink, but he'd have to stay locked in the equipment shed for a little while longer.

They gathered up the power drill, folder, laptop, and camcorder and carried everything outside. Gabriela and Catherina waited, seated at the wrought-iron table on the rear patio.

"Did he confess to what he did to me?" Catherina demanded.

"Not in so many words, but yes," Harjo replied, texting on his cell phone.

"What are you doing?" Sedillo demanded.

"Letting Fallon and Istee know what we learned about El Jefe. What's next for you?"

"I'm taking what we've got to an assistant U.S. attorney in Houston I trust. A second copy will go to Samantha Hodges in El Paso."

Gabriela glanced at the equipment shed. Juan was pounding on the door to be let out. "Are you finished with him?"

Sedillo nodded.

"Then you both need to leave now," Catherina said.

Harjo looked up to see Catherina holding a broom, anger in her eyes. "Don't do anything foolish," he admonished.

"We're just going to even the score," she replied calmly.

Sedillo ignored the comment, slipped the camcorder memory card into her pocket, and smiled at Harjo. "Get your truck and let's go."

The electronic gate swung open as they left the compound. Harjo resisted the impulse to look back. They were out of the colonia and on pavement when Sedillo spoke.

"Don't even ask," she snapped.

"About Juan's fate? I wasn't planning to. What's all this about you dying?"

"True enough," Sedillo replied. She settled back against the headrest. "No more questions. Drive me to San Antonio. I'll catch a flight there. After that, do what you have to do."

Harjo clamped his mouth shut, thinking that sympathy for those who were dying was frequently nothing more than a balm for the living.

CHAPTER 13

Harjo pulled into a passenger drop-off space outside the San Antonio airport terminal and glanced at Sedillo. "Good luck in Houston."

She smiled. "Do you think I've got enough for the agency to go after Gilberto?"

"You've opened a big crack in the Lorenz cartel that wasn't there before."

Sedillo took her hand off the door lever. "That's not a resounding yes."

An airport cop on the sidewalk waved at Harjo to get moving. He flashed his shield, the officer nodded and stepped away. "An assistant U.S. attorney you trust may have the juice to get things started, but . . ." Harjo shrugged.

"I've thought about that."

"Also, it could turn around and bite you in the ass."

"I know."

"If it does?"

"Unless they fire me, I'll work this case until I drop."

Harjo leaned close. "And when exactly will that be, Agent Sedillo?"

Sedillo smiled. "You're persistent, I'll give you that. Under six months and counting, if I'm lucky. And please don't ask me more questions. It's a very depressing subject."

"Fair enough."

"What about you?"

"I'm heading back. There's a lot that Juan didn't tell us. I need to do some reconnaissance before I decide on my next move."

Sedillo nodded. "I thought so. You're going to be in deep shit for this. There's no way I can justify your involvement."

"I volunteered to help—end of story," Harjo replied. "I'll email you a corroborating statement about our interrogation. Look for it when you land in Houston. Anything you want me to leave out other than we threatened Juan with death, drugged him, psychologically destabilized him, and left him in the hands of two very angry, revenge-filled women?"

Sedillo smiled and opened the passenger door. "Oh, what monsters we are. You might say I convinced Juan it was in his best interest to confess and that the interrogation took place in an abandoned building outside Eagle Pass. I'll fill in the blanks."

"Good enough."

She grabbed her bag and the camcorder and stepped out. "What are you going to do back in Eagle Pass, Agent Harjo?"

"Consider my options."

Sedillo laughed. "Goodbye, Bernard."

"Adios, Maria."

He merged into traffic, watching her in the rearview mirror standing curbside until she was out of sight.

———

The San Antonio car dealer, a middle-aged man named Carl with skinny legs and no butt, looked aghast when Harjo drove the pickup truck onto the lot. Once Harjo explained the vehicle was only cosmetically trashed but not damaged, Carl took a closer look, decided Harjo was right, and relaxed.

"You turning it in?" he asked.

"Exchanging." Harjo pointed at a 2007 black Pontiac Grand Prix at the back of the lot with a sale sticker of $1,995 on the cracked windshield. "How many miles on it?"

"Over a hundred and sixty thousand, if you believe the odometer, but it's not a rental."

"Does it run?"

"Yeah, but for how long I can't say. Motor seems okay, rubber is not so good. I wouldn't speed in it."

Harjo inspected the car. He looked under the hood, opened the trunk, cranked the engine, and drove it around the block with Carl in the passenger seat. It stank of stale tobacco smoke and the upholstery was pockmarked with cigarette burn holes.

"I'll give you sixteen hundred cash if you throw in license plates that make it look registered and include a decent spare."

Carl looked pleased. "Deal, but the law says I got to verify you have insurance."

"I'll sign a waiver promising to provide that information tomorrow."

"That'll work."

In the trailer that served as Carl's office, Harjo did the paperwork for the Grand Prix. "I need a haircut. Where do you go?"

Carl handed him the keys. "Benny's Village Barbershop. Turn right out of the lot, go straight two miles. It's on your left in a strip mall. Come back anytime."

"You bet I will," Harjo replied.

He gassed up at a nearby convenience store and found Benny's, a two-chair establishment that had posters of stylish-looking young guys with great haircuts on the wall.

"Cut it all off," he told Benny.

Benny gave Harjo's long hair a close look. "All of it?"

"Buzz-cut it and then shave my head."

"Whatever you say."

When Benny finished, Harjo almost didn't recognize himself in the mirror. He paid cash, tipped big, and walked out whistling. New car, new look. A light rain dampened his shaved head. The pitter-patter on his noggin felt particularly unusual.

He decided to drive to Del Rio, where he wasn't well known, and spend the night. It was an Air Force town, which kept the place thriving. He'd cross into Mexico in the morning and head west to Piedras Negras. He'd stayed before in Del Rio at the All-American Motel, a mid-century, veteran-owned establishment that displayed a sign on the office door: PROTECTED BY SMITH & WESSON. It was a clean, no-frills mom-and-pop place, perfect for an anonymous good night's sleep once the late-night Amtrak train left the station. He hoped it hadn't changed hands, been renovated, gone downhill, or been demolished. He was no fan of the cookie-cutter national motel chains.

With luck, the Pontiac wouldn't let him down.

———

Inside the terminal, Sedillo imported the memory card to her tablet, attached the files to an email, and sent it to Samantha Hodges in El Paso, along with a note that read:

I'm about to deliver the attached recording to Assistant U.S. Attorney Sheila Shapiro, DEA Houston. I don't know if the district office has

*a bad cop or two on the Lorenz Drug Cartel payroll, but I'm playing
it safe. We've had our differences but I know you're ethical and can be
trusted. Watch the interview. It could help the agency dismantle the narco
trade in Piedras Negras.*

M. Sedillo

She deleted the sent message. At a concourse electronics store, not sure
if she was being paranoid or simply cautious, she bought an inexpensive
point-and-shoot digital camera, a new memory card, and imported
the camcorder recording to the camera. In the privacy of a stall in the
bathroom, she removed the memory card and threw the camera in a
trash bin on her way out.

Before the airplane's cabin doors closed, Sedillo called Assistant
U.S. Attorney Sheila Shapiro, and made an appointment to see her
late in the afternoon—Shapiro's only free time. As the plane taxied
to the runway, she sat back wondering what kind of reception she'd
get at the office once the substance of Juan Garza's deposition became
widely known.

———

The Houston office sat on an access road to Interstate 610, known
locally as the Inner Loop. The building next door housed the offices
of the consulate general of Russia. Sedillo had often speculated how
many listening devices were pointed in both directions, and what
high-tech jamming apparatuses were in place to combat spy-shop
eavesdropping.

But that wasn't the question in her mind as the unmarked DEA
vehicle transporting her to the airport pulled out of the secure parking structure. She wondered if the two agents with her, the driver and
a DEA pilot in the passenger seat, were really going to fly her back
to Eagle Pass or drop her out of an airplane without a parachute ten

thousand feet above the Gulf of Mexico. Time, and not much of it, would tell.

Her ten hours at the Houston office had been the most grueling, depressing, eye-opening experience in her career. Attorney Shapiro turned out to be less than trustworthy and more concerned with her next move up the DOJ ladder. After watching the recording, she immediately called in the higher-ups. What began as an intelligence breakthrough into the Lorenz drug cartel became an interrogation designed to discredit and malign Sedillo.

Why did she allow Bernard Harjo, a suspended agent, to assist her? Why did she fail to report his presence in Eagle Pass to her immediate supervisor? Was it possible Harjo falsified his corroboration of the events as she reported them in order to help her story? Why did she refuse to reveal the location of the Garza interview? What were her reasons for withholding the important intelligence information Wanda Cantu had attached to her suicide note? Where was Juan Garza now? Where was Special Agent Harjo? Why did she fail to transcribe the recording into a written statement and secure Garza's voluntary signature?

Her tablet, department smartphone, and the camcorder were seized for examination and analysis. They withheld the results of the mandatory lie detector test she'd been forced to take. They took her sidearm. She was advised to seek legal counsel. She had not been body-searched, so the memory card with the copy of the interview remained tucked inside the waistband of her slacks.

Pending further review, she was to be returned to Eagle Pass with orders to carry out administrative duties only. A senior agent with narco-trafficking experience would be detached to supervise all ongoing fieldwork. Internal Affairs would be dispatched.

There weren't too many different ways to look at the farce. Either the Lorenz drug cartel had penetrated deeply into the Houston office, or career-building was more important than crime-fighting. Realistically, it was likely to be some of both.

The fixed-wing turboprop took off into the night sky, moonlight shimmering on the water below. She'd text Harjo on her personal cell when she got home, give him a heads-up, and ask if he'd be interested in her next, and possibly last, scheme.

———

Harjo woke up, showered, and looked in the bathroom mirror. Tiny fuzzy hairs showed on his bald head. He looked decidedly strange and vowed to grow his hair back ASAP when he got home to El Paso.

He ran his electric razor over his skull, shaved, dressed, and crossed over to Ciudad Acuña to have breakfast at his favorite Northern Mexico restaurant, El Patron's Comida. The house special of chilaquiles was his favorite. Done right, the fried corn tortillas covered in red chile with cheese, sour cream, and sliced onion along with a side of beans couldn't be beat.

He finished his meal and a second cup of coffee before turning his phone on. Sedillo's text message popped up. She was home after being shafted by Houston. Was he interested in one more extracurricular activity, this time in Piedras Negras?

The phone rang as soon as he put it down. Samantha Hodges wanted a word.

"Harjo?"

"What can I do for you, Samantha?"

"Don't come back to El Paso and don't go to L.A. Lay low for a while. Not satisfied with taking control of the Las Cruces double homicide, the CIA has assumed oversight of the Lorenz cartel investigation. They say Mexico is their turf, not ours. They're looking for you and Agent Sedillo, supposedly for follow-up questioning."

"Did you watch the Juan Garza deposition Maria sent you?"

"Yes, and I don't know how you and Sedillo will get out of the mess you've created. Washington is screaming for your heads."

"At the time, taking down a narco-trafficking kingpin didn't seem such a bad idea. Thanks for the heads-up."

Harjo disconnected and sent a text to Maria on the burner phone he'd bought at the Del Rio Walmart last night. He asked if she knew the CIA was on her tail and where she wanted to meet.

Her response was brief. Yes, but she'd eluded surveillance. Look for her in the immediate area outside Gilberto Garza's Plaza Mercado.

What did she have in mind? he wondered.

Fallon and Istee had left voice messages asking for elaboration about the El Jefe information he'd sent by text. Using the burner phone, he called them individually with additional details about Estavio Trevino's tie-in to the Lorenz drug cartel and Sammy Shen's family.

"Be careful," he warned them both. "Langley has taken over again. I'll be in touch when I resurface."

On his way to the Pontiac he crushed his cell phone under his heel and threw it into the bushes behind the parking lot. He'd be a little harder to trace, but not by much.

Federal Highway 2 from Ciudad Acuña to Piedras Negras was a heavily traveled major road along the border. Hopefully he'd make the drive without too many delays and backups.

———

Gilberto Garza's Plaza Mercado was off Zaragoza Street in an older area of the city close to the river. It was popular with tourists and Americans seeking cut-rate medical and dental services, including low-cost prescription drugs. An unimposing concrete block warehouse in origin, the mercado had been given an antiquated look with thin exterior brick facing and a slanted red tile roof with a portico that extended over the sidewalk. Inside were vendor stalls and booths offering Mexican arts and crafts, colorful clothing, handmade leather goods, hats, trinkets for the tourist trade, and imported goods from Central American countries and the Far East. Photographers, guitar makers, weavers, and potters hawked their wares. Several food booths serving Northern Mexican cuisine were popular breakfast and luncheon spots for locals and visitors alike.

Bright banners hung from fabricated ceiling beams, and high windows, punched through the block walls, allowed sunlight to pour inside. Slowly rotating old-fashioned ceiling fans created a cooling breeze.

There were booksellers, music vendors, toy makers, and jewelers. At a low-cost electronics stall, Harjo bought two cheap burner phones. Everything was designed and staged to look festive and bright. It was about as authentic as a Hollywood movie set.

To familiarize himself, Harjo wandered through the mercado twice before circling the neighborhood in the Pontiac. He spotted Sedillo parked in her personal vehicle several blocks away, beeped his horn, and motioned her to get in.

"Nice wheels," she said, giving the Grand Prix a critical once-over. "And I love the new haircut."

"I'm upping my game, hoping for a promotion," Harjo said as he pulled into an empty parking space. "You doing all right?"

Sedillo nodded.

"What happened in Houston?"

She laid it all out. When she finished, Harjo briefed her more fully on Samantha Hodges's warning about the CIA's latest move. "We're in it up to our necks," he added. "So what's the plan?"

"I want to search Garza's office. If we can find physical evidence connecting him to the Lorenz drug cartel, that could get us off the hook."

Harjo smiled. Although it would be an illegal search, the idea had instant appeal. "What if we've been compromised and he knows that he's been outed?"

Sedillo shrugged. "Then he probably knows I've been stripped of my police powers, you're on suspension, and the CIA wants to talk to us. He just might be complacent enough to think everything is under control."

"And just how are we going to do this?"

"Every weekday when he's in his office he goes home at two for his main meal of the day and returns at four p.m. He stays for an hour or two and then often joins friends for a drink or stops at the cathedral to visit with the monsignor. Frequently, he'll make a quick trip to the fast-food restaurant in Eagle Pass he co-owns or visit his grocery store. He's home usually by seven."

"Why not do it when the place is closed?"

"After hours, there are four heavily armed security guards on the premises and two city cops on permanent stakeout outside. When the Mercado is open, only Garza is there, as far as I know."

"How do we get in?"

"His office is at the rear of the building. It has an exterior door to the parking lot. We'll wait for to him to leave and be gone before he returns."

"If we want a clean in-and-out we have to recon everything. Lookouts, CCTV cameras, bodyguards, security devices."

"I'll do the search, you stand lookout." Sedillo opened the car door. "We better get started."

Harjo touched her elbow to hold her back. "What if you find nothing?"

"Plan B is under way," she replied. "We can't trust DEA or the CIA to do what's right, so I decided to go elsewhere for help. A classmate of mine at the academy left DEA several years ago to take a criminal investigator position with Treasury in the Office of the Inspector General. I got in touch with her and asked if she'd be interested in shutting off a narco-trafficker's laundered money spigot. She jumped on it."

"How is she going to do that?"

"Garza's partial ownership of the Eagle Pass fast-food joint gets her foot in the door. With the facts I gave her, she's started a tax-filing search on Garza, including corporate and individual taxes, offshore accounts, and foreign investments. She'll freeze whatever money she finds and go after his property as well."

"That will take some time to accomplish," Harjo noted.

"It's not my preferred solution," Sedillo conceded.

"We could just wait for Garza to return and shoot him."

Sedillo laughed. "We don't have a get-out-of-jail card for that."

"We don't have a legal leg to stand on for any of this," Harjo corrected.

"After we do this, I'm resigning."

"I thought you might."

"And you?"

"If I can get to him, I plan to have a nice chat with Juan's uncle Luis."

"I'll help."

"No, you won't." He handed her a burner phone. "Use this. Let's go to work."

———

They split up on foot, staying in contact by cell phone. Harjo wandered in and out of nearby buildings, checked rooftops where he could, poked around stores, and walked down alleys. He studied the parked vehicles, the pedestrians, the local cops loitering at an intersection. He looked at second-story windows for suspicious activity, inspected lampposts for cameras, and bought some over-the-counter painkillers at a pharmacy.

Sedillo browsed the Mercado, noting the distinctive glass-domed ceiling-mounted CCTV cameras, the electronic locks on the office,

supply closet, and janitorial room doors. She waited until it was unoccupied and visually swept the woman's bathroom. She casually studied
the vendors located close to Garza's office, looking to spot any telltale
sign they might also be muscle or protection. She bought a Virgin of
Guadalupe medallion on a chain and a pair of sterling silver hoop earrings. At one of the food booths, she had a cheese taco, a small bowl
of posole, and chatted with the cook.

After two hours, they switched, and spent the day watching until
Garza left to go home to eat. They reconvened in Harjo's Pontiac.

"What's this?" he said, taking the shopping bag from Maria's outstretched hand.

"An accessory for the car and a pair of earrings for you, to comple-
ment your new look."

Harjo chuckled as he peered inside. "For me? You shouldn't have."
He hung the Guadalupe medal on the rearview mirror and put the earrings in the empty ashtray. "I'll wear them later."

"Can you get me into Garza's office?" Sedillo asked.

"Absolutely. He met somebody outside the rear entrance. Using
my phone camera, I recorded him entering his door access code after
he'd finished talking. He looks and acts exactly like the upstanding,
law-abiding citizen he pretends to be."

Sedillo watched the recording with interest. Agency photographs
of Garza were at least five years old. He was stocky, thick in the waist,
with a receding hairline and bushy, unruly eyebrows. His features
were benign, soft. A large diamond-studded Knights of Columbus ring
sparkled on his right-hand ring finger. "Not very villainous-looking,"
she agreed.

They exchanged reconnaissance information. Nothing inside the
Mercado appeared worrisome. None of the vendors looked like mas-
querading thugs. On the streets there were no signs of sentries or
lookouts. Rooftops and second-story windows were clear of activity.

Toughs weren't lounging in parked cars. Cops didn't seem jittery or on edge.

Harjo checked the time. By now Garza was at home sitting down for his comida. "Let's do this."

—————

Garza's car was gone from the Mercado parking lot, and there were fewer vehicles than previously. Inside, foot traffic had fallen off.

Sedillo and Harjo scanned customers and vendors as they passed by the stalls and booths. Some were unoccupied, with bins full of unwatched merchandise easy pickings for the nimble-fingered. Outside, the street seemed unusually quiet. There were no cars at the intersection waiting for the light to change. A stray cat wandered out of an alleyway and padded slowly down an empty sidewalk. There were no customers visible through the drugstore window across the street. The cop car that had been parked at the corner all day was gone.

"Something's wrong," Harjo said. He took Sedillo by the arm and steered her away from the Mercado. "It's a no-go."

"There's nobody after us," she protested.

"Yet," Harjo replied, pulling her along in the direction of her vehicle.

Out of a building half a block down the street, two punks emerged, closing quickly with semiautomatics in hand. Behind them, two more popped out of a dentist's office, similarly armed.

Harjo pulled his weapon. "I hope you're carrying." He glanced over to see a Colt Pocket 9 in her free hand. "On the count of three, drop prone and start shooting at the punks in front of us. I'll take the boys to our rear."

They hit the pavement simultaneously. Sedillo put one down. Harjo killed one and his buddy fled. Sedillo was reloading when Harjo shot the approaching gunman in the face.

He yanked Sedillo to her feet. "To your car. Let's go."

They ran full-tilt, the sound of an approaching vehicle making them sprint even faster. They turned the corner with Sedillo's car in sight a block away. The sound of screeching wheels made them duck into a recessed doorway. They listened for a long minute. There were no footfalls, only the low grumble of an idling engine.

"Does your car have a remote start?" he asked in a whisper.

Sedillo nodded and pressed her vehicle transmitter. The blast blew the car off the pavement onto its side and sent glass shards flying halfway up the block.

"That's what I figured," he said.

"Damn it, I liked that car!" Sedillo complained, fire in her eyes. "The Pontiac?"

Harjo shook his head. "Too risky. Let's head for the bridge before Garza's goons realize we're not dead."

They used the black smoke from the explosion as cover and made it through the neighborhood to the Gran Plaza, the gateway to the city that bordered the Rio Grande. A modern, well-maintained open space with large sculptures, benches, walkways, large shade trees and grassy meadows, it teemed with people strolling the grounds, photographing each other, and enjoying the cool late afternoon sunshine along the river.

They stopped briefly to look for pursuers before joining a line of pedestrians entering the adjacent walkway of the old two-lane international bridge that crossed the Rio Grande.

They moved as quickly as possible, sidestepping around much slower walkers and parents plodding along with dawdling little children. As Harjo began to ease past an older man with a cane, the man's head erupted in blood and brains. He collapsed against Harjo, who caught him just as a second bullet tore into Maria's chest.

He dropped the old man to the walkway, pulled Sedillo behind the body for cover, and tried to shield her as best he could, waiting for the next round that would take him out. The sniper was firing from Eagle Pass, but Harjo had no idea where.

"Don't." Feebly she tried to push him away. "Go. Go now."

People were screaming, running, crouching, prone on the ground, squeezing past, stepping over the dead man on the walkway. The shooting had stopped.

"I'll get you across. You're going to be all right." To move him out of the way, a young man kicked Harjo hard as he ran past. Harjo wanted to kill him.

"I'm all right," she answered with difficulty, patting his hand, smiling. "This is better than doing chemo. I hated that idea."

"You can make it." They were on the American side of the bridge. He could see the emergency lights and hear the sirens of a fire rescue vehicle on its way, weaving across both lanes of traffic.

Sedillo shook her head and coughed up blood. "Too much damage. I'm hemorrhaging inside. I'll be dead before the medics get here. Leave, Harjo."

He cradled Maria's head in his lap. "I'm staying here with you."

"That's a very nice thing for you to do," she said sweetly, before she died.

———

When the paramedics arrived, Harjo told them he didn't know either of the victims and retreated to Piedras Negras before any cops appeared asking questions. Half dazed, he walked to where the Pontiac was parked, expecting to see a burned-out hulk. Except for four flat tires and destroyed wiring in the engine compartment, it was intact. The Guadalupe medallion was missing, but the earrings were still in the ashtray. He fished them out. Inside a manila envelope left on the front seat were photographs of Gabriela and Catherina, naked and stretched out on tarps with their throats cut. Harjo couldn't tell if they'd been scalped, but he guessed they'd been raped multiple times.

He popped open the trunk. His bag with personal items and extra clothing was missing, but under the spare tire he recovered a second handgun, extra clips of ammunition, and a much-needed packet of emergency money.

He threw the car keys in the trunk, slammed it shut, and walked away. It was time to disappear. Buying a bottle of whiskey and finding a place to stay would be easy. Overcoming his anger about Sedillo's assassination and the brutal murder of Gabriela and her daughter would be the challenge.

To survive and be effective he had to chill, and he knew it.

CHAPTER 14

The citizens of Las Cruces and Doña Ana County rarely com-
mitted murder. When they did kill each other, the clearance rate was
astronomically high, simply because most of the victims and perpetra-
tors knew each other. Sometimes very intimately, sometimes only in
passing, but well enough to let the police connect the dots.

While any garden-variety murder investigation short of a voluntary confession is filled with the normal yet demanding routine of
interviewing witnesses and gathering evidence, it quickly falls off the
front page until an arrest returns it to the spotlight. But the gory murder and ritual scalping of two victims at a local hotel and the killing
of the night manager who'd reported it had captured national media
attention. Sensationalism sold, and it was a big news story, not about
to go away.

Thrown-together television specials anchored by investigative
journalists aired nationally; ex-FBI talking heads on cable news shows
pumped out criticism about flawed investigative police work; local and
state politicians called for larger law enforcement appropriations to

combat crime; and the Chamber of Commerce scrambled to remind everyone that Las Cruces was a wonderful, warm, sunny retirement haven for boomers.

The continuous media coverage of the murders gnawed at Clayton as a constant reminder of his failure to solve the crimes. But having the Feds take over was the right thing to do. The case was too complex, the scope too far-reaching, and the resources of the sheriff's office too insufficient to mount a massive, drawn-out investigation.

Rational justifications aside, Clayton couldn't completely let it go. Back on duty, he'd been handed a number of fresh assault cases—currently the most popular felony undertaken by the citizens of Doña Ana County—which kept him busy. In those spare moments Clayton could wrangle at work, he continued to search the web for information about Estavio Trevino. At home in the evenings, he kept at it when Grace was occupied reading the latest offering of one of her favorite novelists or watching a popular PBS television cooking show.

Two bits of information that came his way upped his enthusiasm to keep trolling. The German Federal Police had interviewed Herman Joseph Arensdorf, the prisoner Interpol had identified through their facial recognition program as a possible relative of Anico's. DNA testing had confirmed it. Arensdorf and Anico were second-degree relatives.

Additionally, Arensdorf had told the police that his older sister, her husband, and their young son had disappeared over thirty years ago during an extended Mexican holiday and were never heard from again. That meant Anico was Arensdorf's nephew. Decades-old missing person reports filed in Germany and follow-up attempts by Mexican law enforcement to locate the family confirmed the prisoner's story. Online, Clayton searched Mexican newspaper archives for further specific information. He finally stumbled upon an old Chihuahua newspaper story about a German couple and their young son. The family had snuck away from a guided tour in the Mapimí Biosphere Reserve and gone off to explore on their own. When they failed to return by dusk, the police mounted a search of the immediate area at first light. They were never located. However, a single set of fresh tire tracks were discovered matching the couple's vehicle that led from some rocky terrain to the paved highway. Believing the family had left the area to continue their journey, local officials suspended the search.

Clayton called the Chihuahua State Investigation Agency Records Section for information. They located and faxed him a copy of the investigation into the family's disappearance. It included a supplemental notification from the Múzquiz PD that their rental camper had been found abandoned and burned on the outskirts of the city. The VIN in the engine compartment block had identified the vehicle.

Clayton checked his file. Múzquiz was the city closest to the Mexican Kickapoo Tribe. And wasn't El Jefe's ranchero supposedly located near the fringes of the Bolsón de Mapimí? It was simply too much of a coincidence. Did Trevino kill the couple, take their child, and destroy the evidence? It seemed possible, but why take the child? Did he have some twisted scheme to raise the boy as his own?

On the off chance that Trevino had contact with other Kickapoo tribes, Clayton scanned through the websites of both the Oklahoma and Kansas bands. He found nothing there. He moved on, searching the local town newspapers near the Kickapoo reservations, fishing for feature stories about the tribes and their members. In the archives of a small Oklahoma paper, he discovered an article about a recent warrior healing ceremony held for two tribal veterans lately returned from Afghanistan.

Except for the casino, the reservation had been closed to visitors during the ceremony. It had been conducted by a highly decorated veteran and healer known only as "Bear."

According to Harjo, Bear was Trevino's Kickapoo nickname. Was he both a medicine man and an assassin? If so, it made perfect sense to

Clayton. Among the Apaches, some of the most famous warriors, past and present, were also healers and singers. What some people might see as a contradiction fit nicely into Clayton's Apache worldview. He was grudgingly impressed.

Hadn't Harjo mentioned something about Trevino disappearing from the Mexico Kickapoo Tribe for six years? If Clayton recalled correctly, six years was the longest enlistment period allowed by each branch of the armed forces. If the healer had been Trevino, he may well have honed his killer skills in the military. Was he Special Forces, an Army Ranger, a long-range sniper, a SEAL, or a Delta Force member? Maybe none of the above.

The article noted that the two combat veterans—both mentioned by name—had returned to active duty the day after the ceremony ended, but there was no mention of their unit assignments. Clayton called and spoke to the reporter who had filed the story. She was unable to tell him where the soldiers were stationed and added she had been warned by the tribal chairman not to interview or photograph the healer. She'd taken his word that the healer was a decorated combat veteran and hadn't attempted to verify it. She finished with a complaint about how difficult it was to get good copy from the Kickapoos. They just weren't that forthcoming.

With the lead a dead end, Clayton tried the tribal chairman, who met his email requests and voice messages with silence. He tried a few members of the tribal council and got the same results. He understood their reticence. It mirrored how Apaches often dealt with outsiders.

His effort to track down the two soldiers through various armed forces and veterans websites met with no luck. On his lunch break at the office, he called Kerney's wife, Sara, at the ranch, explained what he needed, and asked for her help. Retired from the Army as a brigadier general after a twenty-seven-year career, she had knowledge and contacts unavailable to him.

"Aren't you supposed to be off that case?" she asked.

"I can't stop picking at it," Clayton replied.

Sara laughed. "You and Kerney," she said with amusement. "Two of a kind. I'll see what I can do."

"Thank you, General," Clayton replied.

"Stop that," she ordered good humoredly. "No more 'general' stuff, okay? Anything else?"

"That's it."

"Give my love to Grace."

"Will do. Tell Kerney I'll call over the weekend and catch him up."

"He'd like that. We've both been following the news."

"Other than football, crime is America's favorite spectator sport," Clayton observed.

"How depressing," Sara replied.

He disconnected, stuffed his half-eaten sandwich in a desk drawer, and left to find Alonzo Ortiz, a drunk who'd assaulted his best and oldest alcoholic friend outside a homeless shelter for refusing to share his bottle of cheap whiskey. Apparently, for some, the tie that binds can only be stretched so far.

The weekend was looming, and Grace would be teaching a Saturday continuing education workshop for preschool teacher aides. He'd have the entire day free to devote to learning more about El Jefe, Estavio Trevino, Bear, or whoever the hell he really was.

———

At his hacienda, Trevino did all the essential background work needed to prepare for his next target, and this time it was personal. The Internet had made it easy to gather basic facts about almost any person on the planet. Very few people lived lives that were private enough to keep even a curious tech-savvy amateur at bay.

He started with the people in Istee's life. His wife, their two children. His mother, father, and half-brother. His father's wife. He soon knew where everyone lived and had recent photographs of all of them, which he memorized. He pieced together readily available personal histories of the family and turned them into brief biographies. Istee's early years at Mescalero, his college years in Silver City, his law enforcement experience, and the misstep that tarnished his reputation and caused his resignation from the New Mexico State Police.

The same with Kevin Kerney's wartime service in Vietnam and his citations for gallantry. His rise through the ranks in law enforcement, retiring as Santa Fe chief of police. And his reputation as a cop who apparently was more willing than most to use deadly force.

He found particularly interesting his wife's brilliant military career and her decorations for bravery under fire. Educated at West Point, rising to the rank of one-star general, and commander of the Military Police Corps, she was a true woman warrior. Trevino was impressed.

Their son, Patrick, a star high school student and athlete, had received a congressional recommendation for an appointment to West Point and an early admission to MIT. About to graduate from high school, he was a young lion poised to leap into manhood.

What Trevino found most interesting about Kerney was his wealth. Some years ago, he'd inherited a large tract of northern New Mexico real estate worth millions from the estate of his mother's best friend. He'd used some of it to buy a ranch outside of Santa Fe, had given a very small chunk to Istee to pay for his children's college educations, and dabbled in raising and training a small herd of fine cutting horses. He'd wisely invested the rest.

Trevino wondered how much Kerney might be willing to pay in ransom for the return of his kidnapped half-Apache son. The thought gave him pause. Kill Istee outright or kidnap him, get the ransom, then kill him?

Istee's wife and mother were strong Apache women. In photographs,

Grace, his wife, oozed a self-confident refinement. Her achievements as a teacher and mentor spoke of high intelligence. Istee's mother, Isabel, a retired head nurse and tribal elder, looked to be a woman one could learn much from.

All that he discovered about Istee's children told him they lived fully in the modern world yet retained close ties to their native roots. Not only was the daughter a head-turner, she was an athlete and scholar. The son, a medical school student, was serious and brilliant.

Trevino had read up on the Apaches and was intrigued by their matrilineal family structure, which was far different from that of the Kickapoos. Regardless, there was a tribal identity and strength about them similar to that of his own people. He appreciated the evident pride they had in their heritage.

All that aside, Istee's family were potential pawns that could be put into play if necessary. A lot depended on a final plan. That wouldn't happen until he'd finished reconnoitering them on their home ground.

He turned away from the whiteboard that was filled with his research notes and photographs and opened a satellite program on the computer. He entered and saved all the primary locations for the family. He'd study them more before leaving for Juárez in the morning. There he'd load up on the necessary weapons and equipment—all untraceable—buy an inconspicuous vehicle, and meet with Lieutenant Ulibarri of the Texas DPS before crossing over to El Paso for the short drive to Las Cruces.

It was about to begin, and he was ready.

———

In the ten years Roger Ulibarri had been selling confidential police information to El Jefe, he'd met the man only twice. At his first meeting in Juárez, he'd handed over current intelligence information on a Mexican with dual citizenship living in El Paso, the son of the federal attorney in charge of criminal investigations in the state of Chihua-hua. His body was found two days later scalped and dumped outside his father's home. The lawyer resigned his position immediately and moved away.

The second meeting with El Jefe took place recently when Ulibarri delivered the corpse of a man killed in a shoot-out with a police officer in Mescalero, New Mexico. At that time, he'd tried to break away from El Jefe's control, only to be subtly threatened with severe consequences if he made such an attempt. He left feeling if he'd asked any questions about his bizarre smuggling of a corpse into Mexico, he never would have returned home.

Over the years, except for those two meetings, Ulibarri had pro-vided El Jefe the information he wanted by cell phone. Now there was to be a third meeting, again in Juárez.

El Jefe's instructions for the meeting were specific. Ten o'clock at night, at a closed diner on the corner of an intersection in an older downtown neighborhood. He was to enter through the unlocked rear door.

Ulibarri's headlights illuminated the badly chipped yellow-and-orange-painted building as he swung into the small parking lot. A large Coke sign on a steel pole towered over the structure. Below it the name of the joint was missing from an empty rectangular frame. It was nothing more than a dark, abandoned converted lunch shack.

He entered through the rear door to the sounds of mice darting around the kitchen floor and found El Jefe waiting behind a shuttered customer order counter that faced the sidewalk, his features barely dis-cernible in the glow of a corner streetlight.

"You're on time," Trevino noted pleasantly.

"As you asked," Ulibarri replied, relaxing slightly.

Outside, the sounds of an approaching garbage truck emptying dumpsters clanged and thumped its way down the street.

"You have always done as I've asked, and I appreciate that."

Relieved, Ulibarri smiled in the darkness. "Thank you."

"And now you must do one more thing for me."

"What's that?"

Trevino's perfectly placed shot stopped Ulibarri's heart, and he collapsed dead on the floor.

Outside, the garbage truck ground to a halt, the engine idling. Rapid footsteps followed. Two men appeared, wrapped the body in a blanket, and carried it away. The metallic sound of the truck's hydraulics emptying the dumpster followed and then the truck drove away.

Trevino stayed in the darkness of the corner until he heard Ulibarri's car leave the parking lot. Sometimes remaining untraceable made for regrettable acts.

CHAPTER 15

Grace and Clayton had finished a light Friday morning break- fast when Sara called. Grace picked up.

"I'm sure you know Clayton is still fussing around with that horrible double homicide case," Sara said.

"He fiddles with it when he thinks I'm not looking," Grace replied with a pointed glance at Clayton. "Has he roped you in on it?"

"Yes, but he asked nicely," Sara replied. "I have information for him."

"I'll put him on."

"He won't like it."

Grace passed the handset to Clayton, who tried to look guileless.

"Did you find the subjects?" he asked.

"I not only found them, but I've saved you from spinning your wheels any longer. I spoke to the commanding general of the Army Criminal Investigation Command, who agreed to have both soldiers interviewed by Army CID special agents at their duty stations. One soldier is with the Seventy-Fifth Rangers, the other with the Tenth

Mountain Division. Based on their religious beliefs, they refused to answer any questions about their participation in the Kickapoo warrior healing ceremony. Without a legal basis to question them further, you're out of luck. And given the fact that neither soldier broke the law, don't waste your time."

"Nothing breaks easy with this case," Clayton complained. "Thanks for trying. I really appreciate it."

"You're welcome, but don't hang up. Kerney wants a word."

Clayton punched the speaker button.

"Why are you still monkeying around with this?" Kerney chided. "It's out of your hands."

Clayton nodded, looking directly at Grace. "I know, I know. You're right. I'm stopping, promise."

"Good. If Grace is listening, make sure he keeps his word."

"I will."

"Doesn't anybody trust me?" Clayton groaned theatrically.

Kerney guffawed. "You get no sympathy. Keep in touch."

"Ten-four," Clayton said with a laugh. He put the handset in the cradle.

Grace kissed him. "That's better. Now I have one less thing to worry about."

"I don't see how. I'll always be obstinate."

Grace kissed him again. "Go to work."

———

There was much Trevino wanted to learn before striking at the man who'd killed Whistling Bear Who Paints with Clay, and he planned to do it invisibly. In El Paso, he shopped at three sporting goods stores, purchasing all he needed to camp rough in the high-country forests outside of the towns and cities he would reconnoiter. He loaded up on wilderness survival food and ingredients to season whatever edible critters he trapped or killed. He would move camp frequently, re-provision at various stores and gas stations outside his zones of concentration, avoid all improved campsites, and stay away from the hiking trails and old logging roads that drew adventurous outdoor enthusiasts.

Although it wasn't yet hiking and camping season, with night temperatures still cold and deep snow covering the high mountain trails, it was best to remain cautious. He studied detailed geological survey maps and memorized escape routes out of the locations he'd selected as campsites.

In town, his only visible footprint would be his ten-year-old dull gray Jeep Wrangler, which wouldn't draw undue attention in the expanding automotive world of the pickup trucks, sport utility vehicles, and four-by-fours Americans seemed to love. There would be no trace of him to be found at any hotels, restaurants, or local establishments. He had no fixed schedule, no timetable. He'd take as long as needed.

Initially, he'd thought to subdue Istee, drug him, and bring him to his hacienda, but he soon discarded the idea. One small mistake or oversight might bring the outside world to his doorstep, and that he could not allow. Everything would happen north of the border. He'd yet to decide whether to attempt a kidnapping and ransom, or simply kill the man slowly and leave his disfigured body where it would easily be found. Either way, money or not, Istee would die.

On his first night, Trevino camped on the banks of a wide, dry arroyo outside a small ranching community in the Sacramento Mountains south of the Mescalero Apache Reservation. He'd followed a nearly impassable, muddy old ranch road to the abandoned ruins of a house tucked in a slot canyon. Snow covered the higher peaks and clung to the north face of the foothills. By evening it was pleasantly cold, a nice change from the often dry and dusty Sierra Madres of Northern Mexico.

In the morning, he'd visit the Apache homeland to see where Fernando had been killed. He'd say prayers, offer tobacco so that his hunt would be successful, and take a look around the reservation. From what he'd seen so far, the mountains that were home to the Apaches held much beauty.

———

Twice a month, Isabel Istee served as a docent at the Mescalero Tribal Cultural Center and Museum in the village center just off the highway that cut east and west across the homelands. It was a small museum, low to the ground, round in shape, protected by large shade trees at the entrance.

She liked the morning shift best, arriving early to make sure all was in order, walking through the displays of tools, weapons, clothing, and the wonderful collection of old baskets. She dusted and straightened as necessary, put out stacks of brochures about Apache history and culture, and prepared the bank deposit slip for the voluntary contributions made by visitors the day before.

As she often did, Isabel had driven, but today she was in her brand-new all-wheel drive SUV, with her ten-year-old Pekingese, Chapo, in his car seat next to her. It had been fifteen years since she'd gotten a new car, and she was quite pleased with herself. Well behaved and quiet, Chapo loved to sprawl near the museum front door and greet visitors with a tail-wag.

The museum opened at eight and there were rarely any visitors until midmorning, which gave Isabel time to sit undisturbed with her needlepoint. She was about to start in on a complex pattern of Navajo blanket triangles when Chapo came and asked for an outside.

She stepped out with him under the tall trees fronting the museum. A low sky masked the sun and muted the morning gray. A man stood alone a short distance away, holding a buckskin bundle secured with rawhide strips under one arm. Chanting softly in a language Isabel could not make out, he turned slowly in a circle, sprinkling something onto the pavement.

His face was shaded by a hat and she couldn't see his features. She wasn't sure he was Apache. She'd heard of no cleansing ceremony to be held at the site where Clayton had killed the intruder who'd been outside Blossom Magoosh's front door. Any such ritual would surely have included Clayton, and he certainly would have told her about it.

If not Apache, what tribe? she wondered. *What kind of ceremony?*

The man stopped when he saw her, stood very still for a moment, retreated to a nearby Jeep, the wheels caked in mud, and drove away.

Relieved of his burden, Chapo signaled he was ready to return to sentinel duty inside. Isabel walked to where the man had been standing, knelt, and picked up a sample of the sprinkled substance. It was tobacco, one of the sacred plants, and it appeared to be homegrown.

Isabel had been told of other people who had stopped to view the crime scene. A reporter writing a follow-up newspaper story for a weekly, some of Blossom's curious relatives and neighbors interested to see where the shooting had occurred, a graduate student documenting police shootings on Indian reservations. But that was nothing like what she had just witnessed.

Clayton was off the case, the investigation taken over by federal agents. She'd call him at home in the evening and ask if he knew anything about what had just happened.

———

Trevino wasn't happy the woman had seen him outside the museum but wasn't unduly concerned about it, either. Her face veiled by the shadows of the trees, he could only see that she was petite. An older woman, he guessed. She'd made no attempt to speak to him, probably because she'd been surprised. Hopefully, she'd pass him off as some weirdo and let it go at that. He hung around the area out of sight for a while on the off chance she'd called the cops, but none showed.

He drove some of the major paved roads on the rez to get familiar with the area, his appreciation of the land growing with each new vista. He cruised past the ranch area, the fish hatchery, and circled the village center before visiting the impressive resort and casino a few miles outside of the town of Ruidoso.

In town, he parked behind a block of retail stores and entered the GPS coordinates for Isabel Istee's residence. Since he was in the neighborhood, he'd scout her location. He'd do the same with Istee's gringo father Kerney, his wife Sara, and his son Patrick as well as the two Istee children and the deputy's wife. Where did they go? What was their routine? Once he knew how to get to everyone, only then would he be prepared to act.

He'd spend one more night in the Sacramento Mountains, drive to Santa Fe, and camp in the nearby national forest. He was interested to see Kerney's ranch up close.

He reviewed Isabel Istee's profile on his tablet. Never married, retired nurse, former tribal council member. Her house was on a heavily treed hillside at the end of a long driveway behind the Mescalero Public Health Service Hospital. She had one dog and drove an older-model Chevy Blazer.

He decided to make a quick run-by and then continue cruising the rez before returning to camp.

———

Isabel's shift at the museum ended at ten a.m. when eighty-six-year-old Blanca Tapaye arrived to relieve her. Considered one of the most treasured tribal healers, she always dressed traditionally while at the museum. Today she wore a long denim skirt, a flowered blouse, and had a handmade shawl draped over her shoulders. A beadwork necklace made by her grandmother with dozens of sparkling tiny mirror pendants hung around her neck.

At eleven, a busload of fourth-graders from Alamogordo were scheduled to tour the museum and listen to Blanca talk about the long-ago days. She liked to tell the story of how the necklace could be used as a signaling device to warn the people far away of approaching white-eyed strangers or the hated pony soldiers.

Isabel asked Blanca if she knew anything about the ceremony she'd witnessed outside the museum earlier that morning. She described it in detail.

"I know nothing about it," Blanca replied. "Was he a singer?"

"I could not see him clearly," Isabel replied.

"Was it Junior Second?"

Older than Blanca, Junior, bent and frail, was the most famous singer of them all. "No, this was a much younger man."

Blanca shook her head. "Then he was not of the people. This was a bad power you saw. Did it speak to you?"

"No. As soon as he saw me, he left."

"Good." Relief flooded Blanca's voice. "You have not been harmed."

Isabel picked up Chapo, who was ready to leave. "I am glad to know it."

"We will meet again," Blanca said in Apache.

"Our paths will meet again," Isabel agreed.

In her new SUV, just for the fun of it, Isabel drove to town. She picked up some good olive oil and balsamic vinegar at a specialty food store and returned the more leisurely back way home past the resort and casino. As she turned onto the road to her house, a muddy gray Jeep Wrangler passed in the opposite direction.

She slowed to look at it through the rearview mirror. Unlike New Mexico vehicles, which had none, she'd glimpsed a front license plate but couldn't make out the state. Maybe it wasn't a real plate at all, just one of those that advertised or promoted something like EAT MORE BEEF or JESUS LOVES YOU.

On a road where she could name the owners of every other vehicle, the Jeep didn't fit in. As she turned up her driveway, she remembered the man outside the museum had retreated to the same type of vehicle. It gave her a creepy feeling.

Glad to be going home, Chapo barked once.

———

Seeing the SUV on the road surprised Trevino. It had been parked outside the tribal museum, but he hadn't thought anything of it. As the vehicle turned up Isabel Istee's driveway, his concern turned to alarm. That wasn't the vehicle listed on her profile. Had she bought a new car? Was it a friend come to visit? Was it possible she'd watched him perform Whistling Bear Paints with Clay's favorite dance? It was the last act on earth his spirit would witness. Without it, he would not be welcomed into the spirit world, freed from all cares left behind.

He had to know who the driver of the SUV was. The slightest chance he might have raised suspicion was unacceptable.

He considered driving to her house, pretending to be lost, scoping out any vehicles, and asking for directions. Maybe with a White Eyes that would work, but in the tight-knit, insular Apache community of Mescalero, probably not.

He decided to return to camp before his presence became more obvious. Tomorrow he'd find a way to put his eyes on Isabel Istee. Perhaps he would kill her.

That would even the score. Take away somebody Istee loved. The single mother who'd raised him, who adored him. The mother he still honored and cherished. The idea had appeal.

He took the quickest way out of the village and arrived at the entrance of the old ranch road to his campsite. Fresh tire tracks led toward the abandoned ranch house ruins, which were two miles in. However, several rutted roads branched off along the route. Perhaps his camp hadn't been discovered. He'd proceed and see if the tracks veered away.

At the junction of the last fork in the road, the tire tracks continued on. Trevino stopped and killed the engine. If he had a visitor up ahead, there was no sense warning whoever it was that he was coming. He put his Glock 9mm in a coat pocket, left the Jeep, and circled on foot behind the old ruins. At the base of undulating foothills one mile in, he caught sight of a four-by-four pickup truck, engine running, parked next to his campsite. The man behind the wheel was talking on a cell phone.

Trevino considered taking a shot at his head, but at fifty yards the distance was too great for the Glock to guarantee a sure kill. He decided to play innocent. He stepped out into plain view from behind a partially shattered wall and waved at the man in the truck.

The man got out of the cab clutching a lever-action Marlin hunting rifle. In the hands of an experienced hunter, it was a weapon of great accuracy.

Bulky in a winter barn coat and wearing a felt cowboy hat, the man looked to be middle-aged. "Is this your camp?" he yelled.

"Yes, it is."

"Get over here," the man growled.

"What's the problem?" Trevino asked as he moved forward. He stuffed a hand in a coat pocket and gripped the Glock.

"You're trespassing."

"This is public land," Trevino replied, drawing close.

"I lease it, and you crossed my land to get here."

"I meant no harm."

"Like hell. You outsiders come here, shoot my livestock for the fun of it, leave your trash to blow in the wind, cut down trees, start fires, and I can't do a damn thing about it unless I catch you in the act. Well, this time I did, and I've got a deputy coming to arrest you."

Trevino moved closer. "That's not necessary. I'll pack up and leave."

The rancher leveled his Marlin at Trevino's chest. "You'll do no such thing. Stay put."

Trevino raised his hands skyward, stepped forward, and smiled remorsefully. "I'll pay whatever fine you want. Right here, right now. Just tell me how much."

Surprised by the offer, the rancher lowered the Marlin. "You ain't got that kind of cash."

"Five hundred?" Trevino countered. He stuffed his hand back in the pocket with the Glock. "I can do more if you want."

The rancher shook his head. "No, I want your dumb ass in jail. Teach a lesson to others like you."

"I'm sorry you said that." Trevino cleared the Glock from the pocket and shot the man twice in the head.

As he approached the body, a cell phone in the rancher's truck rang. He stopped to listen when the call went to voice mail. The deputy had found the jeep and was a mile out.

Trevino picked up the Marlin, climbed into the bed of the rancher's truck, hunkered down, and sighted the weapon down the ranch road. Given where and how the rancher had lived, he figured the weapon was zeroed in at about a hundred yards, but he couldn't be sure.

The deputy's SUV came into view, emergency lights flashing, which Trevino thought unnecessary and comical in such a remote, unpeopled space. He waited until the vehicle closed to under a hundred yards and shot the deputy twice through the windshield.

The SUV plowed off the road into a rusty water tank and flipped up, hood in the air, before crashing back down on its wheels.

Trevino approached cautiously. The deputy was dead. He'd taken one shot through the neck, the second one high in the chest. On a clipboard he'd written the make, model, and license plate number of Trevino's Jeep. Maybe in a hurry he hadn't called it in.

The police radio crackled. A dispatcher asked for the deputy's location. Trevino reached in through the shattered windshield and grabbed the clipboard. There was no time to finesse the situation.

He broke camp in a hurry, loaded everything in the rancher's truck—including the dead man's Marlin and cell phone—drove to his Jeep, transferred the gear, and set the pickup truck on fire. He was on the pavement long before he heard the wail of sirens in the distance.

Ten miles out, along an empty stretch of a two-lane state highway, he stopped, cleaned his prints off the rifle and the cell phone, and threw them into a culvert.

It was time to go home. He never, ever should have done wet work north of the border.

———

At a Juárez chop shop, Trevino traded the Jeep Wrangler for one of the owner's personal vehicles, an older Dodge Ram truck with seventy-seven thousand miles. The seller got a great deal and Trevino got a vehicle with legal papers and plates that shouldn't raise any Texas cop's interest. He dumped all his camping gear except the Glock in a garbage bin behind a vacant gas station, crossed back into El Paso, and merged with the heavy I-10 traffic heading eastward.

Eagle Pass was about five hundred miles and eight hours away, but Trevino wasn't in a hurry to get there. He needed time to think. Killing the rancher and the deputy sat heavy on his mind. They were innocent civilians, dead by unfortunate circumstances. Messy. That wasn't who he was.

He'd gone off-kilter with the Goggin-Nautzile job. Too greedy for the big money Lorenz had offered for the hit, too agreeable about scalping them both for the bonus payment. Taking out the money-hungry hotel night manager Cosgrove had just been a matter of cleanup, always part of the job, and nothing to stick in his craw.

He'd been stupid to work outside of Mexico, stupid to let vengeful feelings about Clayton Istee cloud his mind. He was the one who'd sent Whistling Bear Paints with Clay to his death, not the cop who'd shot him.

He had to stop and think. The small farming town of Van Horn sat on I-10, an hour away. He'd get a room there, have a meal and a good night's sleep, and head out in the morning on U.S. 90 through pretty country not yet spoiled by too many people.

The idea of adopting Jose Hernandez's son, Little Bear Den Near Cattails, started to sour. Who was he to take a child from a father? To raise him to tolerate loneliness, thrive on violence, be wary of everyone? He'd already done that with Fernando. It was time to stop.

The tribe had let him do just about anything. But was it out of respect or fear? Trevino laughed out loud at the stupidity of the question.

He could do one good thing for his people, buy the Mexican hunting ranch closest to the tribal lands and give it as a gift. It would provide abundant wildlife to hunt and keep Kickapoo traditions, ceremonies, and rituals alive. He'd have to put everything he owned into it, but it could be his legacy.

He'd been cruising in the right-hand lane at the speed limit, big rigs roaring past him one after another, vehicles weaving in and out to pass, gathering precious seconds on the way to somewhere.

Trevino decided he needed a new somewhere. One that was more balanced.

CHAPTER 16

Despite promises made and good intentions, Clayton was unable to completely let go of the Goggin-Nautzile homicide investigation. The killing of DEA Agent Sedillo at the Piedras Negras border crossing, Agent Harjo's disappearance into Mexico, and Isabel's report of the strange ritual outside the tribal museum continued to fuel his obsession with the case.

The ritual had all the earmarks of an indigenous ceremony, right down to the native tobacco his mother had found at the scene. Could it have been conducted by El Jefe?

Was it El Jefe that Isabel had seen driving on the road to her house? Who later that day killed a rancher and deputy sheriff responding to a misdemeanor trespass call? Virtually no evidence had been left behind at the crime scene. That made no sense, unless the killer wanted to shield his identity, which was exactly why the Las Cruces hotel night manager had been killed.

Occasional telephone calls from Special Agent Fallon, asking if he had any word from Harjo, made the case harder for Clayton to walk away from. He'd never met Fallon but could tell by the man's voice his concern for Harjo's welfare was genuine and deeply personal.

When he could sneak the time, Clayton kept trolling the Internet, concentrating on veterans websites, armed forces unit reunion events, veterans conventions and conferences, chat rooms favored by former military personnel, looking for anyone asking about an old comrade or a training classmate called Bear. All in vain.

Did he keep working the case because of vanity? To redeem himself for the fuckup with the state police that cost him the job and marred his reputation? Had regaining honor become a conceit? Sometimes psychology, no matter how insightful, wasn't helpful at all.

━━━

There are nameless enclaves in the world where people have lived for years, in some cases centuries. They are not on any maps, old or new, and there are none of the usual mapmaker symbols to lead you there. Extreme outdoor adventure enthusiasts exploring the wilderness sometimes stumble upon these unknown outposts. They are often never heard from again.

Such places dwell in the realm of legend and myth. Lost tribes, outlaw bands, forgotten civilizations, survivalists preparing for the apocalypse. Thriller movie stuff. But for those who are hunted, they are places of refuge. For others, the enclaves are their home grounds.

High in the Sierra Madre Oriental Range, Harjo had found his way to Los Ladrones, a string of stone-and-stick shacks clinging to the side of a steep canyon hidden deep in the mountains. A perennial stream furnished clear water, the surrounding forest supplied wood, and crops grew in the rich strips of bottomland.

Thirty-seven men, women, and children lived there, all of them indigenous. Harjo thought perhaps they were descendants of a party of Seminoles who'd crossed into Mexico in the middle of the nineteenth century. Supposedly all had returned to Texas before the start of the Civil War. But his attempts to question them about their origins were met with polite silence. Nor would they tell him how Las Ladrones— The Thieves—got its name or where their money came from. They seemed to always have enough to buy essentials and necessities.

They only spoke Spanish around him, but once in a while he caught snatches of a guttural language he didn't understand. They were handsome, brown-skinned people, small in stature. They dressed in a combination of handmade simple loose-fitting attire and store-bought clothing, mostly muted colors.

Harjo had learned of Las Ladrones years ago from a grateful CI who'd been born there. He'd helped Harjo take down a drug dealer running a string of prostitutes in Juárez and El Paso. In appreciation, Harjo got the man legally into the States and away from the remaining sex-ring gangsters trying to kill him.

For three months Harjo had been staying in Las Ladrones with the CI's oldest sister, Felipa, and her family. In her late sixties, Felipa was short but with such a straight posture that she seemed taller than her five-feet-two-inch frame.

The family called him "The Bald One." Every day he went to work with the men of the village, cutting and hauling wood from the forest, hunting game that roamed the high mountains, and quarrying rock used to repair and rebuild the small houses, which were prone to damage from occasional landslides that cascaded down the steep canyon walls.

He learned how to secure loads of firewood onto the burros, dry-stack stone walls, and cut rock with a hammer and chisel. Soon he was climbing out of the canyon without needing to pause and catch his breath, and easily kept up with the men as they moved quickly through the forests. He lost weight, gained muscle, and had regained his endurance and energy from a decade ago. He never felt better.

Frequently, one or two of the men packed up tools and bedding and disappeared from the village for weeks at a time, returning with money and sometimes semiprecious stones used for barter and trade. There was no mention of where they'd been or what they'd done, but Harjo had a suspicion they were mining gold and selling it.

Once a month, Felipa, her oldest children, and several other families trekked across the mountains to a remote one-room schoolhouse where vendors from the nearest town, over twenty miles away, came to sell food, clothing, and supplies to the Las Ladrones. The traders were not allowed closer to the village. Those who tried were forever barred by the villagers. Harjo wanted to go on one of the treks but knew better than to ask. No outsider could know of his presence.

He slept on the floor of Felipa's house in the corner of the single room covered with a thin mat. He continued to shave his head, grew a beard, which he kept neatly trimmed, and worked sunup to sundown with men who rarely spoke to him. Except for Felipa, the women of the village also shied away. Only the younger children were free to be with him, often following him around or including him in their favorite stick-toss game. One fourteen-year-old girl, Rosita, eyed him speculatively. Harjo tried to stay away from her, but she always seemed to be patiently waiting nearby after her chores were done. He figured she was simply curious to learn more about the outside world, but she never approached him to ask.

After his fourth month, Harjo was asked by Guerrero, the oldest male in the village, to join him for dinner. Over eighty years old by Harjo's guess, he lived alone in the largest house in the settlement. Harjo figured him to be the tribal leader, but nobody showed any deference to the old man. And as far as Harjo could tell, Guerrero never gave any orders or seemed interested in village affairs. He took a lot of long naps in the sun on a stool outside his house.

Guerrero cooked and served a meal of beans, tortillas, and coffee, and they ate in silence until the last bit of food had been wiped clean from their bowls.

"You must leave," Guerrero said. Legs crossed, he lit his pipe and leaned back against the wall. "Tomorrow."

"Have I behaved badly?" Harjo asked, somewhat surprised.

Guerrero shook his head. "No, Rosita is much too interested in your world, and that cannot be allowed to continue."

"She hasn't asked me a thing," Harjo said. "We've only exchanged greetings."

"You are a distraction. She is of age to marry and it is Felipa's wish that you depart."

"I didn't know Felipa was Rosita's mother."

"She's not. Felipa leads us all. She has in mind a husband for Rosita. Tomas, whom you know."

Harjo nodded. Tomas was no more than sixteen. "A fine young man."

"You will stay here tonight with me and be guided out in the morning. Your belongings have been left outside my door."

"I must thank Felipa for her kind hospitality," Harjo countered.

Guerrero waved off the request. "She knows of your gratitude. You will stay here until you depart."

"As you wish," Harjo said.

"We have come to enjoy your company," Guerrero said.

"I give many thanks to all for allowing me to stay so long."

"You saved my son's life, for which we will always be indebted."

Surprised, Harjo responded with a smile.

At dawn after breakfast, Harjo was led away from the village by Julio, an armed guide, and his large, tail-wagging black mutt called Perro. They followed a trail hidden deep in the forest Harjo had not spotted. For two days they hiked and camped in the mountains until finally late in the third day they reached a summit that looked over a wide desert valley cut by an empty paved road.

Julio pointed north. "Walk one day and you'll come to a small town. Take Perro with you. When you get there, send the dog back to me. I'll wait here for him to know you arrived safely."

"What if Perro doesn't want to leave me?" Harjo asked jokingly.

Julio smiled through his broken teeth. "Then I will find him waiting for me next to your dead body. But do not worry, you'll be safe. You look like a poor Mexican. No one will ever suspect you're an American policeman."

"Thanks for the compliment."

"What will you do now?" Julio asked.

"Settle an old score," Harjo answered.

Julio smiled again and offered his hand. "A good thing to do. Buena suerte."

"Adios."

Julio whistled once and pointed at Harjo. Perro raised his ears and wagged his tail in acknowledgment. By the time Harjo and the dog were halfway down mountainside, Julio had disappeared into the tree cover.

———

It had not been easy for Trevino to negotiate with Ricardo McCabe Gabaldon. The descendant of a nineteenth-century New Zealand immigrant who'd recently bought over a quarter million acres that bordered Estavio's ranch, Ricardo acted as if he were a Spanish aristocrat. Not only did he snub those he considered inferior, which included the Kickapoos, he had denied the men of the tribe permission to hunt on his land. For those two reasons alone, Trevino disliked being in Gabaldon's company.

Looking to expand his empire, Gabaldon had twice approached Trevino offering to buy his land. Twice, Trevino had turned him down. Fortunately, he didn't have to wait long for a third offer, which came a month after his return from New Mexico. Unfortunately, it took two months of Gabaldon's nitpicking to reach an agreement on a purchase price and closing date.

With the deal completed and money in hand, Trevino put his personal possessions in storage, moved out, gave his workers substantial severance pay, turned over the hacienda keys to Gabaldon's ranch manager, and temporarily returned to live at Colonia de los Kickapoo as a guest of Caballo Galindo.

He brought Consuelo, his Mexican housekeeper, with him. She would live with her sister, who was married to a tribal member.

Soon after his arrival, he told Galindo that he'd decided not to adopt Jose Hernandez's son.

"That will please Jose," Galindo said. "Does he know?"

"Not yet. You haven't asked me why."

"It is clear you are starting something new."

"It is good to shake off the dust of the past," Trevino agreed.

He explained that with the sale of his land and money he'd invested from his work, the purchase of the San Rodrigo Hunting Ranch was about to go through. The land would become part of the colonia and would be owned by the tribe.

"There are many deer on the ranch," he added with a smile.

"Welcome news for all of us," Galindo said happily. "When the time comes, we will have a fiesta at the San Rodrigo to celebrate. Will you continue to live here with us?"

"I've no plans to go away again," Trevino replied. "There is a comfortable cabin on the San Rodrigo. I will live there as the caretaker."

"As chief of the hunt," Galindo corrected. "Will there be no more need for murderer's ceremonies?"

"That is my hope," Trevino said.

"I am glad to hear of it."

In the morning, Trevino approached Hernandez outside his house. "Little Bear Den Near Cattails will stay with you. There will be no adoption."

Hernandez smiled with relief, his eyes tearing. "Thank you. I had a dream that you had turned into a black bear and would not take him away."

"What else did you see as your spirit wandered?"

"Nothing bad. Eat with us tonight."

"Gladly."

Trevino went to his father's old house, long empty and closed up, where he'd stored everything from the hacienda he didn't wish to keep. He opened the door and began carrying out various dressers, tables, chairs, lamps, small appliances, dishes, pots, pans, and glassware. He manhandled a sofa through the door and the desk from his library. He dragged out a large rug and unrolled it on the ground. By the time he'd finished emptying the house, people were already picking through the offerings of the impromptu free flea market, smiling and chatting as they carried away their new possessions.

As he went to his truck to drive to town, the sight of it gave him a good feeling.

———

Clayton was at his desk when Frank Rodney entered the bullpen with a stranger. A younger guy, obviously a cop, who looked Native American. He was tall, fit, and carried himself with an air of confidence. Clayton guessed he was Navajo and some kind of Fed.

Rodney stopped at Clayton's desk. "This is Special Agent Danny Fallon."

Clayton stood and shook Fallon's hand. "I was supposed to team up with you in Mexico to capture El Jefe."

"A fine and admirable venture," Fallon said sarcastically. "Flawed but workable."

Clayton smiled at his flippancy.

Rodney remained stone-faced. "He wants to look at your file on El Jefe and visit the crime scene where the Otero County deputy and rancher were gunned down. I've cleared it with the Otero County SO and the state police. An officer will meet you there."

He looked pointedly at Clayton. "You've got one day to assist Special Agent Fallon."

Fallon sat in the chair at the side of Clayton's desk. "I'm sure that's all the time I'll need."

"Then I'll leave you two to it." Captain Rodney walked away.

Clayton grabbed a thick file from a desk drawer. "Is this about El Jefe or Agent Harjo's disappearance?"

"Both."

"Official or unofficial?"

"I'm on leave, but I didn't tell your captain that."

"What makes you think Harjo's alive?"

"He's too big a fish to kill without making some noise about it. And he's hard to kill. If he were dead, his body would have been dumped where it could have been easily found and we would have heard about it. It's less showy than the way they gunned down Agent Sedillo in daylight on the crowded Piedras Negras bridge, but it's the same narco-trafficker code. Be a Norte Americano federal agent in Mexico and we will kill you."

"There are a lot of different ways Harjo may have died." Clayton handed over the file. "None of them so attention-grabbing. Take all the time you need. I'll answer what questions I can."

Fallon zeroed in on the shooting at the Mescalero village and the early morning ceremony Clayton's mother had witnessed days later.

"Why do you think it was El Jefe that your mother saw?"

"It was clearly an indigenous ceremony. Not unlike what we do in Mescalero to send someone safely on his way to live among his ancestors."

"That doesn't mean El Jefe performed it."

"Stay with me on this," Clayton urged. "After the CIA took over the case, they wanted a second forensic look at the body, which had been sent to a funeral home for cremation. Instead, it had been claimed by someone posing as a family relative. The funeral director never reported it to the police. He'd falsified some documents to make it look legit, but finally admitted he'd been bribed to do it."

"How does this connect to El Jefe?" Fallon inquired.

"Granted, the dead man was the son of the murdered German couple, but it's not unusual for non-natives to be adopted into a tribe. The Kickapoos, like many others, do it."

"You think El Jefe adopted and raised him as his son," Fallon said.

"Perhaps after killing the couple, although that's just a guess. How the boy came to him, I don't know, but tell me how else a German raised as a Mexican would be sent, locked and loaded, to follow the exact route Nautzile and Goggin took on their way to Las Cruces?"

"There are other plausible scenarios," Fallon countered. "The most obvious, he was El Jefe's servant. Bribing the funeral director for the body was just another example of covering his tracks. Part of his MO."

"That's possible," Clayton replied. "I read up on Kickapoo burials. If he had been adopted into the tribe, custom required that he be buried in a cemetery with family members. It is still a common practice among all the Kickapoo nations."

"Have there been any recent burials at the Mexican tribal cemetery?" Fallon asked.

"Cemeteries," Clayton corrected "There are three. But to answer your question, I don't know."

"Was it El Jefe who claimed the body?"

Clayton shook his head. "The description of the man provided by the funeral director doesn't match what we think El Jefe looks like, but it could have been a disguise. Personally, I don't think so."

Fallon paged through the file and stopped at the section that dealt with the newspaper article out of Oklahoma reporting a warrior healing ceremony for two returning tribal veterans conducted by a highly decorated Kickapoo veteran known only as "Bear."

Fallon held up a copy of the article. "What's this?"

"Remember, Harjo told us El Jefe's nickname was Bear. There's a Bear Clan in the Kickapoo tribe. That could account for the nickname. I spoke to the reporter who wrote the story. She told me the tribal leaders would not let her photograph or interview the healer. I followed up and got the same rejection. Maybe it's about keeping the outside world at bay, or maybe it was El Jefe protecting his identity."

"He's a warrior-healer," Fallon speculated. "I didn't think of that. So we need to find an ex-combat veteran Kickapoo healer nicknamed Bear who just might be El Jefe. That's a huge chunk of research to tear into, but a damn good idea."

"I've ground to a halt," Clayton said. "Partially because I've been ordered to, partially because I promised to, and partially because I've gotten nowhere."

Fallon cocked an eyebrow.

"Okay, I still poke around every now and again," Clayton confessed.

Fallon put the article back in the file folder. "I can't let go of it, either. You ready to take me to the crime scene?"

Clayton stuffed the file in the desk drawer, called the state police district office to say they were on their way, and stood. "Let's go."

———

Sergeant Carla Olivas, recently promoted and transferred out of criminal investigations back to patrol, was waiting for them at the old ranch ruins. Clayton had once been her boss. He congratulated her on the promotion and introduced her to Agent Fallon.

Carla grinned and shook Fallon's hand. "I'll walk you through what we know, if you like."

"That's why I'm here," Fallon replied.

"You saw the burned-out pickup truck coming in," Olivas said. "Did you stop?"

"We did," Fallon replied. "Was forensics able to collect anything worthwhile?"

"No, but several weeks ago a highway maintenance crew found the Marlin rifle that was used to kill the deputy and the rancher's cell phone in a culvert ten miles away. They were both wiped clean."

She took them to four evidence markers placed on the ground that formed a rectangle. "This is where the perp slept, out in the open, for one night only. We know this because nothing indicates he used a tent and he left very few footprints."

Olivas stepped to a marked circle of rocks. "He wore very expensive hiking boots, made by a company in Mexico City. Size nine, medium. He kept a cold camp. He didn't gather wood and used a small propane camp stove. Forensics found a small piece of foil probably torn from a single-serve coffee or freeze-dried meal packet."

"Did you locate a latrine trench or a pit?" Fallon asked.

"No." Olivas guided them to evidence-marked tire tracks. "This is where our perp parked his vehicle. Size, type, and make of the tires are consistent with a high-clearance four-by-four. Wheel-to-wheel measurements match nicely with a Jeep Wrangler, like the one Detective Istee's mother saw at the tribal museum."

"This was the camp of no ordinary hunter caught trespassing out of season," Fallon said.

"Exactly," Olivas said. "And he was an excellent marksman, to boot. Clean kills of both victims. No shell casings left behind."

Fallon turned to Clayton. "Any word on the Jeep?"

"No, it's probably somewhere in Mexico or has been chopped for parts."

"Any other evidence?" Fallon asked hopefully.

Olivas shook her head. "That's it. Are we done here?"

Fallon nodded. "Thanks for the tour, Sergeant."

"You're welcome. I'll follow you out."

———

As they bumped and churned their way over the ranch road with Olivas in Clayton's rearview mirror, Fallon asked if he wanted to go to Mexico with him to find Harjo.

"Are you married, Fallon?' Clayton countered. "An ex, maybe? Some kids?"

Fallon smiled. "No, and I hear you. You got people to take care of, family counting on you. Harjo's the same as me, not much family to boast of or worry about."

"You're his family," Clayton proposed.

"And vice versa. He's the big brother I never had."

"When do you leave for Piedras Negras?"

"In the morning."

"How about if I knock off early and buy you a beer?"

"I'd like that. Think you can get Sergeant Olivas to join us?"

"She's married and gay."

Fallon laughed. "Wouldn't you know it? All the pretty ones are taken."

CHAPTER 17

Harjo arrived at the small village, and Perro took off on his way back to Julio. He rested at a cramped restaurant and bar carved out of an old house and drank a cerveza, his first in months. He ate a big meal, loitered overnight, and bought supplies in the morning before returning to the mountains, where he started a slow trek to Piedras Negras. He kept his bearings with a hand-drawn map Julio had made to guide his way.

His days in the high country were tranquil and filled with solitude. No talking, no heightened tension, no need to guard against a slip of the tongue that could unmask a false identity. He encountered no one along the way and decided Julio had sent him along an old smuggler's trail.

Frequently his thoughts turned to Maria Sedillo. Who could he tell how brave she was? How smart? What a damn fine agent she had been?

He was still determined to avenge the murder of his nephew. But thanks to Sedillo, he had another target as well, Gilberto Garza,

Lorenz's brother. Would it be easier to get to Lorenz through Garza, the respectable, upstanding, God-fearing citizen? If so, he'd kill them both.

On the outskirts of Piedras Negras, at a cheap motel with a busted neon sign that flickered on and off, he rented a room and walked along the shoulder of the road to the nearest bar, a working-class establishment sandwiched between a convenience store and a gas station. A couple of miles down the highway the heart of the drug-infested city pulsed along the banks of the Rio Grande, spewing fear into the night. Harjo didn't want to go near it. Compared to Las Ladrones and the Sierra Madres of eastern Mexico, even the fringes of the narco-controlled city were depressing enough.

The cantina customers were mostly truckers, construction workers, day laborers, and some recently repatriated detainees from Texas ICE holding facilities looking for work before traveling south or plotting their next crossing.

Harjo felt right at home in the crowded bar, and after several late afternoon drinking sessions he made acquaintance with some regulars. One of his new drinking buddies was Benito Jimenez, a barrel-shaped man with an infectious smile and an appetite for beer, who owned a yard-maintenance and landscape company.

Harjo kept his cover story short. Born in Mexico, raised in the States, he worked construction without a green card until a traffic stop got him deported. He used his personal history to flesh out any needed details which would be easy to remember and made mention of his new skills in stonework and woodcutting.

In a casual, inoffensive way, Jimenez liked to brag about his family and his work. He had six school-age kids—four girls, two boys—a stay-at-home wife, and owned a government-built house in a blue-collar neighborhood. He ran his one-man yard and landscape company by hiring occasional day laborers for the bigger jobs. During his free time, he helped coach his older son's soccer team, and was in the process of slowly adding another bedroom to his house. Almost completed, the project had been under way for two years.

His business was growing. He'd picked up several new customers in an exclusive part of town and was in desperate need of a stonemason to fill in for a worker who'd suffered a recent back injury.

"Dry-stack work?" Harjo asked.

"Sí, they want stone planting beds built on two sides of a backyard patio with stairs leading down to a new hot tub they just installed. I need someone who I can trust to work alone, so I can take care of my other customers. Can you do it?"

Harjo jumped at the offer but told Jimenez he didn't have any transportation.

"I'll pick you up," Jimenez said. He added that the materials and tools needed were already at the job site.

"Gracias," Harjo said.

"I'll come by three, four times a day to check on you," he added. He finished his third cerveza and stood. "Bring a lunch. I get an early start. Be ready by seven."

Harjo chuckled. "Now you sound like a jefe."

"I am your jefe." He clasped Harjo's shoulder and smiled. "You work hard for me and we'll get along muy bueno." He lumbered out a little tipsy, leaving the tab for his cervezas to Harjo to pick up. Counting out the money from his dwindling reserve, he realized he'd forgotten to ask what the job paid.

———

Trevino entered the basement meeting room at Shen's restaurant, where Lorenz, Sammy Shen, and Juan waited. According to rumor, Gabriela and Catherina had been murdered for the grievous deed of turning Juan into a eunuch. Although false, it had enraged Juan, who'd gleefully raped both women before having them killed.

Longwei was absent.

Trevino sat directly across from Lorenz, who'd asked him to come. "Why have we gathered?"

"We understand you've sold your land and hacienda and purchased a hunting ranch," Sammy said. He'd bought the information from a drunk Kickapoo for a fifth of cheap whiskey.

"It's public knowledge." Trevino glanced at Juan, who stared silently back at him.

"Did you need an extra million dollars to close the transaction?" Lorenz interjected sharply.

Trevino leaned forward in his chair. "Are you accusing me of stealing from you?"

Lorenz's expression softened. "I'm sorry if I sound harsh. Forgive me. I'm just hoping you'll find and return to me what is rightfully mine."

"I never promised to get back your money, Luis. That wasn't our agreement. But as an act of goodwill, I sent my son to see if he could find it. He was killed as a result. Let us consider our losses even, although mine were far greater."

Juan continued to remain silent. Trevino wondered if his tongue had been removed rather than his private parts. Ludicrous, he decided.

Sammy intervened with a sympathetic smile. "We understand it is hard to lose someone close. But our predicament is a question of reputation, mine included. Unless we have the money back, it will be seen by our competitors as a weakness in the way we conduct business."

"Not my problem," Trevino replied flatly.

Lorenz lounged back comfortably and smiled broadly. "All we're asking is that you make a good-faith effort to find and return my money. If you agree, succeed or fail, we'll consider the matter closed."

"Another effort on your part would demonstrate to our competitors that nothing is forgotten or forgiven," Sammy explained pleasantly. "Whatever the outcome, it will remain private, just between us."

"Unless you have other commitments, we'd like you to start right away," Lorenz said.

"I cannot do as you ask." Trevino stood and looked pointedly at each man. "And I have no desire to do so. Our business arrangement ends here and now. I'm retiring, so to speak. Let us part amicably, although I caution you against any notion of retaliation."

They took his warning in stony silence.

"As you wish," Sammy finally whispered through thin lips.

"Very well," Lorenz added.

Trevino climbed the stairs. Did they really think he was such a patsy? They couldn't have made their desire to kill him any more transparent if they'd tried. Now it was just a matter of waiting to see how it would play out.

Regrettably, it wasn't quite time to put his weapons away.

———

Longwei came down from the restaurant where he'd been mentoring an attractive young Chinese waitress recently smuggled into the country from Liaoning Province. Once again, she'd learned one of Longwei's privileges of ownership while bent over the desk with her skirt up in his small office.

"Is El Jefe still our friend?" he asked with a contented smile, settling into his chair.

Lorenz shook his head. "No."

Longwei drummed his fingers on the arm of the chair. "Then we must deal with him, but not immediately."

"Why not?" Juan inquired, unconvinced.

"Because he'll be wary and on guard for a time," Sammy said. "Let him settle into his cottage on the hunting ranch and get comfortable. Then we will strike."

Juan shook his head. "I disagree. We can't wait too long."

"Be patient," Lorenz counseled.

"He can easily take out anyone we send against him," Juan noted.

"We'll swarm him with men, killers all," Lorenz proposed. "Fifty of my officers will seal off the hunting ranch so he can't escape. A coordinated surgical strike will be sufficient. No government official or reporter will blink an eye about a nameless squatter found dead in a cabin on a neglected hunting ranch."

Juan's eyes brightened. "Let me do it."

Lorenz looked at Longwei, who nodded and reached for the telephone. "Let us ask Juan's father for his concurrence."

———

Carmen Garza stepped into her husband's private study, placed a tray of his favorite appetizers on the coffee table, poured two glasses of wine, and joined him on the couch.

It was their ritual each afternoon. They relaxed and talked of the small events of the day, surrounded by the impressive assemblage of various civic and religious honors that decorated the bookshelves and walls.

"Who called?" she asked.

"Longwei," Gilberto replied. "Trevino has refused our offer and wishes to retire. We need to make it permanent. Juan wants permission to handle it."

"Personally?"

"If possible, I would imagine. However, Luis has a plan in mind that should keep Juan safe and deflect public attention."

"Excellent." Carmen paused to sip her wine. "Still, Trevino is formidable, and I worry about Juan's impulsiveness. I don't want him doing something foolish and getting hurt again."

"Nor do I. I will make sure that Luis has two of his best men with Juan at all times to restrain and protect him if need be." Gilberto patted Carmen's hand. "It is time for Juan to step forward in the family business. He's earned the right."

Carmen nodded. "I know."

"Then we are agreed?"

Carmen sighed. "Yes."

"Good." Gilberto picked up the phone.

———

Danny Fallon crossed into Piedras Negras with a list of local bars he'd researched on the Internet. He took a cab to the airport and rented a car for a week. Only interested in dives and local hangouts, he'd immediately crossed off establishments that catered to American tourists. If Harjo were to be found in the city it would be at a working-class bar where only Mexicans gathered. Such cantinas were gold mines of local knowledge as well as great places to hide if you knew how to fit in.

While his list was in no way complete, one bar would lead to another and then another. He'd cover them all if necessary before moving on to the next city on his list, Múzquiz, south of Piedras Negras.

Fallon skipped over the downtown bars close to the river—too obvious to bother with. With a city street map in hand, he spent the majority of the day learning his way around. It was always handy to know the best escape routes.

He had a little over three weeks of leave time and the thought that Harjo might not want to be found nagged at him. He cruised past the heavily guarded police station, wondering if there was one uncorrupt officer inside the building. Probably not. He pictured Lorenz inside, running the family drug empire, caring nothing about the murder and mayhem he created on the streets of the city.

Thugs, punks, and gangsters were everywhere downtown, easy to spot on street corners and in their slow-cruising cars. DEA intelligence now ranked Piedras Negras as the fastest-growing narco-trafficking center along the border. It would soon kill the heart and soul of the city, much like what had happened to Juárez and Tijuana. No wonder ordinary people wanted to escape from the chaos that overwhelmed them and find a safe place in the States for their families.

The first bar on his list was a grubby tavern with gaudy Day of the Dead skeletons—human and animal—painted on the walls. Salsa music blared from overhead speakers. One draft beer and two indecent propositions later, Fallon was out the door. No sense hanging out with the gay guys.

———

The stonework job was in a gated hillside community with a guardhouse at the entrance. Large homes on expansive lots were all completely surrounded by a tall steel security fence. Jimenez's client, the owner of an international trucking company, met them when they arrived to walk them through the work to be done. Wearing a thousand-dollar suit and expensive wing-tips, Senor Miguel Valencia gave Harjo a critical once-over. Deferentially, Jimenez introduced Harjo, who removed his ball cap and acted as subservient as possible.

The house, starkly modern with thick concrete and stone walls offset by large windows and wide sliding glass doors, was both imposing and inviting. Although it was nicely landscaped, Harjo guessed it had been recently constructed. The planting beds that Valencia's wife wanted built matched the stone used in the construction of the house and would bracket the covered patio, which contained a complete top-of-the-line outdoor kitchen.

Senor Valencia went over the design plans. Harjo eyed them speculatively. If he worked very slowly and carefully, he just might be able to pull it off. Psychologically, he felt up to the challenge of building something that couldn't be messed with by prosecutors, thwarted by bungling agency bureaucrats, sabotaged by uncooperative witnesses, or torpedoed by hung juries. Making something that would last held enormous appeal.

After the trucking czar and Jimenez left, Harjo carefully measured the dimensions, staked the corners, and ran the string lines, before slicing through the lush green grass and turning over the first spade of earth.

By noon he'd finished trenching for one planter. Jimenez had been by twice and seemed satisfied with his work. He sat under the shade of a palm tree, ate lunch, and drank from a pitcher of ice water and a large plastic glass the housekeeper had thoughtfully put out for him. He finished his last tortilla still hungry. Tomorrow he'd bring more food.

Two women stood behind the patio doors watching. The angle of the sun made it impossible to see them clearly, but Harjo figured it was the trucking czar's wife and her housekeeper.

He stood, went to the pallets of rectangular and square stone in various sizes, and started sorting through the rocks for the best ones to use as the foundation. Thanks to his stay in Los Ladrones, he wasn't sore or tired. He decided to do one planter at a time so his progress would be tangible and keep him motivated.

Using a wheelbarrow, he carted loads of stone to the trench and laid them out in two long rows. When finished, each twenty-foot-long planter would stand three feet tall and be thirty inches wide. Laying the stones was an art of precise placement, requiring a keen eye and close concentration. He cleared his thoughts and began.

By the time of Jimenez's third supervisory visit Harjo had almost forgotten that he'd returned to Piedras Negras to kill some very bad people.

———

Halfway through his second day on the job, the housekeeper brought Harjo a pitcher of iced tea and lingered for a few minutes.

"I'm Lupita," she said. Tall and round, she looked to be in her sixties.

"Bernard," Harjo replied, raising his glass of iced tea. "Gracias."

"Por nada." Lupita glance at the patio doors. "My senora thinks you are working too slowly."

So far, Harjo had a third of one wall up, which he thought was damn good progress. "Is she in a hurry for me to finish?"

"Sí. Once you are done, she wishes to have a big party and invite the neighbors, muy importante people."

"Big shots," Harjo commented.

Lupita nodded.

"I'll try to work faster," he promised.

The patio doors opened, and two women stepped out. One young with every hair in place, the other much older, matronly-looking.

"Lupita, Senora Garza stopped by to visit," the younger woman said. "Bring us coffee in the living room."

"Right away," Lupita replied.

The women retreated inside.

"A neighbor?" Harjo ventured.

"Sí," Lupita answered, hurrying toward the house.

It had to be *Carmen* Garza, Gilberto's wife, Harjo thought. Suddenly he was no longer interested in building dry-stacked walls.

He forced aside the distraction. He had no weapon, no phone, no vehicle, and no way of knowing which mansion of the two dozen or so inside the compound Carmen and Gilberto Garza inhabited. He needed to find that out first and discover what additional security they had, human or otherwise. Then he'd assemble what he needed to pay the Garzas a visit.

———

Over the last decade, the hunting ranch had been neglected and virtually abandoned. Many of the dirt roads that had been cut in the topsoil to accommodate hunters were now overgrown trails. Artificial ponds built to attract waterfowl had failed and wetlands along live streams now flourished, bringing back water turtles and catfish. Grasslands once leased by a rancher and seriously overgrazed had rebounded and spread.

There were two entrances with locked gates and the property was fenced, but not secure against the migration of animals or the intrusion of humans. A good population of deer roamed freely, and quail and mourning doves thrived. Amazingly, Trevino had caught sight of several weasels once thought to be extinct in the region. There were squirrels, rabbits, and coyotes, but no sign of bears or cougars. He thought it improbable either would return, although he longed for it to happen.

He spent a week cleaning out the caretaker's cottage of the vermin that had moved in and killed all the snakes around the building, usually a woman's chore. He made necessary repairs to windows, doors, and the leaky roof, stocked up on food and supplies, cut and stacked a cord of wood to dry, and outfitted the cottage with a few pieces of furniture he'd kept from the hacienda.

Deer in a nearby clearing kept him company, browsing on twigs and leaves at a tree-lined thicket. The small herd consisted of an old doe, three very pregnant ones, and two frisky one-year-old fawns. With mating season still a long way off, there were no bucks sniffing around. The deer appeared unconcerned by Trevino's presence, moving slowly in and out of view, only mildly interested in the occasional noise that he made.

There were no power lines to the cabin. A gasoline generator supplied enough electricity to pump well water to use in the kitchen and
the small bathroom barely large enough to turn around in. The small
scale of the place with its wood cooking stove that kept the place warm
at night was cozy and comforting, although he had no plans to sleep
there right away.

For defense, Trevino installed solar-powered wireless driveway
alert systems at both ranch road gates, which he kept padlocked. He
added solar-powered motion sensors a few yards out on either side of
the entrances in case unwanted visitors chose to ignore the gates and
crash through the fence. At the cabin he mounted a battery-operated
CCTV camera over the front door and another at the back of the building. He programmed his smartphone to monitor all the devices. Close
at hand was a handheld police radio he'd purchased at a premium from
a semiliterate Piedras Negras uniformed officer who had reported it
stolen from his patrol car.

It wasn't a perfect early warning system, but it was better than none
at all. For now, he'd cook, take his meals, and shower at the cottage,
with weapons within reach for the invasion by Lorenz's henchmen that
was sure to come, and soon.

For survival, he set up three concealed field-of-fire locations away
from the cabin, each stocked with a sniper rifle, assault weapons, a
large supply of ammunition, water, and night-vision goggles. He'd bed
down at the one farthest from the cabin and wait for the attack. When
it came, he would either engage or retreat depending on what Lorenz
threw against him.

If he was still standing when it ended, he'd mapped and marked an
escape route to follow. Once he was safe, blood would be spilled. Only
the question of where to start remained unanswered. He'd think about
that later. For now, he felt tranquil and contented. The ranch truly felt
like home. A place where he could live close to his people, his tradi-

tions, his culture, and his language, yet be apart. Where he could come and go freely without the constant need to hide. Here, he'd hunt, grow crops, and be Kickapoo again.

It was the best thing he'd ever done.

———

Jimenez picked Harjo up Friday morning and told him it would be his last day on the job. The injured stonemason had recovered enough to return to work and needed the money. He'd start back on Saturday and work through the weekend.

"He's worked for me for a long time," Jimenez explained apologetically. "He wanted to start today, but I told him no because it wouldn't be fair to you and you needed to make money also, just like the rest of us."

"I appreciate that," Harjo said with a smile. "Because I thought you were going to fire me for being too slow."

Jimenez chuckled. "Rich people don't know nothing except hurry, hurry, do what I want, and here's ten pesos."

"Did they complain?"

"Only un poco. The wife."

"You told me you have another job close by, maybe with Senor Garza. Could you use me there?"

"Garza?" Jimenez roared with laughter. "If only. How did you hear of him?"

"Lupita, the housekeeper."

"Now, that would be a job I'd love to get. We drive by his place every day. The one with the twelve-foot brick wall with all those huge planters filled with flowers out in front. He's got a full-time grounds-keeper. No, my other job here is for a wealthy old widow who just wants her lawn cut, the leaves raked, and never tips."

Staying in character, Harjo shrugged. "The rich, always so stingy. Do you know of any other jobs?"

Jimenez shook his head. "No se. What will you do?"

"Go home. Cross the border." For Jimenez's protection, Harjo said no more. He needed to cut all ties with him.

"I'll buy the beers tonight," Jimenez offered.

"Bueno." After the cervezas, he'd move out of the motel. "By the way, how much will my pay be?"

Jimenez pulled to the side of the road and consulted his cell phone. "A little more than two thousand pesos."

Harjo did the math. Four ten-hour days had earned him a few bucks over a hundred U.S. dollars. He smiled appreciatively. "Okay."

"You're lucky to have a place to go to in the States," Jimenez said. "But I'll miss your company."

"Me, too," Harjo replied sincerely.

———

Each morning, Harjo had paid for his motel room in advance. After beers with Jimenez, he returned to his room, packed his few things in a cheap canvas tote bag, and left the dingy motel through a side door. He walked along the slender shoulder of the roadway toward downtown Piedras Negras with the din of traffic clattering in his ears.

Hidden under the waistband of his jeans was a money pocket he'd worn since entering Mexico with Agent Sedillo. It contained enough dollars to buy a gun on the street, a burner cell phone, some meals, and necessities, but not much more. Certainly not a vehicle. Although greenbacks were a common enough currency in Northern Mexico, Harjo had used them sparingly to avoid drawing unwanted attention. When the job was done and his money gone, maybe he'd have to steal a getaway car.

First up was finding another place to stay. Since leaving Los Ladrones, Harjo had stopped shaving his head, which was now covered by a thick stubby fuzz. At the motel, he'd cut off his beard except for the mustache. With his new look, it was time to drop out of sight again for a while.

At an Internet café, Harjo paid for an hour of computer time and found an ad for a furnished room to rent in an area three miles from the local airport. Or, less expensively, he could rent a bed in a dormitory-style room that accommodated four guests. The photographs looked copied from old magazines, suggesting the place was guaranteed to be a real dump.

He bought a burner phone at the counter, called, and booked the furnished room. It would cost him half a day's wages in pesos. He faced a long hike on an increasingly cold night, but he was up for it. Walking was always good for heavy thinking, and he had some serious obstacles to consider.

How could he breach Garza's estate without detection, given the security cameras and sensor lights on top of the twelve-foot walls? He also had to get by the gated guard station at the entrance to the subdivision.

Would it be better to go after Lorenz in the secret basement room under Longwei's restaurant? He needed to scout out those safe houses before deciding. He also needed a way to know when to strike. There was no sense doing any of it if his quarry wasn't present. If he got Lorenz, could he take out Gilberto? Or would that be too much of a reach?

He set out on the empty downtown sidewalk, hoping he looked too down-and-out to attract any potential muggers. Although slugging some cranked-up punk for his handgun would be a satisfying way to close out the evening.

CHAPTER 18

Clayton was eating lunch at his desk when Captain Rodney rang and ordered him into his office. The smell of nicotine hung in the air, signaling that he'd just returned from one of his frequent smoke breaks.

"You're still playing with the Goggin-Nautzile case," Rodney noted, looking only slightly peeved.

"I haven't tried to hide it," Clayton replied. "But it's not been on the clock. I give it a few minutes before shift, and if my desk is cleared I put in some time after work."

"I know that. Do you have anything new?"

"I've formulated some assumptions about El Jefe to use as a baseline. Active-duty soldiers and veterans tend to remain loyal to their units and branch of service. Marine vets stick together. Air Force, Army, and Navy the same."

Rodney nodded. "I get it. So what?"

"So, to narrow down my search, I'm assuming El Jefe served in the Army, like the two soldiers who went through the warrior healing ceremony. Remember, the newspaper article reported the officiant had been a decorated combat veteran."

"Isn't being a Kickapoo enough of a strong bond without an Army connection?" Rodney countered.

"Maybe, but they all came from different, geographically separate tribes in Oklahoma, Kansas, and Mexico. Granted, there's interaction between them, but I've got nothing that tells me the three men knew each other in civilian life or on active duty. However, Jefe's proficiency as a killer strongly suggests extensive military training."

"Your assumptions have big holes," Rodney commented.

"That need filling," Clayton concurred. "But according to General Brannon, my father's wife, the two soldiers are posted at different Army units, the Seventy-Fifth Ranger Regiment and the Tenth Mountain Division."

"How does that fill a hole?"

"Perhaps their reluctance to reveal the healer's identity is nothing more than normal Kickapoo reticence with outsiders. Or there's an important military connection between the three of them of a somewhat special nature."

"The strong bond of brothers in arms," Rodney speculated.

"Exactly," Clayton replied. "I'm not saying they all served together at the same time, but they share that common bond of combat and pride in their unit."

"So where does that take you?"

"Given the sketchy intelligence we have on El Jefe, I'm assuming he's fifty to fifty-five years old, unmarried, and served one six-year active-duty enlistment as a young man. I set a ten-year parameter for his service, 1983 to 1991, to adjust for any margin of error. Then I took a look at conflicts during that time frame that put major troops on the ground, and narrowed it to four: Grenada in 1983, Operation

Just Cause, which was the 1989 invasion of Panama, Operation Desert Storm in 1991, and the Battle of Mogadishu in Somalia in 1993. Only two of those conflicts put boots on the ground from both the Tenth Mountain Division and the Seventy-Fifth Ranger Regiment, Desert Storm and Somalia. I'm assuming El Jefe served in one of those units during both operations."

"*Black Hawk Down*," Rodney said. "I read the book, saw the movie. Those troops got their asses kicked, won a shitload of medals. But back up, what makes you think El Jefe is in his fifties?"

"The murder of the German couple in Mexico occurred almost thirty years ago. Assuming their two-year-old child was adopted by El Jefe, do the math. El Jefe enlists at seventeen, is honorably discharged at twenty-three, and soon after his return home he finds and adopts the boy."

"I'll go with that," Rodney said. "It's all good speculation, but how is it going to get you to El Jefe?"

"His nickname is Bear, and I'm betting it was his moniker in the service. A lot of veterans who served in combat units hold annual reunions and gatherings to revive old friendships, remember fallen comrades, and recall their good and bad wartime experiences. There are hundreds of such events posted on various social media sites monthly. There are also chatrooms expressly for vets of different units. I'm betting former service members from the Tenth and Seventy-Fifth are no different. Somebody out there who served in Somalia or Iraq remembers a fellow soldier named Bear. I'll adopt a fictional identity as a relative who has lost contact with 'Bear' and wants to find him."

"And if you do find him?"

"I'll write out a criminal complaint, get an arrest warrant, and ask for a travel voucher so I can go get him and take him down. Screw the Feds."

Rodney smiled. "He's a dangerous man. You'll need backup."

"Care to go with me?"

Rodney snorted. "If you make this happen, Detective Istee, I'm going, invited or not."

———

At every bar, cheap motel, fleabag hotel, and greasy spoon in Piedras Negras that Fallon visited, he worked his cover story. He was searching for his crazy uncle who weeks ago abandoned his travel trailer in Eagle Pass and disappeared into Mexico. He described Harjo to everyone he talked to, not expecting to get anywhere with it. Harjo was expert at changing his appearance and Fallon could only guess how he might now look. So, he settled in at the local bars and took every opportunity to talk about his crazy uncle who liked to run away and hide from his family. How worried everyone was back home. How heartsick his family was.

Three solid days and nights of buying drinks and telling his sad tale about his lost, loco uncle had Fallon at bars on the outskirts of the city, where the beer was cheap, the talk friendly, and no narco thugs hung around. The customers had dirt under their fingernails, wore sweat-soaked, battered cowboy hats, baseball caps, and dusty clothes, and drank their cervezas with a congenial chatter that had Fallon thinking maybe Mexico was more than just rapists, criminals, illegal immigrants, gang members, and dope fiends trying to endlessly surge across the border intent on destroying the American way of life.

At one such cantina along a highway, down the road from a sleazy motel with a defective neon sign that buzzed and flickered relentlessly, Fallon talked to a plasterer named Lorenzo who had tiny splotches of dried concrete on his denim work shirt.

"He likes to hang out in cantinas," Fallon concluded as he finished his spiel about his lost loco relative. "Have you noticed any new hombres like that?"

"This one viejo came around for a while. Worked for Benito Jimenez a couple of days."

"An old man?" If true, it was a new disguise for Harjo. Fallon was impressed.

Lorenzo, who was twenty-two, shrugged. "Yeah, beard, tall but skinny, hair almost shaved off. All fuzzy, just growing back. Haven't seen him in a while. He was staying at the motel up the road."

"Is Jimenez here?" Fallon asked.

Lorenzo scanned the crowd. "Don't see him."

"But this viejo worked for him?"

Lorenzo nodded. "Stonework. Benito owns a lawn and landscape company."

Stonework? Fallon pondered. Another new wrinkle. "How do I find Benito?"

"He's my mother's neighbor."

"It could be my tio." Fallon motioned to the bartender. "Let me buy you a cerveza."

Lorenzo smiled and a gold front tooth glistened. "Okay."

Fallon bought several rounds for Lorenzo before leaving the cantina with Benito Jimenez's home address in his pocket. At the motel with the broken neon sign, a two-hundred-peso tip to the room clerk confirmed Lorenzo's description of the bearded, fuzzy-headed viejo. He'd stayed there almost an entire week, checking out two days ago.

Out the door and in his rental car, Fallon felt jubilant about finally having a lead. But he got turned around twice trying to find Jimenez's house, and finally, after getting directions from a convenience store clerk, pulled up outside. He rang the bell on the gate of the security

fence that enclosed the small front yard and waited. After a few minutes, a wary man came outside and asked what he wanted.

"Are you Benito Jimenez?" Fallon asked. "I'm trying to find my
lost tio. Lorenzo said he may have worked for you recently."

Jimenez relaxed and approached. "Sí, Marcos. I met him at the cantina. He got arrested in Texas and ICE deported him. Said he would
be going back home soon."

Fallon repressed a smile. Marcos was Spanish for Harjo's murdered
nephew's given name. "Tall, thin, with a beard and hair real short?"
Fallon queried.

"That's him. Good worker, slow but good."

"Did stonework?"

"Sí."

"Did he say where he'd been before you met him?"

"A place somewhere south, but he never said where."

"What else can you tell me?"

Jimenez opened the security gate. "Come inside. I am glad to do
whatever I can to help you find your tio."

———

Fallon left Jimenez's house knowing Harjo was deep undercover, without backup and living poor. Was he still on mission? Did he have
money? Weapons? Transportation?

He couldn't stay buried forever. He would have to surface to gather
intelligence. He'd need access to the use of a computer, a burner phone,
the Internet. Fallon's phone search listed three Internet cafés in the city,
all open late at night.

He struck out at the first two on the list and reached the downtown
business just before closing. It smelled of stale pastries, bad coffee, and
cigarettes. The kid on the late shift, a teenager with slicked-back hair,

remembered a thin, old guy with real short hair and a mustache who'd been in a couple of nights ago. Harjo must have lost the beard, a smart move when changing locations.

"He also bought a cell phone," the kid added.

That was good enough for Fallon. "Which computer station did he use?"

The teenager pointed to a booth in the back corner. "Won't do you any good. We delete search histories on all the machines every night."

Fallon handed him a twenty-dollar bill. "Mind if I have a go at it?"

The cash disappeared into the kid's pants pocket. "Don't take too long. I gotta close up."

The fairly new desktop had good speed and memory. Fallon did a quick search for free programs to restore deleted history, downloaded software that provided access to the hard drive, and began searching. Over the past three days, several thousand websites had been visited. Sorting through to find what Harjo might have been looking for would take a little time.

The overhead lights in the café dimmed.

The kid hovered nearby. "I'm closed. You have to leave."

Fallon held out another twenty. "Give me half an hour."

"Okay."

He was close to handing over another twenty when he found a website search for local rooms to rent. He entered the URL and smiled. It was for a dump with Photoshopped pictures near the airport that rented four beds in a dormitory room and two adjoining private rooms. All shared a bath. He wrote down the physical address.

"You know where this is?" He read the address to the kid.

"Sí, the man you're looking for asked me for directions there. It's a bad place, lots of drunks and bums and crazy people."

"Perfect," Fallon replied. "How do I get there?"

———

Harjo was in his room eating spaghetti out of a can when Fallon walked in.

"Sorry for barging in," he said. "Your door doesn't have a lock."

Harjo looked at him without expression. "Do you have any money? Weapons? A vehicle?"

"Nice to see you, too," Fallon replied. The room was the size of a big closet with a twin bed, a straight-backed armless chair, and a small side table with a lamp, the only light in the room.

"You're looking well. I like your digs."

Harjo dropped the empty can in the wastebasket. "How?"

"The Internet café."

"Figures." Harjo waved at the chair. "It was the first time I came up for air. Sit, if you're here to help. Otherwise leave."

Fallon sat.

Harjo smiled. "It's good to see you."

"Because I have money, guns, and a car?"

"That, too."

"I'm assuming you have a plan."

Harjo perched on the edge of the bed. "Half of one, or maybe not."

"Meaning?"

"Do I kill just one of the brothers or double down and kill them both?"

"You said Lorenz had to go."

"He may be the hardest one to get to. The two tunnels from the safe houses to the basement room at Longwei's restaurant are under constant surveillance. Police headquarters is a virtual fortress, and Lorenz lives surrounded by his favorite thugs and assassins."

Fallon made a time-out signal. "Back up. You're talking about things I know nothing about."

Harjo grabbed his bag and his coat. "Not here. You've blown my cover. We need to find another place to stay."

————

They broke through the fence on a moonless night deep in the darkest hours, multiple vehicles thundering down both ranch roads, police radio traffic confirming that Trevino was sealed in and trapped. He burrowed as far as he could underneath the brush cover that concealed him, listening to the handheld through an earphone. Had Lorenz sent the whole damn police department plus his cartel assassins and thugs to kill him? If so, should he consider it a great honor? Or was it a farce put on by bullies?

He'd expected the attack. Earlier in the day, he'd been tailed from town to the ranch. On the dirt road leading to the ranch there had been fresh signs of frequent vehicle traffic. Late in the afternoon a helicopter had flown over the cabin. It was enough of a warning. There was nothing he could do but wait it out and hope to remain undiscovered. As he listened to Juan barking orders, he wondered if Lorenz had put him in charge of the operation, or if he'd volunteered. Trevino figured the latter. To be able to brag that he'd killed El Jefe would be irresistible to Juan, even if it took a hundred men to help him do it.

The handheld was a godsend that fed him fresh information of Juan's strategy. Juan had established his HQ at the cabin with two bodyguards to protect him. Teams of four men each had been sent out on foot searches in the four major compass directions. Cops were stationed on the ranch perimeters a thousand yards apart with orders to shoot to kill. A five-thousand-dollar bounty would be paid to the lucky cop who got him. Same for the sixteen men stumbling around the ranch in the dark, their flashlights bobbing in the night.

A shot rang out a good half mile away. Juan and his bodyguards converged on the action only to discover the shooter had killed one of their own. A second shot exacted justice for the blunder. Surely, Juan pulled the trigger, a jefe's prerogative. Given enough time, Trevino wondered if they just might kill each other off.

Several times, searchers came close but were called back when a concealment site was located, and everyone was ordered to search in another direction. It skewed the hunt far enough away from Trevino for him to consider making a run for it. But as an open target it would be too risky. He'd decided to stay put.

Time passed. Trevino relaxed and cleared his mind. He worked best with a calm and steady hand. He patiently waited for the inevitable attack, hoping to take more than a few with him. But as the terse radio exchanges dwindled, with Juan occasionally snapping orders redirecting his troops and demanding updates, Trevino sensed a diminished danger.

At daybreak, Juan called everyone in and soon the growling of engines filled the air, dispersed by the sudden arrival of windblown rain that quickly turned into a torrent. Trevino didn't move until all he could hear was the rain.

Slowly, he pushed aside the soaked layers of brush that had covered him and stood in the downpour, scanning for targets. Two startling explosions roared like rolling thunder. Smoke and flames rose from the direction of the cabin.

He bent low and zigzagged to the edge of the small pasture near it. Roofless and fully engulfed in flames, it sizzled and smoked in the pouring rain. Nearby, his truck was nothing more than twisted, red-hot metal and melting rubber, licked by dwindling flickers of burning gasoline.

No longer calm and steady, Trevino turned and retreated into the woods. His rage didn't subside until he reached Colonia de los Kickapoo.

CHAPTER 19

After Danny Fallon left for Mexico, Clayton kept hoping he'd call with news about Agent Harjo. Days of silence followed, and although there was nothing he could do about it, the situation gnawed at him. His call to Fallon resulted in a message that his voice mail was full. Twice more he got the same result.

He wanted Fallon to know, since he'd raised the question, that he'd accessed a recent satellite image of the Mexico Kickapoo village that clearly showed a recent burial in one of the three cemeteries. If El Jefe was back on his home ground, he and Clayton might be able to make a plan.

During shift hours his caseload kept him busy. He cleared a road-rage incident where a seven-year-old girl had been shot in the head and killed by an angry driver cut off in traffic. Eyewitnesses supplied the suspect's license plate number and his ex-wife provided the name of his current girlfriend.

With SWAT backup, Clayton arrested the man at the woman's trailer in Radium Springs, a small town in the northern part of the county. It had been a quick-and-easy one-two-three investigation capped by the suspect's voluntary confession. But Clayton got no satisfaction from the bust. He couldn't shake the image of the blood-covered little girl slumped over in her car seat. It had been an epically senseless, stupid crime.

His sporadic efforts to find El Jefe through websites, chat rooms, and social media sites proved to be beyond ridiculous. The delusion that he was computer-literate became more obvious with each failed attempt to navigate through the various website security roadblocks that restricted access to pages he wanted to surf for information. Rather than drop it completely, he solicited the help of the department's one-man cybercrime unit, Deputy Alex Pruitt.

A former university soccer forward who had a master's degree in computer science, Pruitt stood six-three. He spent his free time pursuing a doctorate part-time and competing in regional triathlon events.

Clayton bought Pruitt lunch at a popular burger joint near the university and briefed him on his pathetic online efforts to find El Jefe. He gave him all the case information he'd accumulated, including the initial investigative reports and his handwritten notes, and pleaded for some help.

Pruitt smiled sympathetically at Clayton's dismay. "You've got to understand how to surmount the little tricks coders and web builders use. I bet gaining back-door access to the Internet sites you've pinpointed won't be hard."

He paused to squirt more mustard on his green-chile cheeseburger. "I'll create a fake identity and build a creditable profile. Give me a day or two to put it together."

"What about government websites?"

"Tougher," Pruitt acknowledged. "But there are other ways to tap government data."

"I really appreciate this," Clayton said.

"No problem. I'll give it what time I can. How do I log my hours?"

"The Goggin-Nautzile homicides."

"Is Captain Rodney in the loop?"

"I'll mention your involvement to him."

"That'll work. I thought the Feds yanked the case away from us."

"Not the case, just the investigation. It happened on our turf and since the murders remain unsolved, I'd be negligent to stop working it."

Pruitt smiled. "I admire your persistence."

Clayton shrugged. "Thanks, but it's more a genetic defect than a positive attribute."

Pruitt laughed. "I think I suffer from the same preexisting condition."

———

Early in the investigation while he was still working the homicides, Clayton subscribed to a Piedras Negras news website. He'd fallen into the habit of checking it daily, hoping something pertinent would pop up highlighting drug cartel operations or police corruption reports—anything that might dovetail with the case. No such luck.

Local Mexican journalists knew to keep away from such stuff to avoid assassination. Consequently, the website concentrated on benign local news with occasional op-ed pieces about the pressing problem of illegal immigrants from Central America pouring into the city trying to cross the border. Clayton scanned through the articles quickly, always disappointed.

Except for a predawn Saturday morning at Isabel's house where the immediate family had gathered for the weekend. Clayton rose early, made coffee, and accessed the news service website on his phone. A headline story jumped out at him.

Suspicious Fire at Recently Acquired
Kickapoo Hunting Ranch

An unoccupied cabin and late model pickup truck were destroyed by fire at a hunting ranch recently purchased by the Colonia de los Kickapoo tribe. A spokesman for the Coahuila state police confirmed the cause was suspected arson. Only heavy rains in the area kept the fire from spreading. Tribal representatives in Eagle Pass and at the colonia declined to comment. The investigation is ongoing.

No surprise there. The Kickapoos could be as closemouthed as Apaches. Generally, Clayton approved, but this time he wished they would have been a little more forthcoming. Why was it torched? What was the motive? Somebody knew something.

Photographs released by the Coahuila state police showed the burned-out, partially collapsed shell of a building and the twisted metal frame of the truck. It took a lot of heat to contort forged steel.

He surfed for more information about the fire and found a blog devoted to news, commentary, and opinion about Mexican drug cartel operations. It included a forum where members could anonymously report accounts of cartel roadblocks, shoot-outs, murders, kidnappings, and other atrocities. On it was a seemingly benign posting about a convoy of twenty-five cartel and Piedras Negras police vehicles seen leaving the city the night of the fire.

A second posting by a different source noted the discovery later that night of a Piedras Negras police officer who'd been lynched and left dangling from a railroad trestle. The body had been removed by a squad of Coahuila state police called out to investigate the fire near the Kickapoo colonia.

Too many coincidences, Clayton thought as he closed the blog and looked up to see his sleepy-eyed son Wendell appear at the table and slide into a chair. It was his first trip back from Albuquerque since the new year break from med school.

He nodded at the drip coffee maker on the counter. "Did you make the coffee?"

"Yeah, why?"

"Because then I can have some." Wendell rose, poured a cup, and returned to the table. "Grandma's is pure poison."

Clayton laughed. "Don't you let her hear that."

"Never. You're up early."

"Couldn't sleep," Clayton replied. A strange dream had yanked him awake. He'd been floating above the tribal museum looking down on the lifeless body of the man he'd shot. He had no idea of what to make of it. Had the ceremony Isabel witnessed been a Kickapoo ghost sickness spell cast on him for the shooting?

Maybe he needed to seek Blossom Magoosh's counsel. Ghost sickness he didn't need.

Thinking about Blossom made him think about Lucy. She'd given Blossom money for the girls, promised to fix her roof and buy a new stove. And Lucy had told her old high school teammate, Houzinnie, that she wanted to return home, start fresh, and make things right with the casino. Only two hundred thousand dollars would've solved that problem.

Ruling out the obvious was a basic tenet of good police work. Had he dropped the ball by believing a stolen two hundred K was sufficient reason to have a sicario mutilate and kill Goggin and Nautzile? That was a disconnect Clayton needed to reconcile.

It suddenly hit him it had been a recovery mission that had led to the shooting outside the museum. That's why the man had followed Lucy and Goggin's exact route from Eagle Pass to Mescalero. But for what? It had to be the million dollars.

"Earth to Dad," Wendell said, shaking Clayton out of his preoccupation. "Come in."

Clayton stood up. "Sorry. Thinking about work. How about we bust out of here and get some breakfast?"

"Won't Grandma be upset?"

"She'll handle it. We deserve some guy time together. I'll leave a note."

"I'm game," Wendell said.

———

Oscar's Diner on the highway north of Ruidoso served the best breakfast in the county. Clayton and Wendell arrived early enough to grab a window table with a view of the grassy valley enclosed by steep pine-tree-covered hills. The diner was a former vacation cabin and the walls were filled with homey sayings carved on wooden planks, along with a gallery of framed photographs of the resident cats that had prowled the premises over the past three decades.

They both ordered Oscar's famous scramble, a combination of whipped eggs, ham bits, chopped onions, and diced peppers all mixed together with hash-brown potatoes.

They ate, dawdled, and talked, mostly about Wendell's highs and lows in medical school. The classes he loved, the demanding professors who sometimes vexed him, the hours spent in the library devouring hundreds of pages of text, and a pretty classmate he'd taken to studying with.

Clayton didn't press on the pretty study mate, and Wendell didn't elaborate.

"Will you and Mom ever move back to Mescalero?" he asked.

"We think about it," Clayton replied. "Why do you ask?"

"You seem real settled in Las Cruces."

"We moved there for you and your sister."

"And your job."

"That, too. Think we've become too urbanized?"

Wendell laughed. "In Las Cruces? Impossible. But you must know Mom and Grandma want the family to move back to the rez."

"Will you and Hannah be coming along?"

"That's not fair," Wendell replied with a slight grimace. "I've a long way to go before I'll have the freedom to decide where I can wind up. Same for Hannah."

"I take it back." Clayton waved at the waitress for the check. "Want to go treasure-hunting with me?"

"For what?"

"I have my suspicions. While you were packing away breakfast, I remembered something somebody said that I want to follow up on."

"Where are we going?"

Clayton paid the bill. "The Old Ladies Village."

———

Houzinnie's mother had lived at the edge of a cluster of houses sequestered away from the tribal center. No longer did old ladies live there alone in the failed government attempt to destroy the Apache culture. It was neither picturesque nor tidy but had a particular Apache informality about it that Clayton loved. Dogs lazed about, trucks were up on blocks awaiting repairs, and unfinished house additions open to the elements weathered unattended. It existed on Apache time, more rhythmic, less methodical.

The front yard of the vacant house was filled with windblown litter that clung to a riot of overgrown dry weeds. A pile of old rotted-out porch railings stood stacked at the side of the gravel walkway. On the roof, a television antenna attached to a tall pole flapped precariously in a gusty breeze.

The front door was locked, but a kitchen window at the side of the house was unlatched. Wendell volunteered to crawl through it.

"What am I looking for?" he asked as Clayton hoisted him up.

"Anything that doesn't belong," Clayton replied.

"That's a big help." He clambered through the window and opened the back door.

The house was dark, dusty, and smelled of mildew and dead mice. The electricity had been shut off, so Clayton used his flashlight to inspect the refrigerator, an older-model wood cookstove, and all the kitchen cabinets. There was a small, locked freezer on the enclosed back porch. He pried it open and got a strong whiff of ammonia. Everything had been cleaned and emptied.

The yellow wall-mounted telephone next to the kitchen door had Wendell shaking his head in disbelief. "That's an antique." He picked up the receiver. There was no dial tone.

"They didn't have phone service here until the 1990s," Clayton explained.

"You're kidding me."

"It's a fact. Let's keep looking."

Clayton inspected the two small bedrooms and the single tiny bathroom. There was nothing on the closet shelves, hidden in the toilet tank, or in the empty medicine cabinet above the sink.

"There's water and plumbing," Wendell noted. "But where's the hot water heater and the furnace?"

"The fireplace and cookstove supply the heat for the house. If you wanted a warm bath you boiled a pot of water."

"Unbelievable," Wendell said. "People lived this way?"

"Some of the elders still do, they prefer it."

"I didn't see a firewood pile outside."

"Houzinnie probably told the neighbors to come and take it when she moved her mother out."

"Well, at least Houzinnie's mother had television."

Clayton laughed. "If the weather cooperated, maybe she could pull in an over-the-air station for a couple of hours."

"That's insane." Wendell glanced around the empty front room. "There's nothing here."

"Be patient," Clayton counseled. "We're not finished."

Clayton inspected the fireplace chimney before moving on to the kitchen stove. With a pocketknife he uncoupled the flue above the stove, dislodging a puff of soot that floated down to the floor, where he spotted fresh, deep gouges. The stove had been recently moved.

"Help me pull this away from the wall," he said.

They jockeyed it out and a satchel stuffed behind the stove dropped to the floor. Clayton zipped it open. Inside were neat bundles of Ben Franklins.

Wendell's eyes widened at the sight of so many hundred-dollar bills. "Good god, how much?"

"From the heft of it, I'd say a million." Clayton zipped the bag closed and replaced it behind the stove. "Help me push this back."

"What?"

"We were never here. You don't want to get arrested for breaking-and-entering, do you?"

Wendell shook his head. "What about the money?"

"It's not ours." Clayton closed the kitchen window, ushered Wendell out the back door, and locked it. "It belongs to the tribe, and it would be better if we didn't find it."

"That's it?"

At the car, Clayton tossed him the keys. "Not quite. You drive."

On the way back to Isabel's, Clayton called his cousin Selena. "Sorry to wake you up so early, cuz."

Selena yawned into her phone. "This better be an emergency, Clayton."

"It is, in a way. You know that campaign you started to raise money for a summer youth drug prevention program? An anonymous donor has left a large contribution behind the cookstove in Betty Yuzos's old house."

"Are you serious?"

"Better go get it before the persons who hid it change their minds. See you soon, and don't tell anyone." He disconnected and put his phone away.

"Why Selena?" Wendell asked.

"Because I can trust her to do the right thing with the money."

"Where did it come from?"

"Drugs," Clayton said. He would love to tell Harjo the money had been recovered. Maybe, soon, he could. "You're to say nothing about this, understand?"

Wendell grinned. "That spoils all the fun."

Clayton rubbed his son's shoulder and leaned back. "It was fun, wasn't it?"

CHAPTER 20

The Gulf Coast storm that doused the fire at the hunting ranch stalled over the colonia, bringing much-welcomed rain. Trevino sat with Caballo Galindo in the front room of his house watching the splatter of wind-driven drops against the windowpane. Outside, rivulets of rainwater snaked down to nearby family gardens where soon corn, beans, and squash would be planted. Beyond in the pasture, livestock stood, heads lowered against the storm, enduring the onslaught of stinging rain.

"Perhaps we'll have a good harvest this year," Galindo commented. "We will dance for more rain."

"A good thing to do," Trevino replied.

"Will those who tried to kill you come for you here?"

"I don't think so. It would not be wise, and they know it. I will leave soon after the storm breaks. Perhaps those who travel to town could mention my absence the next time they go. That should divert their attention from the colonia."

Galindo nodded. "Where will you go?"

"Not far."

"And the hunting ranch? Who will care for it?"

"I see no reason to rebuild the cabin right away. A summerhouse would be adequate for now. A volunteer might stay there until I return."

"More than one volunteer I think," Galindo replied. The rain had intensified. He rose to look out the window. "Having a few of the younger families living there would give protection to the land. They could plant crops to attract waterfowl, patrol to keep poachers away, remove the debris from the fire, clean some of the streambeds. There are several younger couples interested in such endeavors. I will ask Eagle Pass to pay their stipends."

"That would be ideal."

Galindo turned away from the window. "Good. Will you return?"

Trevino hesitated. Galindo was politely asking if he would survive. "There are people who are not good of heart. You know what I must do."

Galindo smiled. "We will have a feast upon your return. The storm will soon pass. Join me now for a meal, and we will talk of more pleasant matters."

Trevino stood, his earlier rage calmed by Galindo's unspoken affection and concern. "It would be my pleasure."

After a hearty meal and an enjoyable conversation about the hunting ranch and its rich potential, Galindo conducted a private departure ceremony for Trevino. He called on Kitzihiat, god of the Kickapoos, to look after him on his journey, and puffed tobacco smoke in each of the four directions so that Trevino might be protected wherever he might go.

Outside, with the sun breaking through a thick cloud bank, Trevino gathered up a small handful of saturated soil, wrapped it in a bandanna, and put it in his pocket. It would help bring him home.

He started out on foot for Piedras Negras. It would take him several days to complete the journey, traveling cross-country, avoiding all towns and settlements. He needed to arrive unannounced and unexpected if he had any chance of success against Juan Garza and Luis Lorenz.

For the first time in many years, he contemplated a different future. He wanted to survive to see it.

———

Deputy Alex Pruitt worked one Sunday a month to make up for the time he took off during his regular duty schedule to attend graduate seminars at the university. In a year he'd be ABD—all but dissertation— and freed from coursework evermore.

The SO headquarters was unusually quiet, which meant there were no major crimes, traffic crashes, or public safety emergencies happening in Doña Ana County. At least not yet. Today he was at his desk ready to take a first serious stab at finding Bear, the suspect's nickname in Detective Istee's double homicide case. He reviewed the profile parameters supplied by Istee for his baseline search. They included the subject's ethnicity, approximate age, length of service in the U.S. Army, calendar years of his active service, and the likely units he'd served in.

Pruitt had never served in the military and wondered if Istee's focus on two major conflicts involving U.S. Army units was too restrictive. He accessed a comprehensive list of all armed services combat engagements or military advisory operations between 1983 and 1993. There were boots-on-the-ground conflicts in Grenada, Panama, Iraq, and Somalia, and a smaller number of special ops actions in Bolivia, Honduras, Colombia, Bolivia, and Peru. That might be a sufficiently large enough parameter to sample.

He spent time reviewing general information on the outfits where the military killer elites dwell. Delta Forces, SEAL teams, Special Forces, Ranger Regiments, and U.S. Air Force and Marine Corps rapid response and engagement units. No need to broaden the base, but to make sure he didn't miss anything he went to the Department of Defense website and clicked on a link that provided an eye-popping alphabetized list of sites for every imaginable armed forces organization, corps, and command. Simply sorting through them to rule out all irrelevancies would take many hours. Best to stick with the special ops units.

Pruitt paused. Federal government websites had excellent firewall protection, especially for those relating to national security. Hacking one wouldn't be easy or simple. Additionally, it would be a federal crime under the Computer Fraud and Abuse Act. If he got caught it could cost him his job, his pending Ph.D., and any chance for a successful career out of law enforcement later on.

How far could he get with the word "bear"? According to an online blog, the origin of the word had nothing to do with the animal, but was a surname likely derived from an old Anglo-Saxon word for a grove or a swine pasture. In addition, the spelling could be fluid. Beara, Bere, and Beere were common variations. Interesting but hardly helpful. Entering the word alone in a search engine would be useless.

Istee had already done a very comprehensive Internet search for Estavio Trevino, supposedly El Jefe's real name, which was uncovered by DEA Special Agent Harjo during the interrogation of Juan Garza. Pruitt dug a little deeper, searching through Mexican websites and Spanish-language social media platforms. There were Mexican Kickapoos with the same surname, which added credence to the information, but no Estavio Trevino who fit the working profile. He replicated Istee's search just to make sure nothing had been overlooked. It had been thoroughly done with no missteps.

He created an online identity to use to query potential targets. He'd be a civilian relative searching for a lost uncle called "Bear" who'd disappeared after his discharge from active duty. He'd fill in the blanks as to his uncle's name, service branch, and dates of service once he had a list of targets to query. If he had any.

He searched social media sites for any current armed service members surnamed Bear. More than a dozen popped up. As expected, none fit Istee's working profile.

Pruitt was having fun. The assignment was different from anything handed to him in the past. He was trolling for a secretive assassin instead of child predators, swindlers, porno freaks, fraudsters, sex traffickers, credit card thieves, and website hackers.

Istee had probably been smart to narrow his focus, but Pruitt wasn't quite ready to concede the point. He downloaded a Department of Veterans Affairs directory of service organizations and began visiting websites.

Three hours passed with nothing meaningful to show for the effort. He went for a workout in the department's weight room and fitness center, took a fast shower, ate lunch at his desk, and pondered what to do next. Were there any organizations or associations of former service members of the Seventy-Fifth Ranger Regiment and Tenth Mountain Division? He found one of each and began a careful review of their websites.

The Seventy-Fifth had a guest page where visitors could post comments, reminisce, and search for former comrades. There were no postings by Estavio Trevino or someone nicknamed Bear, but a year-old entry galvanized Pruitt's attention:

I've written a book about my experiences serving with the 1st Marine Expeditionary Force in Somalia, *Confessions of a Marine Sniper.* You can order a copy by writing to me at the address below. Send $12.95 which includes postage. I'm also looking for an Army Ranger nicknamed Bear, who saved my life in a roadside firefight with Aideed forces that went bad in Bardera. He was a SFC and Native American I think, but that's all I know about him, except he was Airborne with the 75th, and was one hell of a warrior. I wrote about what he did in the book and would love to send him a copy. Please contact me if you know where I can find him. Thank you.

Smitty Winters

In addition to an address, Smitty had included his phone number. Pruitt called, told him he was writing a dissertation on the Somalia 1990s United Nations multinational relief operation, and asked to have a copy of the book sent by next-day air.

"I've got a publisher lined up and will give you full credit for anything I use from the book," he added. "I'll pay by credit card or check."

"Hell, I'll give you a copy and pay the shipping myself," Smitty replied. "Got twelve unopened boxes of them gathering dust in the garage."

"No, I'll pay," Pruitt said. "Let me give you my credit card information and mailing address."

"Shoot."

Pruitt rattled off the information. "Did you ever hear from that soldier who saved your life?"

"No, but a buddy he served with in the Seventy-Fifth called me," Smitty replied. "Said he heard Bear was doing fine and living in Mexico. Had dual citizenship or something like that."

"Did this buddy give you Bear's name?"

"He said he couldn't do that. Something about black ops and national security. Wouldn't give me his own name, either."

"When did you get that call?" Pruitt asked.

"Two weeks ago. That's why I got excited when you called. Thought maybe it was Bear."

"Do you have the number stored on your phone?"

"Yeah, I kept it." Smitty read off the number.

Pruitt wrote it down. "Thanks. Did he say anything else that would be helpful finding Bear?"

"Nope, but I sure hope he gets in touch with me. Saved my life. You'll read about it in my book."

"I look forward to reading it." Pruitt thanked Smitty again, hung up, and googled the telephone number. The call had been made from Piedras Negras, Mexico. Had the caller been Bear? Wouldn't that beat all?

For all his mucking around mired in the web of the military Internet jungle, progress had finally been made. Pruitt typed a quick update, sent it to Istee's SO email address, and shut down his computer. He reread Smitty's post. Did "SFC" mean sergeant first class? He didn't think it meant System File Checker.

He considered dialing the Piedras Negras phone number and decided against it. That was Istee's call to make. Pruitt stood, stretched, and turned off his desk lamp. It was time to go home.

———

Early Sunday supper concluded with Clayton and Wendell at the sink on KP duty while Isabel, Grace, and Hannah chatted at the kitchen table. Isabel rose to answer a knock at the front door and found a stern-looking Selena Kazhe clutching a black satchel.

Startled by Selena's serious demeanor, Isabel asked, "Is something wrong?"

Selena forced a smile. "No, I mean yes. Is Clayton here?"

"In the kitchen."

She followed Isabel, dropped the satchel on the table, and glared at Clayton. "Why did you do this to me, cousin?" she demanded. "I couldn't sleep all last night. I can't keep this."

"What is it?" Grace asked.

"A million dollars," Wendell said gleefully as he dried the last pot.

Clayton shook his head. "I wish you hadn't said that."

"He told me where to find it yesterday morning," Selena explained. "Told me to use it to fund the youth drug prevention program."

"Generosity is one of the four Apache laws," Clayton noted gravely, hoping to get off easy.

Hannah unzipped the satchel and squealed in disbelief at the sight of the money. "Where did you find it?"

"At an undisclosed location," Clayton interjected before Selena could answer.

Isabel sat, peered at the bundles of hundred-dollar bills, and scowled. "What did you do, Clayton?"

Clayton dried his hands and joined the women. "Good police work," he replied casually. "Deductive reasoning."

His mother crossed her arms and sighed.

"How come Wendell knows about this?" Grace inquired.

"He was my able assistant."

Wendell lowered his head to avoid his mother's gaze and slid into the empty chair next to Clayton.

Hannah fingered a bundle of hundreds. "What do we do with it?"

"Turn it in and it will be sucked up by the bureaucracy," Clayton warned. "It will sit in a special account for years drawing interest until the government declares it unclaimed and transfers it to the public till."

He looked at Selena. "It's drug money stolen from a narco-trafficker, a man who peddles death and kills without remorse. I thought of you because it should be used for something good here at Mescalero."

"We just can't keep a million dollars," Grace proposed.

"Why not?" Isabel countered.

Her response caught Clayton by surprise. "Yeah, why not?" he echoed. "No serious law has been broken. I have no police powers here. This is purely a family matter."

"How would you use it?" Isabel asked Selena.

"For our youth. Drug abuse prevention, college scholarships, counseling services, promoting our Apache language and culture. Whatever our young people need to retain their tribal identity and succeed."

"What if an anonymous donor gave the money to me with the stipulation that it be used for just those purposes?" Isabel queried.

"Gave it to who?" Grace asked incredulously.

"Me," Isabel repeated. "I can make regular deposits into a special account. I doubt tribal administrators or council members will question my word. In fact, we'll say nothing about it publicly unless we're asked."

"Brilliant!" Hannah said, her smile lighting up the room. "If anyone can pull it off, it's you."

Isabel looked at everyone. "Are we agreed?"

Everyone nodded.

"In order to work, this conversation has to stay in this room and never be mentioned again," Clayton cautioned. "Understood?"

Nods made it unanimous.

"Finally, we get something back from the White Eyes," Wendell noted.

"The drug lord is a Mexican," Clayton corrected.

Wendell shrugged. "Gringo or Mexican, it doesn't matter."

Clayton laughed. "You're right. Now all we have to figure out is where to safely keep the money."

Selena zipped the satchel shut and smiled at Isabel. "In a large bank safe-deposit box, of course. Isabel and I will go to town tomorrow morning."

"Can we use some of the money to buy Blossom a new stove, fix her roof, and put some aside for the girls?" Isabel asked.

"I think that's the perfect place to start," Grace said.

Isabel clapped her hands together. "Good, now I won't feel like such an outlaw."

Clayton grinned and slapped Wendell on the back. "What have I always told you? The women rule."

"Isn't that the Apache way?" Wendell replied.

CHAPTER 21

Throughout his shift, Clayton continually glanced at his desk phone and the lined writing pad beside it with the Piedras Negras phone number Smitty Winters had given Pruitt yesterday. The urge to dial the number had tugged at him for hours, but first he wanted to read Smitty's *Confessions of a Marine Sniper*. At least the part about how Trevino had saved the jarhead's life.

It was a paperwork day and the seemingly endless amount of it should have fully occupied his attention. But he kept looking at the door waiting for Pruitt—who'd promised to check for its delivery at his apartment—to walk in with the book in hand. At five-thirty, Pruitt showed up and handed Clayton the opened package.

"I couldn't resist," he said with an apologetic smile. "I had to read what Smitty wrote about El Jefe. The guy was a kick-ass warrior back in the day."

"I bet he was." Clayton pulled the thin book out of the overnight envelope. "I owe you big-time for this."

"No problem," Pruitt said. "You know what they say: eat, sleep, read. My ex-wife practiced that daily. That's why we're divorced." He waved goodbye on his way out the door.

Clayton examined *Confessions of a Marine Sniper.* A paperback slightly over a hundred pages, it had been self-published through an Internet company. The cover design consisted of the Marine Corps emblem of the eagle, anchor, and globe in the center with an outline of a prone Marine rifleman below. The title ran along the top with Smitty's name, followed by *MSGT, USMC, Ret.* at the bottom.

On the back there was a photograph of the author and a brief bio about his thirty years of service in the Marine Corps and his major combat decorations.

There were sixteen chapters. Clayton turned to the one titled "Bardera, the Bird, and the Bear."

> *We'd been working roadside checkpoints for about a week in an area outside the town of Bardera, a major relief distribution hub. The main road into the interior was in piss-poor condition with potholes, crumbled pavement, and washouts that could almost swallow a truck, blow out tires daily and crack axles. Just about every convoy suffered delays and breakdowns, especially along several really bad stretches, which we had to constantly patrol.*

Clayton skimmed ahead. Smitty went on to write about how they were not allowed to disarm civilians and could only shoot if a gun was pointed at them or if the weapon was a machine gun or larger. The brass even required them to carry reminder cards of what they could and could not do. Smitty called it BS.

He talked about the men in his team and how excited they'd been to ship out from Camp Pendleton and the disappointment they felt about not being allowed to go to war. He described the terrain as an empty desert of rolling plains with scrub brush, thorn trees, and occasional isolated hills. He wrote about the starving people, nothing more than walking skeletons, staring empty-eyed, barely able to slap away the swarms of flies that hovered around their heads.

Duty consisted of a dull routine in hot and dusty days and cold and windy nights spent removing broken-down vehicles from the roadway, guiding vehicles around hazards, guarding precious emergency food and cargo in the disabled trucks, escorting convoys to the distribution centers, and patrolling for rebels in the immediate area. Occasionally a Special Forces bird would overfly a convoy to keep any possible hostiles or bandits off guard.

At dusk during a swirling dust storm that had slowed a large convoy to a crawl, the Marine escort vehicle was hit by an RPG, wounding Smitty, who was the senior NCO, and Micky, his eighteen-year-old driver, and knocking out all radio communication. At the same time, the armored personnel carrier at the rear of the column came under heavy rebel fire. Reinforcements were a good twenty minutes out and all fixed-wing air support was grounded due to the storm. Smitty continued his story:

> *Overhead, out of the storm, came a small assault helicopter we fondly called the Killer Egg, inbound to Bardera. It hovered in front of me, one man on the portside bench. It dropped low and that one lone soldier jumped to the ground, rolled, and came up firing at three rebels approaching my position. They all went down as the bird veered away to the rear of the convoy.*
>
> *My left arm was smashed, and I had taken shrapnel in the neck. Mick, my driver, was bleeding and unconscious. The soldier pulled us out of the vehicle before it blew up, dragged us into a roadside ditch, checked our wounds, and asked me if I could fight. I nodded and he handed me his Beretta M9 and took off toward the firefight at the rear. I had the M9 and my own Colt .45 but never needed to use them. Ten minutes*

later the shooting stopped, and the soldier returned to tell me the rest of my squad was okay. He dressed my neck wound and said it was just a nick although at the time it had turned my shirt red with blood and I thought I was gonna die.

Mick had come around. The soldier patched the wound that had grazed his temple and sliced off part of his ear. He checked my vitals, grinned, held out his hand, and asked for his M9 back.

I gave him the weapon, thanked him, and asked who he was. He said to call him Bear. That's the only name he ever gave me. He wore the rank of a sergeant first class and had a Special Forces Airborne patch on his shirtsleeve. He looked like an Indian right out of those old photographs from the nineteenth century.

He asked if we needed to be evaced and I said that Mick and I would stay with my men. He left in the bird as Corporal Evans came up from the rear to give me an action report. It was only then that I learned Bear had taken out another three camouflaged hostiles who had Evans and the rest of my team pinned down in the APC. Bear had found them one at a time, slit their throats, and scalped them.

Sometimes I wonder if I dreamt it. That Bear was just a ghostly memory of something I made up. But then the weather changes and the ache in my left arm reminds me that what happened in Bardera with Bear and the Killer Egg Bird was all true.

I'll never forget that warrior. He would have made a helluva Marine.

Clayton closed the book, wondering if war had changed Trevino into a killer or if he was just naturally good at it. Had the military simply taken El Jefe's raw talent and sharpened his skills? Was it something he'd learned from his warrior tribe?

He glanced at the desk phone again. Maybe the Piedras Negras phone number Smitty had given Pruitt was from a burner phone. Maybe not. What if it had been Trevino who'd called Smitty? Did he think it safe enough to use his personal phone? And if so, why did he call in the first place?

It seemed completely out of character, unless Trevino was reliving the past, taking inventory of his memories of war and of the people whose lives were intertwined with his during those times. Clayton knew that combat veterans and first responders often buried their harrowing experiences for decades only to have them erupt unexpectedly when triggered by a painful event. As a career police officer, it had happened to him. As a combat veteran and cop, it had happened to his father.

Clayton was on his own for dinner, so there was no need to rush home. Grace was at the board meeting of the friends of the public library, Wendell was back in Albuquerque for classes, and Hannah was at an early evening NMSU baseball game with her boyfriend.

He picked up the handset, set the phone to automatically record, dialed the Piedras Negras number, and listened as it rang.

"How did you get this number?" It was a man's voice, stern and demanding.

Surprised, Clayton took a deep breath and said, "Estavio, I'm Detective Istee with the Doña Ana Sheriff's Office. Do you have a few minutes to talk?" He waited for the phone to go dead.

"Smitty Winters sends his regards," he added. "That's quite a story he tells about what you did to save his life in Somalia."

"What do you want?"

Clayton smiled. Trevino hadn't denied who he was. "Right now, just to talk."

"Talk."

"It was you outside the museum, wasn't it? Releasing the spirit of the man I'd shot there to enter the Real World to be with his ancestors. Or were you there to put a ghost sickness on me? What was his name? His ID said Lawrence Anico, but we knew that was fake."

"His name was Fernando. I should kill you for what you did to him."

"I wish it hadn't happened and I am sorry that it did. You were kind to rescue him many years ago after his German parents were murdered in Mexico. Some think you killed them. I don't."

"You've done your homework. Do you have the money?"

"Excuse me?"

"The million dollars. Do you have it?"

"No, I don't."

Trevino laughed. "Someone has it."

"Let's hope they put it to good use, as you have with the hunting ranch you bought for your people. I was sorry to learn of the fire. Has Commander Lorenz of the Piedras Negras Police Department been unable to help you?"

"I am impressed. Enough small talk. What do you want?"

"To get to know you better. That's all, for now."

"To arrest me, you mean."

"You murdered five people in my backyard, Estavio," Clayton said. "Lucy Nautzile, James Goggin, John Cosgrove, and the rancher and the deputy at your campsite. That's a lot of killing. I'm compelled to arrest you."

"The last two were inadvertent, and—like you—I am sorry."

"Did you come back to New Mexico to kill me?"

"Yes, and your family also if necessary."

"I'm happy that you changed your mind. Can we meet? I'd be willing to come to you."

"Come here and I will kill you," Trevino promised.

"I thought we'd gotten beyond that. What name did you use in the Army?"

"Now you sound like a cop."

"Actually, I'm a fan. You've had a life filled with adventure, heroic exploits, and danger. I'd like to know more about it."

Trevino laughed. "We should exchange dossiers, Detective. Although I believe mine to be more extensive than yours. Don't push it, or you might see your entire family dead."

"You were that angry? Why the sudden change of heart?"

"You swim in dangerous waters, Clayton Istee. We have talked enough."

"Before you hang up, how did you arrange in advance to have John Cosgrove assist you at the Las Cruces hotel?"

"Those incidentals are of no consequence. Cosgrove was gullible and greedy, like so many Norteamericanos."

"No regrets about killing him?"

"None."

"What do you know of DEA Special Agent Bernard Harjo's whereabouts?"

"I know nothing about him other than he was to accompany you to Mexico to arrest me. Is he here?"

"I don't know where he is. I hope you will call me so we can talk again."

"There is no need for that. Adios, Detective Istee."

The phone went dead. Clayton listened to the playback. He'd solved the case, gotten a confession, had it all on the record. Okay, he hadn't Mirandized Trevino, so it wouldn't hold up in a court of law. But that didn't matter. The case would never go to trial anyway, and he doubted El Jefe would ever allow himself to be captured alive.

Clayton would love to give it a try. He was itching to know for certain what had made Trevino change from a cold-blooded assassin back into a flawed and imperfect human being.

He made copies of the recording, sent them in an email attachment to Captain Rodney and Sheriff Vasquez, and left for the night, suddenly starving. He needed a green-chile cheeseburger with all the fixings, and he knew right where to get it.

CHAPTER 22

For the equivalent of one hundred U.S. dollars, Danny Fallon paid a month's rent for an old, furnished single-wide mobile home in Zaragoza, a town forty miles outside Piedras Negras. On concrete pillars, it tilted a good three inches off center, sloping from the rear bedroom to the front living room/kitchen area. The surrounding trailers, also rentals, looked no better, and the neighbors were mostly day laborers, drunks, drug addicts, disabled, or plain crazy. They paid no mind to Fallon and Harjo, who crashed on the floor of the mobile home in surplus sleeping bags they'd bought in lieu of using the lice-infected beds.

The water, when it was on, had a harsh, chemical smell to it, but they had no plans to use it. They weren't bathing, shaving, or changing their clothes. Deep cover meant being completely invisible, attracting no attention. They became derelict Mexicans wandering the Piedras Negras streets. They ditched Fallon's rental car on the side of the highway outside of Zaragoza. It was gone on the first morning. As they waited for the bus from Saltillo that would take them to Piedras

Negras, Fallon called from a burner phone to report it stolen to the rental company.

Some days they took the bus, other days they hitchhiked or rode in the back of delivery trucks, paying the drivers pocket money in pesos for the privilege. In Piedras Negras, they bought a clunker at a junkyard along with a rebuilt starter and water pump to keep it running. At night they parked it and took the last bus back to Zaragoza.

They ran random spot surveillance on Lorenz and his brother, Gilberto, looking for possible weaknesses in their protection that would get them within kill range. They worked varied hours to avoid establishing a routine that might signal any telltale interest to watching eyes. To gather intelligence, Fallon used his phone, or they bought computer time at one of the city's Internet cafés.

Frequently they split up to cover more people and places, one on foot, the other in the clunker. They'd switch off to observe in-and-out traffic at the exclusive enclave where the Garzas lived, run surveillance at Longwei's restaurant, and follow the beat cops outside the Plaza Mercado. They never rendezvoused at the same place and never parked the clunker on the same street. Back at the trailer, they averaged four hours of sleep each night.

Nothing seemed particularly promising. The safe houses with the underground tunnels to the basement room in Longwei's restaurant were, as Harjo had described, heavily guarded, and there was nothing subtle about it. Pickups with manned, mounted fifty-caliber weapons in the truck beds were parked outside. Armed guards with automatic weapons roamed the surrounding streets. Few residents dared to leave their homes unless necessary. Several times when Harjo or Fallon attempted to walk by, acting three sheets to the wind, as Fallon liked to say, they were intercepted, cursed, and prodded away by the guards. Not once did they see anyone enter the safe houses, which obviously were no longer in use.

A police patrol car had been posted 24/7 at the entrance to the gated community where Gilberto and his wife lived. That was a new wrinkle for Harjo, who'd seen no cops there while working for Benito Jimenez. At Garza's Plaza Mercado and his popular Piedras Negras grocery store, plainclothes officers roamed the aisles inconspicuously.

Longwei's restaurant had a doorman packing heat. In parked vehicles on the street near the front entrance, two-man surveillance teams kept watch. It all screamed danger.

Trailing Lorenz proved difficult. He traveled with armed escorts in accompanying vehicles and rotated between his three mansions in and around Piedras Negras, staying in them on different nights. All were tucked behind security walls with sophisticated surveillance systems and armed guards at the gates. Who knew how many more goons were posted inside? Fallon figured dozens.

He suggested buying a drone with a camera for a look around the properties. Harjo nixed the idea as a dead giveaway that the brothers were targets.

Breaching police headquarters without a Delta team and heavy air support would have been impossible. More than a fortress, it was the hub for cartel business, guarded by highly trained elite police officers who doubled as Lorenz's assassins, drug mules, intimidators, and rapists. No right-minded citizen would ever go there. Fallon decided no wrong-minded, renegade DEA agents would, either. Harjo didn't quibble.

The cartel's increased show of protection surprised them. What caused it? Were they blown and didn't know it?

Along with the elite cadre of officers who worked for the cartel, there were the street cops, mostly lowlifes who transported product from the interior when not serving, protecting, and shaking down the citizenry and tourists. They patrolled in pairs and were expected to pay kickbacks to their superiors. If they failed out of greed or poverty, many were simply disappeared. It made for a high turnover rate among the department's lower echelon.

Harjo and Fallon lowered their sights and began surveillance on two of Lorenz's lieutenants, Diego Mendez and Vito Torres. Both had the bad habit of sticking to a predictable after-hours routine. Graduates of the San Luis Potosi Police Academy funded by the U.S. government, they were former Mexican federal officers bought and paid for by the Lorenz cartel.

They favored each other's company and frequently drank and ate together at several popular restaurants and bars. They spent time at an exclusive gentlemen's club, drove expensive German SUVs, and owned houses in the same quiet, peaceful neighborhood that attracted professional-class residents. They had no personal security to protect them. Mendez was single, with a string of girlfriends. Torres had a wife and three pre-teenage children.

Ten days in, Harjo called a halt. They had found their weak links. They drove the clunker to Zaragoza, cleaned out the trailer, left the car behind, and took the bus south to Saltillo, the state capital of Coahuila. In a city of nearly a million people, they could safely come up for air and still stay lost among the multitudes.

At the bus station, they cleaned up, changed into fresh clothes, and rented a room in a nice hotel close to the city center. They ordered room service and a bottle of scotch.

When the food and booze came, Harjo poured two liberal shots into glasses, tossed an ice cube into each, and handed one to Fallon. "How much money do we have?"

"I've a little over eight thousand left," Fallon replied, digging into his steak, medium rare, covered in green chile.

"That should cover us, with enough left to get across the border when it's done." Harjo knocked back his scotch, poured another, and sat at the table watching Fallon eat. "I say we go for Gilberto. He's the easier target of the two."

"That's fine, but it won't kill the two-headed snake or put the cartel out of business."

Harjo examined the whiskey in the bottom of his glass. "What more can we do?" he mused.

"I suppose half a snake is better than none," Danny replied, pleased with his riff on the cliché.

Harjo laughed. "Cute."

"I like clichés," Fallon said between bites. "They simplify conversation." He stopped eating and sipped his scotch. "We're gonna need better weapons." All they had were semiautomatic handguns.

"Diego Mendez or Vito Torres will provide them from their arsenals." Harjo took a bite of his mole poblano. Delicious.

"Which one of the scumbags do we kidnap?"

"I'm thinking Mendez," Harjo replied, pushing the beans on his plate off to the side. They were too mushy. "He's single and seems the more arrogant and self-absorbed of the two."

"Thinks himself too important to be fucked with," Fallon summarized.

"Exactly, and therefore sloppy about being cautious. We'll take him at his house."

"And if a girlfriend or two are there on a stay-over?" Fallon inquired. Mendez, the cartel's chief executioner, was a devoted practitioner of ménage à trois.

"No civilian casualties if we can avoid it," Harjo replied. "Mendez is fair game."

"That works for me."

They went over the first phase of the setup. To avoid suspicion, Mendez needed to believe a Piedras Negras patrol officer was knocking at his front door. They'd picked Officer Beltran Diaz to provide the uniform and sidearm. About Harjo's size and weight, Diaz was a lazy, not-too-bright cop who worked the tourist district. He lived with his waitress girlfriend in a small house near a dirt soccer pitch used by neighborhood schoolkids. She was at work when he got off shift, dropped at home by his partner. She didn't return for five more hours. They'd seize him there, take what they needed, tie and gag him, and be gone in under five minutes.

"Then the clock starts ticking," Fallon noted.

Harjo, who wasn't sure if that was a cliché or not, said nothing.

They ate, drank, and talked. The second phase of the operation wasn't quite as clear-cut. The guard at the gatehouse in the subdivision where the Garzas lived was always a trusted off-duty police officer. It was a plum job that more than doubled the officer's official salary. Bribery wasn't an option. Nor was murder.

In cases of emergency, the guard kept a list of security codes for all gated residences inside the subdivision. Fallon had read about it in a blog posted by a Piedras Negras firefighter who thought the policy was stupid. First responders should always have immediate access, he'd complained. Fallon googled the firefighter's name and learned that, a week after the posting, the man had been killed in a hit-and-run. The poor sucker's family probably had no idea why he was dead.

Assuming they could neutralize the guard and the cops in the patrol car stationed at the entrance *and* get the access code for Garza's property, they could only guess what awaited them inside.

"We could be mowed down like ducks in a row," Fallon said, pleased with his latest cliché.

Harjo groaned. "Give it a break. We've seen no police going in and out of the enclave, just what appears to be typical everyday traffic. Homeowners, wives, delivery trucks, housekeepers. No slick-top cop cars or undercover vehicles."

Fallon shrugged. "They could be smarter than that."

"Well, we'll just have to find out." Harjo plopped down on one of the double beds. "Let's get some sleep and worry about it in the morning."

Danny yawned. "Finally, a plan I can relate to."

———

Their first day back from deep cover had Fallon and Harjo quickly morphing back into normal human beings. Knowing it wouldn't last, they made the most of it, sleeping in and capping off a late breakfast in the hotel dining room with a shopping trip to a nearby big-box discount department store. They bought new clothes, two small back-packs, and got haircuts at a nearby barbershop that was right out of the 1950s. There was no resemblance to the two derelicts who had roamed the Piedras Negras streets.

At a sporting goods store they bought ski masks, hunting knives, heavy-duty zip ties to use as handcuffs, duct tape, and a package containing industrial-strength flexible tent repair patches to cover Office Diaz's mouth, which would hurt like hell when pulled off.

They walked part of the way back to the hotel, taking in the scenery and everyday life of the city. It felt like a holiday. Saltillo citizens seemed more at ease than the residents of Piedras Negras, not so pinched-faced and jumpy. Harjo ventured that maybe the cartel wasn't in control of everything in the city just yet. Fallon laughed off the idea.

A mile high and bordered by rolling mountains, Saltillo spread out from its historic core across a valley filled with residential subdivisions and modern industrial parks. In a sad way, it reminded Harjo of Los Angeles, or any other southwestern American city. Fallon refused to be depressed. He stepped to the curb and whistled over a cab.

Back at the hotel, Fallon called Guillermo Maldonado, a used car dealer in Piedras Negras. Earlier in the week they'd checked out a beige

Chevy sedan with eighty-six thousand miles and no body damage. Fallon named a price that ate significantly into their cash and Maldonado agreed to meet them at the airport with the car.

They packed, checked out, and took a cab to the airport, where they hired a pilot with a small single engine four-seat Cessna for the one-hour flight to Piedras Negras. They landed and were met by Maldonado outside the terminal building. He counted the cash, turned over the paperwork and keys, and left in a brand-new truck driven by a smiling senorita who waved gaily at them as they drove off.

"I'd like to have a truck like that," Fallon muttered.

"Not the girl?" Harjo suggested.

Fallon cranked the Chevy's engine. "Maybe both."

———

With different wheels and their new average-citizen disguises, they spent the remaining daylight hours checking and rechecking on all the important people and places essential to their plan. Beltran Diaz and his partner had the same shift assignment. Diaz's waitress girlfriend was on time for work at the restaurant. By sundown the soccer pitch in front of Diaz's house was deserted. The patrol car posted near the guard station to the enclave where the Garzas lived contained the same two shift cops. The regular off-duty police officer running security at the entrance smiled and waved through the residents without a care, signaling all was calm.

Lorenz's lieutenants, Vito Torres and Diego Mendez, left police headquarters within ten minutes of each other and lingered at their favorite watering hole for a good hour before parting company.

"It's going like clockwork," Fallon said with a grin as they left the bar's parking lot on their way to Officer Diaz's house. His grin faded under his ski mask when they arrived, knocked at the front door, and

Diaz's girlfriend answered. She had dyed-blond hair, the sniffles, and was home early with a cold.

"Like clockwork," Harjo mumbled as he forced the woman into the front room, his handgun at her head, hand covering her mouth. Diaz was nowhere in sight. "Where is he?" he whispered.

She nodded at a closed door at the back of the room adjacent to a small kitchen. Fallon moved to cover it. A toilet flushed and Diaz emerged, his hairy belly hanging over the top of his sweatpants.

Fallon dug his piece into the cop's rib cage. "Hands over your head. Speak and you're dead."

Diaz nodded and complied.

They put both of them facedown on the floor, zip-tied their hands and feet, duct-taped their eyes, and slapped patches over their mouths. They dragged Diaz to the bathroom and tied him to the plumbing under the sink. They did the same to the girlfriend in the kitchen. They'd be uncomfortable and miserable but would survive the night.

Harjo dressed quickly in Diaz's uniform, pinned on the badge, strapped on the sidearm, and gathered up his clothes. They were out the door in eight minutes. Way over their time limit, which pissed them both off.

The rode in silence to Mendez's house and found the driveway in front of his garage empty, a good sign there was no playdate happening inside. They parked the Chevy on the street and climbed the stairs to the front porch, past the rows of manicured native plants.

With a peeved look on his face, Mendez opened up to the sight of Harjo in the police uniform. Fallon coldcocked him with the butt of his handgun, yanked him inside, and lowered him onto an expensive modern couch that fit nicely into the minimalist décor of the room, cluttered only by two handguns on the coffee table and an assault rifle leaning against a wall.

Fallon picked up one of the semiautomatics and stuck it in his waistband. "Who says assassins don't have good taste?"

Harjo grabbed the assault rifle. "I like how he's accessorized."

Mendez was a bantamweight, wiry but muscular. They carried him easily to the attached garage, bound and gagged him, and put him in the back of his SUV. Harjo drove while Fallon kept Mendez company. When Mendez came to, Harjo stopped behind a church and Fallon transferred him to the front passenger seat.

Harjo waited until Danny slid into the backseat and stuck his pistol in Mendez's ear. "Here's how you stay alive," he said. "Do as we say or die."

Mendez garbled something through the patch that had been slapped over the gag. Harjo ripped it off and pulled out the gag.

"Son of a bitch," Mendez screamed. Skin around his mouth was torn and bleeding. "Fuck you."

"Kill him now," Harjo ordered Fallon.

"We don't need him?" Fallon asked.

"No, I don't think so."

"Wait a minute," Mendez protested. "I've got money."

Fallon snorted. "Stick another patch over his mouth."

"No! What do you want?"

"You're going to help us pay someone a visit," Harjo said. "You don't have to do anything more than sit where you are and say nothing. Got it?"

"Who are you visiting?" Mendez demanded.

Harjo waved a warning finger. "You're talking."

"Let me shoot him." From the backseat, Fallon ground the muzzle of his weapon in Mendez's ear.

"Okay, I'll shut up."

"Good." Harjo put Mendez's SUV in gear. "Here we go."

———

The police car with the two uniforms was parked next to the gate. Harjo stopped at the guard station, rolled down the window, and nodded to the officer inside.

He gave Harjo a hard, questioning look. "I don't know you."

Harjo smiled and poked his thumb in Mendez's direction. The blood around his mouth had been wiped clean. "Do you know him?"

The man's expression softened. "Of course. Excuse me. Is there a problem?"

"No problem, just a matter requiring some delicacy. Open the gate."

The gate swung open.

"And give us the code for Senor Garza's security gate."

"I'm not allowed to do that."

"You have Senor Mendez's authorization." Harjo turned to Mendez, who'd somehow opened the passenger door. He tumbled to the pavement, hands and feet still zip-tied.

"Shit!" Fallon said. "Shoot the guard." He put two rounds in Mendez's back as the man tried to crawl away.

Harjo shot the guard in the mouth, picked up the assault rifle, and before they could react took out the cops in the patrol car through the open passenger door of the SUV.

Fallon got in the front seat, slammed the door, and took the assault rifle from Harjo's hands. "What do we do now?"

"Fight or flight?"

Fallon pointed the weapon straight ahead. "Let's go."

Harjo gunned the SUV into the enclave, accelerated to Garza's estate, and drove it into the front security gate. It buckled but didn't break. He backed up and hit it twice more before it gave. Motion sensor lights illuminated the long driveway. Harjo gripped the wheel waiting to be shot, Fallon hung halfway out of the passenger window searching for targets.

The front of the house was lit up, lights ablaze inside, but there was no resistance. They pulled down their ski masks, bailed out of the SUV, and stormed the front door. Fallon blew the lock off and they went in low through a long entryway to a large room, where Gilberto Garza, dressed in his nightclothes, stood wide-eyed and empty-handed surrounded by massive Louis XIV gilded furniture.

"Who are you?" Garza asked, his voice shaking.

Harjo shot him dead and watched him fall. "Let's go."

He turned in time to see Carmen Garza come out of an adjoining room. She raised her shotgun. The blast caught him in the stomach.

Fallon killed her. The rounds from the assault rifle slammed her into the wall and turned her housecoat into bloody puffballs floating in the air.

Harjo sat on the carpet holding his innards. "Get out now."

Fallon bent low to lift and carry Harjo to the SUV. "Not without you."

Harjo gripped Fallon's hand to stop him. "I'm not going anywhere. Leave now. Go to my place in El Paso. Do this for me."

Fallon didn't move.

Harjo smiled and coughed blood. Danny's face was out of focus. "Please, do as I ask. I left something for you there."

"Okay, okay." Fallon pried Harjo's hand free and stood.

Slowly, Harjo stretched out on the carpet. It was an ugly room to die in. He listened for the sound of the SUV and didn't close his eyes until he heard Fallon drive away.

CHAPTER 23

Danny Fallon wheeled Mendez's armored SUV out of the enclave, rounds from arriving officers gouging the bulletproof windshield, pinging off the front of the hood. He slammed one patrol car out of the way, running over Mendez's body in the process, and roared down the winding road, sideswiping another responding unit as it rounded a curve. There were two units in pursuit, but the SUV far outmatched them and soon the headlights receded to small dots in the rearview mirror.

Traffic on the police radio reported that roadblocks had been set up on all escape routes. Fallon doubted he could blow through them. To survive, he had to go off-road. He gunned the vehicle between two houses, traveling downslope, taking out a wood fence and a backyard patio set. A steep drop-off ahead would put him upside down on a stretch of pavement. Through the trees below he could see stationary flashing emergency lights signaling a roadblock. He grabbed the assault rifle, opened the driver's door, and bailed out. The SUV careened into an arroyo, tipped over, and burst into flames. Hopefully the cops would stay busy looking for a body, and he'd be far away when they discovered there wasn't one.

Fallon strapped the rifle over his shoulder, scrambled down to the pavement, and took off running uphill, away from the roadblock. He paused at an intersection to a dirt road that climbed to higher ground. Sirens were screaming, the sounds carrying up from the city below. Lorenz had probably thrown everything he had to bring him down. Danny didn't like the idea of being tortured, castrated, and hung from a railroad overpass.

He couldn't go through the police or around them, so he'd go over them through the high terrain and find a place to cross the river into Eagle Pass. Get to El Paso as Harjo wanted.

Fallon gauged the incline. The terrain was child's play compared to what he'd experienced in Afghanistan. He'd parallel the dirt road and stay in the shade of the bordering trees. Outside lights came on in several nearby houses. He started out fast and picked up the pace, crashing through the underbrush. He had no time for caution or stealth.

He ran with the image of Harjo dead on the carpet in Garza's house, his guts spilling out. It was burned in his mind like an impression etched on glass. He never should have left him there. That was wrong. His eyes watered, but he wasn't crying.

———

For several days, Estavio Trevino had watched two deep-cover assets gather real-time intelligence on Lorenz, his brother Gilberto, Juan Garza, and several high-ranking cartel gang members. They were clearly professional, carefully studying and surveying the home turf of each subject. They'd obviously done their homework and knew exactly where to look: Longwei's restaurant, the safe houses, their targets' homes, even the heavily fortified police headquarters.

What they had planned for the street cop they'd surveilled, he could only guess. Some sort of gimmick. Trevino suspected they were Americans. He admired their thoroughness.

He'd shadowed them with great interest until he was almost certain he wasn't their target. But even a kernel of doubt that they might be DEA agents sent to seize him as originally planned made him consider taking them out.

Late one night, he'd tailed them to their rented Zaragoza trailer and spent an hour huddled in the cold debating the proposition before turning away. There was no need for a preemptive strike. Not yet.

Lorenz and Longwei had tightened security in anticipation of his retaliation, and with the murders of Gilberto and Carmen Garza, protection had been further reinforced. No matter where he chose to strike, there would be no easy way in.

As a police commandant, Lorenz had used his position to stifle information about the Garza killings. The weak-kneed news media played along. It was reported that during a home invasion the highly respected couple had been murdered and Gilberto had heroically killed one of unidentified attackers before succumbing. The surviving attacker remained at large.

Bloggers, lacking information, were silent. Reporters on Texas television stations used the crime to highlight the continuing epidemic of horrific murders of innocent people along the Mexican borderlands. On the streets of Piedras Negras, there was whispered talk of three police officers and one of Lorenz's top lieutenants found gunned down outside the Garzas' gated subdivision the very same night of the murders. And a rumor spread about a patrol officer and his girlfriend found dead in their apartment the following day. Cops talking on the QT called it a murder-suicide.

Trevino marveled at the audacity of the assassins. He was pleased he had taken no action against them. But who were they? How did they learn of Gilberto Garza's clandestine role as partner in the Lorenz cartel? Exactly how did they pull it off?

He retreated home to Colonia de los Kickapoo, where Caballo Galindo welcomed him. He asked if it was time to have a feast to celebrate his return.

"Not yet," Trevino replied.

"Ah, I see," Galindo said. "A brief visit."

Trevino nodded. "Yes, and a request. I'd like to have Jose Hernandez assist me for a few days in Piedras Negras, if you can spare him from the colonia."

Galindo raised a cautious eyebrow. "Would he be in danger?"

"Not at all. I need him to watch and report what he sees, nothing more."

"He will willingly oblige."

"Good."

Galindo nodded. "I'm sure you have heard we now have a young family living at the hunting ranch. Their summer home is complete, and they have done much to remove the debris caused by the fire. I will go there next week to dedicate their house. Friends and relatives will go with me and we will feast on a deer harvested from the ranch. The very first."

Trevino smiled. "I am pleased to hear it."

"When will you leave?"

"In the morning. When I next return, my journey will be complete."

"I'm glad to hear you say that."

———

Across the street from Shen's Famous Chinese Restaurant stood the old Hotel Castillo. A long, two-story brick building that harkened back to an earlier, more peaceful era in the city, it had arched windows and a row of large ceramic planters filled with miniature trees on either side of the covered entrance. It was hardly a castle, nor was it a dump. Mexicans coming from the surrounding villages loved it; tourists from north of the border ignored it.

Trevino installed Hernandez in a second-floor front room with direct line of sight of the restaurant's front door. He gave him a burner phone with pictures of Sammy and Longwei Shen, Lorenz, and Juan Garza, and told him to memorize the faces. He handed him a pair of binoculars along with instructions on how to observe without being detected.

"Call me whenever any of these men come to the restaurant," Estavio instructed.

From behind the curtain Hernandez peeked out at the street below. "What if I'm sleeping or hungry?"

"Don't worry, I'll relieve you so you can sleep, and food will be delivered. Only let me or the maid in, but do not leave the room, understood?" Trevino had secured the hotel owner's cooperation with a handsome bribe and substantial tips for the maids.

Hernandez nodded. "Okay."

Two days passed with only Longwei showing up or leaving. Mid-morning on the third day, before the restaurant opened for lunch, Hernandez reported the arrival of all four men, plus an unidentified woman.

"Who did she come with?" Trevino asked. He was staked out two doors down from one of the safe houses that had tunnel access to the restaurant.

"Sammy Shen."

In front of the safe house, two armed gang members lounged at the rear of a pickup, smoking and joking with the gunner of the fifty-caliber mounted in the bed, who perched on the tailgate. The boredom of a dull routine could be lethal. In this instance particularly so.

"Describe her," Trevino ordered.

"Brown hair, maybe five feet four or five, pretty."

Carmella Schuster, Trevino guessed. Her first appearance, as far as he knew. "What's Sammy driving?"

"Blue Audi, parked outside."

"Leave the hotel, destroy the phone, and go home."

"Now?" Hernandez asked.

"Right now." Trevino stepped into the open and killed the three thugs quickly, the pop of his silenced weapon barely noticeable. He used the fifty-caliber to blow open the front door. Inside the house, he killed a man cowering in a bathroom, cleared the rest of the house, removed a timed explosive device from his backpack, and set it at the tunnel entrance to detonate in five minutes.

He sprinted the length of the tunnel to the basement room, crashed through the door, rolled on the floor, and shot the two armed guards before they could pull their weapons. Lorenz and Juan looked surprised when he stood and carefully shot them in the head where they sat, frozen.

Longwei, Sammy, and Carmella were motionless in their chairs. They didn't utter a sound.

"I should kill you all," Trevino said. "But right now I do not have the inclination."

He ordered them facedown on the floor, zip-tied their hands and feet, smashed their cell phones, and fished Sammy's car key from his pants pocket. "What are you driving and where is it parked?"

"Blue Audi, out front."

In the dining room, the waitstaff was setting up for lunch while the armed doorman and a hostess chatted at the front of the house. Trevino killed the doorman as he reached for his handgun, and coldcocked the hostess who came at him with a knife. He ordered everyone else into the kitchen, told them not to move, and set a second explosive at the front entrance timed for three minutes,

He stepped outside, expecting to be gunned down. He was halfway to the Audi when a car veered onto the sidewalk behind him. He turned and shot the driver through the windshield. The car careened across the street, smashed into the planters in front of the hotel, and came to a stop. Trevino shot the thug in the passenger seat before he could get out.

He made it to the Audi and did a tight one-eighty just as a second car slammed into his rear end, crumpling the trunk. He floored it. Ten feet past the front of the restaurant it blew up, shattering plate glass and spewing debris into the street. The concussion from the blast knocked the car behind him onto the sidewalk and into a lamppost.

He reached the outskirts of town with no one chasing him and relaxed behind the wheel. It was time to disappear again into the Bolsón de Mapimí. For several months at the very least. He looked forward to the solitude that awaited him there. Then, when he was ready, he'd return home for good.

CHAPTER 24

The explosion forced Longwei to close the restaurant for repairs. The news media reported a gas leak had triggered the blast, but there had been no injuries. The knife-wielding hostess who failed to stop El Jefe vanished. It was surprisingly harsh treatment for a woman who'd once been Longwei's favorite mistress.

To keep the murders under wraps, Sammy let it be known to the cartel members that Juan and Lorenz were safe but incommunicado for the next several days. Everything remained calm.

That evening, Longwei hosted Sammy and Carmella at his estate outside a small farming village south of Piedras Negras.

"Trevino has done us a favor," he said, accepting tea from his concubine. He'd brought her from China soon after the death of his wife ten years ago. "Now we can take over the cartel's heroin and cocaine trafficking network and use it for fentanyl distribution as well."

"A smart move," Sammy said. "However, Trevino should not be left unpunished. He might find a reason to come back for us."

Longwei waved his concubine from the room. "It's a question of timing. The most pressing matter is controlling the cartel before it breaks into factions and total chaos ensues."

"That will not be without difficulties," Sammy cautioned. "Mexicans like their drug lords to be mestizos at the very least, not Chinese."

"A mixed-blood who is part Caucasian would be more than acceptable," Longwei noted. "Which is why I think Carmella should serve as titular head of the cartel."

"Titular?" Carmella snapped. "I will not serve as your token *anything.*"

Longwei lowered his gaze. "I apologize for my poor choice of words. You will have a voice in all decisions. But we must protect you, as Lorenz did his brother, only be much better at it."

"I'm listening," Carmella said.

Longwei used a remote to turn on a wall-mounted television. "Vito Torres, Lorenz's numbers man, is an accountant by training." A short video of Torres and his family enjoying a backyard barbecue played across the screen. His two young twin sons and a slightly older daughter smiled happily at the camera while his pretty wife looked on.

"He's a perfect choice. Levelheaded, calm by nature, and well regarded by the cartel rank and file. He's a family man, not a killer. If we put him in charge right away, he'll do what we ask of him."

"Are you sure?" Carmella demanded.

Longwei smiled. "Torres has provided valuable cartel information to me for a number of years. You could say that we own him. Or I should say that *you* own him."

Carmella nodded at the concession. "How will we explain the disappearance of Juan Garza and his uncle?"

"A coup led by Torres and a mysterious powerful associate, rumored to be a woman." He smiled at Carmella, who nodded her agreement. "We will move the cartel away from murder and intimidation and make life less hazardous for us all."

"And the sicarios?" Sammy asked.

"We will keep them close at hand as our peacemakers." Longwei rang the bell on the side table. "Let's have a brandy together before this old man goes to his bed."

———

Danny Fallon sat at the desk in Harjo's El Paso house and read through the file he'd found in the top drawer. In it were documents that appointed him executor of Harjo's estate with power of attorney, a signed, notarized property deed transferring ownership of Harjo's mortgage-free house to Fallon, and instructions on disbursing the remainder of his assets to Mark Villalobos's parents. A note left with the documents read:

Danny,

If you're reading this I'm dead. There's not much in the house worth anything, so keep what you like and give the rest away. My sister may want a few things, so check with her before you toss stuff out. I wrote her phone number on the front of the file folder. Call her after you've gone through everything. She's the primary beneficiary on my insurance policy, government retirement benefits, and pension plan, which means you're probably going to have to fill out paperwork swearing to my untimely death. Sorry to put you through the bureaucratic BS. Samantha Hodges, SA in Charge El Paso, can help you get the ball rolling. Use the photographs in the manila envelope if you have to.

No death notice, obit in the papers, press release, or teary-eyed DEA memorial service please. If my body is ever recovered, have it cremated. Make it clear to Hodges and anybody else who asks that these are my wishes. Mail the two addressed letters by overnight express. The one to my sister is just to say goodbye and tell her of my wishes. The one to the woman in Bermuda—well, that isn't your business. One more

thing: my neighbors and good friends, Henry and Fiona Saenz, should
be told that I'm dead. He'll be knocking at the door soon, maybe before
you even finish reading this. Be nice to them and let them be nice to
you. And thanks.
    Bernard

The manila envelope contained a half dozen date-and-time-stamped eight-by-ten black-and-white glossy photographs of Samantha Hodges and a younger man making love. From her expression, she had enjoyed the experience. On the backside, Harjo had written the man's name, along with a notation that the photo had been taken while he'd been a special agent under Hodges's supervision in the El Paso office before transferring to another district.

Fallon put the photo aside and called Harjo's sister. As he explained that Harjo had died in the line of duty while on an undercover operation, he almost cried with her. He reassured her that her brother hadn't suffered and promised to express-mail Harjo's letter to her. It would arrive tomorrow.

He hung up and the front doorbell rang. He opened it and greeted a smiling Henry Saenz, whose happy expression quickly vanished.

———

After consoling the grieving Saenzes for several hours, Fallon mailed the letters and met with a pricey lawyer on how to proceed as Harjo's executor. Back at the house, he prepared a fictitious account of his activities searching for Harjo in Mexico. It took deep into the night to finish it. He ordered takeout from an open-late Chinese restaurant, returned to the house, poured some of Harjo's good scotch to go with it, and ate sitting in the living room watching an episode of a SWAT crime series that was hysterically funny.

Morning coffee revived him along with a hot shower and fresh change of clothes. He finished an early breakfast at a family-run diner and found a used-car dealer willing to buy the Chevy for cash. He rented a car, drove to the El Paso DEA Division, and cooled his heels for a half hour waiting to see Samantha Hodges.

She appeared, brusquely ordered him into her office, sat behind her desk, and launched into a frontal attack. Harjo's corpse had been fished from the Rio Grande south of Eagle Pass. A DEA investigation determined that Fallon had reported his rented car stolen in Piedras Negras prior to the assassination of Gilberto and Carmen Garza. Clearly, he'd been Harjo's accomplice. Admit it now, resign before charges were brought, and avoid the disgraceful mess of a trial and possible prison time.

Red in the face with righteous anger, Hodges paused, glared, and waited for a response.

"Finished?" Fallon smiled pleasantly and placed the manila envelope on the desktop. "My turn. Take a look inside. I have a number of requests, so you may want to use pen and paper."

Hodges looked at the photographs and sank back in her chair, wrath deflated.

Danny spelled out Harjo's final wishes and decisions one by one. He made it clear any death-in-the-line-of-duty payments were to go to Harjo's sister. All paperwork to disburse his retirement and pension funds to his sister was to be expedited, and Harjo's remains were to be brought to El Paso for cremation as soon as possible.

"There will be no memorial services or official announcement of his passing," Fallon added, placing a legal document on the desk. "My sworn affidavit that I witnessed his death should be sufficient substantiation of fact."

Hodges, head buried over a lined notepad, had scribbled down Fallon's bullet points. She looked up and read the affidavit. "Is that all you want me to do?"

"No, I understand you're in line for a big promotion to assistant chief of operations in D.C."

"That hasn't been officially announced."

"It will be soon, I've been told. I want to be posted as resident agent in Eagle Pass effective immediately."

Samantha grimaced. "I can't do that right now."

"Either you do it *right now*, or you can waste away here in Tequilaville until retirement. Make the call."

"You're asking me to completely whitewash your involvement in this."

Fallon grinned. "That's the bottom line. Let's say I was sent under deep cover by you personally to find rogue Special Agent Harjo and return him for disciplinary action. Learning Harjo had been killed and fearing for my safety, you waited until my return from Mexico to reveal the operation."

Hodges shook her head. "That's a stretch."

"No, it's not." He handed her a DEA file folder. "Here are my complete case notes and final confidential report of my effort to locate Special Agent Harjo in Mexico and stop his attack on Gilberto and Carmen Garza. Unfortunately, I was too late to prevent his death. It's all the documentation you need."

Hodges paged through the paperwork. "Unbelievable."

Fallon retrieved the photographs and stood. "Are we good?"

"Leave the photographs."

He dropped them on the desk. "They're yours. Once you've done what I've asked, I'll send you the remaining copies. Promise."

"Break it and I'll destroy you," Hodges snarled.

"No doubt," Fallon noted. "Again, are we good?"

Hodges nodded. "Give me twenty-four hours."

"I'll be in touch."

Fallon stopped at the Intelligence Unit on his way out to get caught up on what was happening in Piedras Negras. Shen's Famous Chinese Restaurant was still closed for repairs. The bomber had yet to be identified. Juan and Lorenz remained in hiding. Vito Torres was running the cartel in their absence. Brains over brawn? Fallon didn't think so, not completely. Controlling the cartel required muscle and the ability to provoke fear. There had to be somebody else pulling the strings. He advised the analyst to have Intel dig deeper. He suggested Garza and Lorenz were dead, killed by Estavio Trevino, aka El Jefe.

"That's pure speculation," the analyst replied flippantly.

"Always trust what the boots on the ground tell you or you'll never win the war," Fallon advised.

"What?" the confused analyst replied.

Outside, El Paso was blinding under a clear sky and hot sun. He had one more stop to make. In the parking lot he called ahead to the Doña Ana Sheriff's Office and set up a meeting with Detective Istee. ETA one hour.

———

Clayton said little during Special Agent Fallon's briefing, surprised to be so shaken by the news of Agent Harjo's death and how it occurred. Was there much of a difference between Fallon, Harjo, and Trevino? The lines seemed blurry. He listened intently as Fallon recounted what he'd uncovered in Mexico with Harjo and his suspicions that El Jefe was responsible for the disappearance of Juan Garza and Luis Lorenz.

"Only Trevino could have pulled it off," Fallon concluded.

"Yeah, El Jefe strikes again," Clayton wisecracked. "You know, I talked to him on the phone."

Stunned, Fallon blinked. "You're kidding?"

"Nope. I tracked him down with the help of our cybercrimes expert."

Clayton handed him *Confessions of a Marine Sniper.* "He talked to the retired Marine who wrote the book. There's a chapter about El Jefe in it."

"How did that get you to El Jefe?"

"First read 'Bardera, the Bird, and the Bear.' It's flagged."

Fallon speed-read the pages, shaking his head in amazement, even chuckling at times. "Unbelievable. So give, how did this get you to Trevino?"

"For some unknown reason Trevino telephoned Smitty posing as Bear's friend to tell him that he was alive and living in Mexico. The call originated in Piedras Negras. Smitty had the number, so I called it."

"I'll be damned. That was smart thinking."

Clayton turned on his desktop computer and played the audio. "Listen."

Fallon sat stock-still until the recording ended. "I need a copy."

"I figured you did." Clayton handed him a thumb drive.

"Do you want a crack at Trevino if I can produce him?" Fallon asked.

"How are you going to do that from your duty station in Vancouver?"

"I'm about to be appointed Eagle Pass resident agent. Again, yes or no?"

"He killed five people in my state. Of course I want him."

Fallon slipped the thumb drive in his shirt pocket. "I'll be in touch." He stood and shook Clayton's hand. "Thank you."

"Good luck," Clayton replied.

He watched Fallon leave, typed up a note of the meeting, sent copies to Captain Rodney and Sheriff Vasquez, and leaned back in his chair. Was it over? Not really. Maybe the Piedras Negras cartel had its head cut off, which was certainly a plus, but there were always understudies waiting in the wings and Trevino still roamed free.

Clayton pushed it out of his head. Too many maybes and what-ifs to worry about. He had cases to work, and Rodney wanted results.

CHAPTER 25

Held in the late afternoon on the rooftop patio of a downtown
Santa Fe hotel, Kerney's surprise seventieth birthday party went off
perfectly. He'd been lured there by his old friend retired state police
chief Andy Baca, under the pretense of attending a meeting about
increasing law enforcement retirement pensions. In attendance were
family members, friends, former associates, and dignitaries. The gov-
ernor made a quick appearance to appoint Kerney an honorary colonel
aide-de-camp on his staff, the mayor read a proclamation declaring it
Kevin Kerney Day in Santa Fe, and the state speaker of the house presented him with a legislative memorial praising his decades of outstanding law enforcement achievements.

Unbeknownst to Kerney, Clayton and his family, including Isabel,
had come up the night before and stayed at the hotel. Sara's parents
had flown in from Arizona. Kerney's ranch foreman, who cleaned up
nicely, and his wife also made an appearance.

Dozens of retired and serving sheriffs and police chiefs from all
parts of the state came to the party, along with a large contingent of

former senior officers who had at one time or another served under Kerney's command. Three former district attorneys, several judges, and a half dozen trial lawyers, including Gary Dalquist, were crowded at the long bar talking politics. Patrick had brought his girlfriend, Jill, to keep him company in the midst of all the old people sipping wine and nibbling hors d'oeuvres. Along with Wendell and Hannah they huddled at a table, snacked, and talked under a clear blue sky with a view of the Sangre de Cristo Mountains as a backdrop.

Knowing her man and aware of his discomfort in the spotlight, Sara stayed close to Kerney until Clayton snuck him away for a private father-son drink in the downstairs hotel bar. They snagged a corner table away from a noisy group of day-trippers up from Albuquerque. Kerney ordered a single-malt scotch and Clayton asked for a craft-brewed pilsner.

"Do you remember how we met?" Clayton asked when the drinks came and they'd finished their toast.

Kerney laughed. "Do I! You cited me for trespassing on Mescalero tribal land. Didn't budge when I showed my shield and asked you to let me off with a warning. No way, I had to pay the fine."

"A good beginning, wouldn't you say?" Clayton joked.

"Little did we know," Kerney mused. "I had no idea you were my son, and you steadfastly believed you needed no father."

"I'm glad it happened."

Kerney nodded in agreement. "Me, too. Are you staying over tonight?"

"Just Grace and me. We're making a long weekend of it. Hannah leaves after the party. She's dropping Wendell off in Albuquerque on her way to Las Cruces."

"Good. How about the four of us meeting for Sunday brunch?"

"I'd like that." Clayton's phone rang. Danny Fallon's name showed on the screen. "I've got to take this." He answered and asked what was up.

"If you want El Jefe, now's the time," Fallon said.

"Explain."

"I've had NSA using voice recognition software from that recording you gave me to intercept Trevino's phone conversations. He'll be at the Eagle Pass Kickapoo tribal community center tomorrow for a feast and celebration. I'll fill you in when you get here."

"Are you sure?"

"Positive. A DEA airplane can be at the Santa Fe Airport in two hours if you're game. Your sheriff says it's your call to make, but he strongly recommends you accept my invitation. You can call him if you like."

"Not necessary."

"I didn't think so. He faxed me a copy of your criminal complaint and the court approved arrest warrants. I'll outfit you with equipment and weapons when you get here."

"Okay," Clayton replied.

"Two hours." Fallon clicked off.

Clayton put the phone down and grimaced.

"Something up?" Kerney asked.

Clayton laid it out. "I've got to do it."

"Of course you do. I'll take you to the airport."

Clayton laughed and shook his head. "You don't get out of your own party that easily. And I can't sneak out of town on Grace without an explanation."

Kerney finished his scotch and sighed. "Reality intrudes once again. Don't get shot up in Eagle Pass and ruin my birthday weekend."

"I wouldn't think of it."

———

At the Santa Fe Airport, Grace gave Clayton a half-hearted kiss and said, "Things have to change."

Motionless, with her arms crossed, she waited until he was seated next to the pilot before walking away with not so much as a good-bye wave.

She was right, of course. Things had to change. And while they'd talked about it, especially with an empty nest looming in the near future, he'd always managed to push the subject aside. That wasn't going to work anymore.

Fallon met him at the Maverick County Airport and filled him in on the short ride to Eagle Pass. Trevino had vanished after the myste-rious disappearance of Lorenz and Garza, whose bodies had yet to be found. Longwei and Sammy Shen were operating the syndicate using Carmella Schuster and Vito Torres as fronts for the organization. Under their leadership, gang violence in Piedras Negras had fallen to a twenty-year low. Citizens were becoming cautiously hopeful about the future.

"That's jim-dandy," Clayton said. "What about Trevino?"

"He went deep into the Bolsón de Mapimí and laid low for a while. Not a peep. I thought I'd lost him. Several weeks ago he made phone contact with the Mexican Kickapoo chief. That's when NSA started recording his transmissions."

"Who is he talking to?"

"Mostly the chief, Galindo. It seems Trevino has decided to reha-bilitate himself. He returned to the village and had what's called an arrival ceremony. From what I understand, it's not much more than giving thanks to their god for a safe return home."

"That's his rehabilitation?" Clayton inquired.

Fallon laughed as he pulled into the resident agent parking lot. "Don't be so skeptical. He also had a warrior cleansing ceremony. Technically, it's known as the murderer's ceremony. Went on for days, with fasting and praying, asking the spirits of his victims for forgiveness. They did some sort of a buffalo thing. You can't get into their version of the hereafter without it. A Kickapoo elder from the Oklahoma tribe conducted it."

"There's salvation for all of us, no matter what tribe," Clayton cracked, not in the mood for forgiveness.

"God knows we all need it, bro," Fallon added.

Inside, they went directly to the conference room. Behind the table was a wall-mounted whiteboard with a hand-drawn diagram of the entrance to the Eagle Pass Kickapoo Reservation. It outlined four vehicles in different locations, numbered accordingly.

Fallon stood in front of the whiteboard. "The Eagle Pass Traditional Kickapoo Tribe manages Colonia de los Kickapoo. In order to officially transfer title of the Mexican hunting ranch to the tribe, Trevino must sign the paperwork in Eagle Pass. He'll do that tomorrow at ten a.m. As you know, only tribal police and FBI have jurisdiction on the reservation, so we'll take him when he leaves."

With a pointer he indicated where the interception would take place. "We'll move when he's a quarter mile off the rez. There will be four units of two-man teams positioned out of sight until I signal to converge."

He tapped the unit marked number 1. "That's us. We'll do the takedown. Long-range target acquisition surveillance will be tracking him constantly. Additionally, two choppers will be airborne with spotters and snipers."

Fallon described the make and model of the pickup truck Trevino would be driving. "He'll be shadowed all the way."

"Will he be traveling alone?" Clayton asked.

Fallon shook his head. "Galindo, the Mexican Kickapoo chief, will accompany him."

"That could get sticky."

"We can't control everything. Every agent knows Trevino is our only target." Fallon put the pointer on the table. "I got you a room at the hotel next door. Check in, freshen up, and I'll buy you dinner."

Clayton smiled. "That's the least you can do."

Fallon grinned. "We're gonna get him."

Clayton studied the diagram. "I hope so."

———

Lying awake in the hotel room later that night, Clayton barely slept, his thoughts jumping from one worry to another. He couldn't image Trevino surrendering peacefully. Scenarios played out in his head. Would he attempt to evade capture? Mount a frontal attack if boxed in? Did he have some alternate escape route that Fallon hadn't considered? Surely he'd try to kill them all—or as many as he could.

He thought about Grace's icy stare when he'd told her why he had to leave Kerney's birthday party. And then watching her abruptly turn away as the DEA airplane taxied down the Santa Fe Airport runway. She'd barely forgiven him for his inexcusable absence at the family gathering to help Blossom Magoosh and her granddaughters speed Lucy Nautzile on her way from The Shadow World of human beings to The Real World beyond, The Land of Ever Summer. He was seriously derelict in his duty to family, and she had every right to demand that he change his ways.

What could he do? He wasn't cut out for a desk job.

Up at six, he did a forty-five-minute workout in the hotel fitness center, showered, dressed, and had coffee and a piece of toast in the breakfast room. His stomach couldn't handle anything more. By seven-thirty a.m. he was with Fallon and six agents from Houston checking out equipment and weapons in the DEA conference room. At eight a.m. dispatch reported Trevino and his passenger were on their way, less than two hours out.

Time slowed for Clayton. After Fallon's final operational briefing, he fell silent in the middle of the nervous chatter that filled the conference room. As the teams left one by one to take up their positions, Fallon held him back for a moment.

"Trevino dead or alive, do you care?" he asked.

"Death is too easy a punishment for him," Clayton answered.

"Don't take any unnecessary risks, okay?"

Clayton headed for the door. "Let's all get home safe."

———

For over an hour they sat in the unmarked unit, saying little, listening to radio reports of Trevino's progress on his way to Eagle Pass. When surveillance announced he had crossed into Texas, Clayton tensed up. His heartbeat quickened and his lips felt dry in spite of the oppressive humidity the vehicle's air-conditioning couldn't completely conquer.

When the truck came into view, he wanted to stop it there and get it over with. He forced himself to relax as it passed by, Trevino just a blur behind the steering wheel.

"Soon now," Fallon said.

Soon became an hour more of waiting. When aerial surveillance reported Trevino and Galindo were exiting the reservation, time stretched out again for Clayton. Almost magically, the truck came into view. As it approached, Clayton could see Trevino clearly through binoculars, his head tilted toward Galindo as if listening to him in a casual, friendly way.

On cue, everyone moved. Fallon spun their vehicle onto the pavement, headed straight at the pickup. A unit cut the truck off from behind. The two remaining units joined up quickly with Fallon and Clayton, spread out like wingmen to form a barrier. On Fallon's command, every vehicle swung into position and stopped. Agents piled out of the vehicles and took cover, weapons at the ready.

Up ahead, the truck screeched to a stop. From behind the protection of the driver's-side door Fallon barked orders to Trevino over a loudspeaker. Clayton wasn't listening. He watched Trevino say something to Galindo, reach across him, and open the passenger door. Galindo nodded, placed his hands on top of his head, and stepped out of the truck. He walked directly to the side of the pavement and waited.

"The chief is unarmed," Trevino shouted through the open window. "He will do as you ask."

Fallon directed Galindo to go to the unit behind the pickup, where the officers frisked him, cuffed him, and locked him in the backseat cage.

"Your turn, Trevino," Fallon said. "Step out of the truck."

"Is Detective Clayton Istee with you?" Trevino asked.

"I'm here," Clayton shouted.

"I'll surrender to Istee, no one else."

"No deal," Fallon snapped. "Take the keys out of the ignition, drop them on the ground, and exit the vehicle with your hands in plain sight. Do it now."

Trevino threw a handgun out the window. "I'm unarmed. Send Detective Istee to me. I'll surrender only to him."

Fallon glanced at Clayton, who was in a kneeling position behind the open passenger door. "We've got a clear head shot. It's your call."

Clayton stood. "I've always wanted to meet El Jefe," he whispered. "Here I come," he called out.

Eyes locked on Trevino, Clayton mentally counted the paces—forty-six exactly—to the truck. He unholstered his handgun. "Keep your hands where I can see them. Open the door from the outside handle and exit slowly."

Trevino didn't budge. "My true name is Wind Stands with Bear Among the Wallows. I wanted you to know that."

"Why?"

"Because you have been a worthy enemy." Trevino ducked and came up holding something in his hand. Clayton fired a second after a head shot blew Trevino's skull against the rear window, blood splatter coating the glass.

Clayton opened the door. Trevino had a cell phone in his hand. His face was unrecognizable.

I can't do this anymore, Clayton thought. He removed the magazine from the semiautomatic, tossed it aside, dropped the weapon, and turned. He was no longer *guzhuguja*—in balance. Forty-six paces back to Fallon's unit wouldn't fix it. He needed to travel a lot farther than that.

AUTHOR'S NOTE

Among many indigenous tribes, including the Kickapoo, native language names have special meaning not generally shared with outsiders. I found very few English translations of Kickapoo names, but discovered each individual receives a name that is eponymous to the totem of the clan to which he belongs. With that, the native language names in the story are of my own invention.